DON'T LET
IN THE COLD

DON'T LET IN THE COLD

KEELY PARRACK

sourcebooks
fire

Published by Sourcebooks Fire, an imprint of Sourcebooks
P.O. Box 4410, Naperville, Illinois 60567–4410
(630) 961-3900
sourcebooks.com

Cataloging-in-Publication Data is on file with the Library of Congress.

Printed and bound in Canada.
MBP 10 9 8 7 6 5 4 3 2 1

For Luka,
who was there from the start.

DAY ONE
October 25

1

6:33 p.m.

THE BLOOD-ORANGE SUN BALANCED FOR ONE dazzling moment, trapped on the mountain ledge. It slipped behind the ridge, leaving us in the hushed shadows of twilight. I wished I could do the same: slip away.

Lit by the car's high beams, the winding road stretched like a ribbon ahead. The glaring brightness made the surrounding landscape seem even darker.

"Are you sure we're not lost?" I asked Mum, glancing at the nothingness around us. "Only it's been an hour since you said we were almost at the cabin."

"It's a Tesla. Teslas don't get lost." Mum flicked back her long blond hair. "I know you're not a big fan of the great outdoors, Lottie, but Oliver's cabin is so lovely. And as he's your stepfather now, it's your place too. There's nothing for you to worry about. It will be fun."

"Yep," I said, thankful that it was too dark to see how close to plummeting off the edge we were.

Vague outlines of tall, dark pines appeared at the sides of the road. We sped by a smaller turnoff, leading deeper into the forest, a sign to a campsite, a lone store—Soto's Shakes & Supplies—a cross by the side of the road, and then nothing but Mum's off-key singing and the squeal of tires as she spun around the corners.

I stared at the first evening stars through the sunroof. They were so bright. Of course, because there was no light pollution. We were driving through endless wilderness. I should have known it would be a rustic cabin, in the middle of nowhere. I'd be trapped there with no escape. My chest felt hollow. I swallowed.

"It will all be better in the daylight, Lottie. Then you'll see how beautifully stunning Tahoe is. Now here we are!" She turned down a narrow road and glided the Tesla smoothly onto a long driveway, stopping abruptly in front of a cabin.

My Frappuccino fell from the cupholder, spilling its dregs onto the white leather divider. I wiped the sticky blob with a crushed napkin.

"Is keeping my wedding gift clean for one day too much to ask?" Mum glared at me.

"Sorry." I licked the chocolate residue that freckled the back of my pale white hand. We'd barely arrived, and I'd already disappointed her.

She sighed.

I waited. I knew what was coming. The talk.

"Lottie, I'm trusting you." She stretched her fingers on the steering wheel to better admire her brand-new wedding ring, glinting in the dark. "It's not like I'm asking a lot. It's only one night."

I hoped my mother's new marriage would last longer than that. I stared at the cabin. It was nestled into the side of a hill, surrounded by silhouetted pine trees, dark shapes against darker shapes. Anything could be out there. "It's just so isolated."

"That's what makes it so safe." Mum smoothed out the creases in her ivory shift dress. "Jade's sweet and extremely smart, like her dad. It will be good for you to spend this weekend together. She's really looking forward to having more time with you."

I seriously doubted that. During the three times we'd met, we'd spoken twice, and both of those were a monosyllabic *hi*. And one *sorry* (not sorry) when she "accidentally" slammed the car door on my foot. "I don't have much choice, do I?" I asked.

"Lottie, it *is* our honeymoon. We'll be back tomorrow, for God's sake. Oliver's planned this lovely time for you and Jade in the cabin. Aren't you excited? I thought you were happy for us."

"I am." It was hard to sound genuine about something that didn't seem real. That morning's city hall wedding was over in less time than it had taken for us to find parking in downtown San Francisco.

"The cabin's fabulous—you'll love it. Anyway, it's not like you've got anything else to do." She tilted the rearview mirror, checking that her scarlet lipstick hadn't bled into her white skin.

"No, and who's fault is that? Moving every six months doesn't exactly help," I pointed out. Every time I'd start to fit in and actually have friends, we'd move and suddenly I'd be a stranger with a weird accent all over again. If I ever forgot about it, I'd be reminded. The novelty of my English accent never wore off for people here. Yes, I'm from England; no, I don't want to say "water" for you, *again*.

"Five schools in two years, and now another, in my senior year?"

"Don't blame me for your introverted personality, blame your dad. You're so like him—always seeing the negative instead of the opportunity. Things will be better now, you'll see." She smiled, all fake cheer and white teeth. I seriously wondered if she was my mum at all. "We're all going to be one big happy family."

I wanted her to be right, but I knew this would be one more in a long line of broken promises. Only this time there was another kid's heart to break as well. "I hope so. I really do. But right now, my special role in this arrangement is being a companion to a fifteen year old. So, sorry if this situation doesn't look that rosy to me."

"Almost sixteen. You only just turned seventeen. There's barely a year between you, and she's way more mature than you're being right now!"

A gust of wind rattled through the car. I shivered. The cold, the mountains, and that sound—for a moment I was back there, holding Dad's calloused hand, trekking up stony trails, wind whipping in my ears, eyes streaming. He called them Father-Daughter Days. I called them Goodbye Days. The next morning he'd be gone, off on another mountaineering expedition, away for months. I'd pretend to be sick to stop him from leaving—he'd always go anyway. So much for happy families.

I swung out of the car and slammed the door.

"Lottie!" Mum hissed after me. "Don't you dare screw this up!"

As usual, so trusting in my abilities. I pretended not to hear, held my head high, and marched up to the cabin's front door.

"You've arrived!" Oliver, my new stepdad, gathered me in a bear hug. "I was worried your mom had got lost." His cashmere sweater smelled of cinnamon and earth.

For a moment I allowed myself to feel wanted, safe, protected. But there was no use pretending. I pulled myself away. "She couldn't resist one last Starbucks stop."

"Well, it's good to finally have you here." He grinned, brown eyes crinkling at the edges, like they were used to smiling. All of his features were smooth and warm—brown skin, round cheeks, smooth, bald head, and his deep voice, which made it sound like he meant every word he said.

I stood there, clutching my battered backpack.

"At least we had time to open up the cabin and check everything worked before you arrived. Lights, power, fire." He clapped his hands. "It always takes a little while for the hot water to heat up when no one's been here for a while, but it should be fine in half an hour or so. Jade's been waiting for you." Oliver moved aside to reveal her, sitting cross-legged on the cream suede sofa in the middle of the enormous living room.

"Hello." I gave a little wave, like that was a normal thing for a stepsister to do.

She gave me a nod and returned to her Switch game. A black curl had escaped her high bun and bounced gently against her brown neck, as her fingers tapped the console. She'd changed out of this morning's sapphire dress into ripped blue jeans and a soft gray cardigan over a teal EXTINCTION IS FOREVER T-shirt. I bet her sweater was cashmere like her dad's. I suddenly felt the weight of my consignment store fleece. It was North Face, probably a nineties original. I fiddled with my oversized watch, stopping as soon as I realized I was acting nervous.

"Don't mind her. She's a little shy, but get her talking about anything nature and she's your friend for life." Oliver grinned at me, as if I was in on the joke and would actually smile back.

Jade gave an aren't-parents-embarrassing eye roll. I gave a small smile, like I agreed. But I'd take embarrassment over disappointment any day.

"Hello, darling!" Mum made her entrance, all flying scarf and crimson peacoat. Oliver swept her up in his arms and twirled her. She flung her head back, squealing in delight.

"Does it drive well? I was getting worried about you."

Mum tilted her head. "I know I said I'd follow you, but it's not like you can get lost when there's only one road. You don't mind, do you, darling?"

"No, of course not. But I think we'd better rush if you want to make our dinner reservations." He looked at his watch. "We're cutting it close."

"Whatever you decide, darling. Popping to the loo, then I'm all yours." Mum dashed by me. "Oh, and the Tesla drives like a dream, but it's almost out of charge."

"Okay, then." Oliver grabbed his jacket. "Guess I'm the valet," he said and went to park the Tesla in the garage.

My throat was dry. I was sinking. I wish I hadn't agreed to this.

8

It was going to be long and painfully awkward being alone with my new stepsister, but at least it was just for one night. I took a deep breath. Maybe Mum was right, maybe this time would be different. It was a marriage, after all. But it was still *her*.

Between them, my parents did not have a great track record for relationships. Dad vanished, leaving no trace on my eighth birthday, and Mum was a one-woman tornado of broken promises. *Never trust anyone* was her motto. *Prepare to be let down* was mine.

I dropped my backpack by the closet and made my way to the fireplace, bumping into the oak coffee table on my way. Nice entrance. The iron chandelier lights flickered high above me for a second, before returning to normal. I stared at the flickering glow of the flames in the fireplace, rubbing my hands as if I were cold. Pretending to be at ease.

"What are you playing?" I could at least act like I was interested.

"*Animal Crossing*," said Jade without lifting her head from the screen.

"Oh." I glanced up at the cathedral ceiling, feeling smaller by the second.

"You're in the guestroom downstairs." She pointed to the stairwell.

"Right. Thanks." I wondered if I could leave out some back door and disappear. Jade would be fine playing her game, and Mum wouldn't even notice I was missing. Not that there was anywhere to go.

Oliver hugged Jade goodbye. "Bye sweetie."

"Bye, Dad. Love ya." Jade smiled.

"Love you too." He kissed her cheek. Like the perfect dad in a television commercial.

I stood there feeling like a total intruder.

"Sorry, Lottie," said Oliver. "I was going to leave you the Land Rover, but I guess we're taking that now. I'm charging the Tesla for you. It will be ready in a few hours. You'll be fine until then. And don't let Jade trick you into letting her drive. She only just got her permit." He smiled.

I didn't dare tell him I hadn't got my license yet. "Just don't disappear on us." It came out sounding more desperate than I'd meant it to.

He shook his head. "Never. I promise."

———

They were ready in seconds, a flurry of coats and hugs, and off they went—the black Land Rover's headlights slicing through the night.

Oliver called out of the car window: "Don't worry about the snowstorm. We'll be back long before then. And Jade knows where everything is!"

"What snowstorm?" I shouted, but they couldn't hear me above their music. "What things?" Oliver was already singing along to Coldplay. Mum's choice, for sure.

I lingered at the front door until the taillights disappeared. A breeze ruffled the branches, sending gentle waves through the surrounding woods. I shivered. The air was too thin, too cold, and too lung-stabbingly sharp. A crow cawed from the top of an overhanging pine. The bird stared at me with black marble eyes. My neck tingled; I had the sensation that I was being watched. I turned and stared at the trees, as if I could make out anything hiding in there. It was so dark, so quiet. Waiting-for-something-to-happen quiet.

A gust of wind shook the trees. I shivered and checked my weather app. My phone was down to one bar. "Jade?" I came back inside, taking care to double-bolt the huge door. "Did you know about a snowstorm coming?"

"It's Tahoe. Sometimes it snows. Dad said not until Sunday." She looked out the window. "It won't be much. Not in October. It will probably just be freezing rain."

"Oliver would have said, right, if it was going to snow badly, like left special instructions, or warned us?"

"He wouldn't leave us here if he thought we'd be in any danger. Stop worrying. It's a ski cabin, built for snow. Anyway, he'll be back in the morning." Jade checked her watch, like it would tell her the exact time he'd be back. "Like twelve hours."

"You make it sound like he's coming back alone."

"No. I didn't mean..." Jade looked startled by my suggestion.

"I know." She was probably counting down the minutes until it was over too. I picked up my backpack and took it downstairs.

The cabin was built into the side of a hill. From the front it looked like a cozy one-story place. But beneath the entrance floor, with the open-plan living area—dining, lounge and kitchen, and observation deck—was the downstairs floor, and it was enormous. Huge windows looked out onto the surrounding wilderness.

There was a den with a deep blue sectional and an enormous TV. To the left of the door was a corridor leading to the bedrooms.

I wandered along, looking into each bedroom.

I threw my backpack onto the bed in the last room at the end of the hallway. I figured since it didn't have a king-sized bed strewn with abandoned outfits, or a neat pile of Tahoe nature guides and AP textbooks on the bedside table, this room devoid of any personality had to be mine—the guest room. Perfect for temporary visitors.

Our whole apartment building could fit into the space of that one cabin, and this was just their vacation house. It wasn't even where I'd be living. According to Mum, that would be in a gorgeous Craftsman home in Menlo Park. It all seemed so unreal. I felt dizzy for a second. Pinpricks of light glittered before my eyes.

So much space for only two people, but originally it would have been for three. Her sparkling eyes gazed out from the family photos dotting the walls—at the beach, in the forest, at the top of the Empire State Building—Jade's mum, looking like Beyoncé's long-lost sister, beautiful and confident. Oliver had a smooth, bald head even then, and there was bright-eyed, dimple-cheeked mini Jade. They leaned into each other, faces shining with happiness.

Jade had lost someone too. Her mom died when she was young, but not too young to remember. Our only commonality—a weight of sadness clinging to us like shadows.

2

9:35 p.m.

"SO, HERE WE ARE THEN." I STOOD IN THE MIDDLE OF the open-plan living area, dwarfed by the enormity of everything— the wall of bookshelves, the eighty-inch flat-screen TV, the huge stone fireplace, and the gleaming steel kitchen. With Mum and Oliver gone, it echoed with emptiness.

"Yup." Jade stretched her legs out on the sofa like she was taking ownership. Staking her claim. My new sister. We were a family just like that.

"Just you and me. In this whole big place." I glanced out the windows. It was too dark to see anything but the bright reflections of two strangers playing house. Anyone outside would be able to see everything we were doing, without us having a clue they were there.

"I'm not shy." Jade sat upright, daring me to contradict her. "I just don't like talking, unless I have something to say."

"I get it." Wise. "Me neither." I flicked my watch. "So…" I could feel myself struggling to connect with her on any level, like I was trying to swim in the sky.

"Dad says you've never been to Tahoe before?"

"Nope." Not really in our budget. "Mum was always too busy to travel, I guess."

"Tahoe's our special place." She paused and looked out the window into the night.

"Don't you find it…" I hesitated.

"Boring?" said Jade. Obviously expecting the worst of me.

"No, not that. Just lonely. I mean, it's so quiet, out in the middle of nowhere. Don't you ever get worried, being so far from anyone else?"

Jade smiled. "I love it out here. It's a good place to experience nature, without being interrupted or interrogated."

My face flushed. I hadn't thought what it might be like for her. "It will be cool to explore Tahoe with you." *It will be cool?* Ugh, she must hate me already.

"There's a lot of wildlife. Hope you like bears and mountain lions." Her amber eyes glinted. Now she was teasing me.

"As long as they're not too close." It was seriously dangerous out there.

"Honestly, Tahoe is beautiful, especially when it snows. And the skiing's amazing."

I'd never skied in my life, and I didn't expect to be around long enough to learn. "Sounds great." I gave a small, tight smile.

She fake-smiled back, then went out onto the deck. The French doors shut with a click behind her. I'd failed at her first attempt to connect. This was going to be hard. But it was only for the night. I could survive this. I sighed, resigned to giving it another shot. It was that or circle around each other for the next ten hours, which almost sounded better.

I followed her outside. The wind whispered through the surrounding trees. I leaned over the railings and inhaled a deep breath of musky pine. Oliver was right. There was nothing like Tahoe mountain air for rinsing out grimy, city lungs. The thick darkness took more getting used to. Things moved in the undergrowth. Invisible things, scurrying.

"It's so dark out here." I was thankful for the light of the moon.

"Sometimes at night, when it's really clear, you can see migrating birds flying over," said Jade, staring up at the sky.

"And I thought you were looking at the Milky Way and watching for shooting stars." I looked up just in time to see one fall. "Wow, there's one."

"Yeah, there's a lot of space action out there." She tapped her fingers on the wooden rails. "That's what Dad always looks at."

"Of course, being an astrologist and all."

"Astrophysicist. He studies stars, not signs."

"That's what I meant." I couldn't tell if she was teasing or actually thought I was stupid. Both, probably.

I focused on the bright stars freckling the indigo sky. There were millions of them all clustered together, staring down at Earth. All those planets exploded, galaxies unraveled, and stars were born light-years away. You could never look up and see the present, only images of the past.

"Hear that?" Jade tilted her head as an owl called from nearby. "Great gray owl. Shoot, I should have grabbed my binoculars."

"Why don't you use that?" I pointed at a telescope. The brass casing winked at me through the window.

"Er, no." Jade crossed her arms.

"Er, why?" It was a glare-off.

She arched her brows. "One, you don't use a telescope to bird-watch. Two, Dad will kill you if you touch it because, three, it was Einstein's and it's priceless."

"Yeah, right." She seriously couldn't think I'd fall for that.

"Okay, I'll prove it." She pushed the door open wide.

I followed her inside. The telescope was locked in a glass case, balanced on the sideboard behind the sofa. I ran my finger over the brass inscription, ALBERT EINSTEIN. "For real? And Oliver uses it?"

Jade hesitated, then gave a half nod. "He had it brought it up here so we could see how Einstein saw the stars with his old telescope, compared to how they look through Dad's modern ones. He thought it would be fun."

"Sounds like Oliver." I doubted "we" included me. "If he was planning to use it anyway, would he really be mad if we set it up tonight?"

Jade pursed her lips. "I can find one of Dad's better telescopes, if that's what you want. You can use that old thing when he's back tomorrow, okay?"

I nodded and stared at it wistfully.

"Look, it's on loan. It's not even supposed to be up here. Dad made me promise not to touch it. So we're not going to." She stared into my eyes, daring me to flinch.

"Got it." I smiled reassuringly. "So, do you want to star gaze with your binoculars and listen for owls? Or maybe watch a movie?" I bet they had all the streaming services.

"You can watch a movie. I'm tracking birds." Jade ran downstairs, reappearing seconds later with a pair of binoculars. She draped the throw from the sofa over her shoulders.

"I'll join you," I blurted without thinking. Still, those stars were pretty amazing.

"It gets chilly out here." Jade paused at the door like she thought I couldn't handle a little cold.

I grabbed the fuzzy fleece blanket from the armchair and turned off the lights so we could see the sky in all its glory. Starlight scattered across the velvet night, sparkling the dark with silver brilliance. Even the clouds that gathered at the edges couldn't spoil the effect.

"Wow"—I pointed—"shooting star!"

"That's a satellite," said Jade. "You can tell by its steady motion." We followed its path across the sky. "Keep looking. I'm sure you'll see another actual shooting star soon."

I wasn't so sure, but I lay down on a lounge chair and focused on the night sky.

"And that's...not supposed to happen." Jade's forehead creased with concentration.

I squinted to where she was pointing.

A crack of emerald opened above us. Fragments of torn rays

rippled along the crack's edge—a hem of phosphorescence. Ribbons of light silhouetted the pine trees and flickered like flames, running up and down the length of a giant undulating curtain, swaying in the magnetic wind. Nothing like a meteor shower.

I jumped up, staring.

"The northern lights." Jade murmured it like a spell.

"It can't be." I stood on my tiptoes, like that would help me see better. "I thought they only happened up north, like Scotland or Alaska."

"Yeah"—Jade paused, forehead scrunched, like she was trying to remember something—"but planetary events can push them farther south."

"Planetary events? Like what?" I was totally relying on her to have accessed Oliver's encyclopedic knowledge of astrophysics through osmosis, or birth, or anything.

"Sun storms can cause auroras like this, that knock out satellites and power grids. It happened in Canada." She sucked the air between her teeth.

"And you know that, how?"

"Dad."

I nodded. I was right. Oliver probably had an episode about unusual auroras on his *Astro Professor* podcast series, and Jade probably knew all of them, word for word. It was weird suddenly being related to a geek celebrity. Like winning a prize in a drawing you didn't enter.

A ripple of fuchsia entwined with the luminous ripples of green and pulsed across the sky. We stood motionless, scared to move for fear of it disappearing like a dream. I'm pretty sure I forgot to close my mouth.

"It's amazing," said Jade.

I nodded. My heart was singing. That moment—I clicked an invisible camera in front of my eye—a frozen image to be captured forever, locked in my memory.

We didn't want to leave the back deck, not while the kaleidoscope of auroras was still dancing, but it was freezing, so we bundled up, and lay side by side swaddled in blankets.

The wind whooshed like waves through the trees. Dark clouds rushed over the mountains, snuffing out the stars, cluster by cluster. The auroras faded, then vanished completely. An owl hooted in the distance. A great gray owl according to Jade.

"We should go in, before we freeze to death." I sat up, shivering in the chilled air.

"That was incredible," said Jade. "I'm gonna call Dad. See if he saw it, too." She rushed inside.

"It is their honeymoon!" I shouted after her.

The air chilled. Something rustled in the undergrowth. I hurried inside, locking the night behind me.

"Jade?" I flicked on the wall switch. The light bulb was out. I made my way to the floor lamp, by the dim light of the fire. That one was out too. In the kitchen, the fridge no longer hummed. The dishwasher was mute. I smacked into the corner of the side table, knocking a stack of magazines to the ground. The fake bear-skin rug felt a little too real. The whole cabin was thick with silence.

"Jade, where are you?" Branches swept against the window. "Jade?" I whispered.

The bookshelves loomed. The telescope glinted from its glass cage. I beamed my mobile phone's light along the wall. A masked frogman, with huge eyes and an angled spear, stared at me from a distressed gold frame.

Jade popped up from the stairwell. "I'm right here. I ran down for my charger."

"I can't get the lights to work." I flicked the hall light switch on and off to demonstrate the lack of power.

"Let me see." Little clicks came from all around the kitchen as Jade turned on multiple switches. She went through the living area, double-checking everything I'd already tried. Then ran along to the bathroom and tried there. "Nope. It's all dead," she said. "Nothing works." Her voice echoed in the dark.

3

10:25 p.m.

THIS WAS NOT SUPPOSED TO HAPPEN. "OKAY," I murmured to myself. It was so quiet and dark. I'd gnawed on my lip and licked the blood away.

"It happened, just like I said. The auroras tripped the power grid." She paused, deep in thought.

"What exactly happened in Canada?"

"A nine-hour power failure. Don't worry. We're fine here."

"Yeah, of course." Nine hours. Just get through the night. "Should we check the circuit breakers?" Please let it just be a blown fuse.

"I'll get the flashlights," said Jade.

Such an obvious thing to do, that I hadn't thought of. "Let's get the torches together," I suggested.

"Torches, like flames?"

"Torches, flashlights, whatever. Same difference." England and America, forever divided by a common language.

"Not exactly," Jade said, but she led the way.

I followed her vague outline to the closet by the front door, tripping over a metal bowl and sending it clattering across the floor. My heart went into a frenzy.

"What was that?" Apparently, Jade's did too.

"A dog bowl?" I picked it up. "I didn't know you had a dog."

"We don't." She sighed. "Mom was allergic. And now Dad just can't."

"Oh." I didn't know what else to say. I placed the bowl back against the wall.

Jade opened the closet door. "It was probably from Uncle Marvin's dog. He stays here sometimes. He brought up the Einstein telescope for Dad last week. He's ex-marine, Dad's best friend."

"I bet he'd know what to do in an emergency." I never imagined Jade and Oliver having an extended family. People I didn't even know were suddenly clinging to the branches of my family tree. Unlike Dad, who deliberately broke free.

I took a sharp breath.

"Are you okay?" asked Jade.

"I'm fine." I wasn't about to explain the memories that snuck up and pulled me under like a riptide.

Jade nodded and turned back to the closet. "Here are the flashlights we use for owling." Four Maglites were neatly lined up in a row on the top shelf. She passed me a satisfyingly hefty one and took another for herself. "Look, it's not an emergency. Even if the power's really out, we have food, fire, and water." She paused, feeling further along the shelf. "That's weird. I thought the emergency radio was here too." A packet rustled in her hand. "Dog treats? They must be for Uncle Marvin's dog too." She tossed them back.

"I'm just not used to this pitch-black dark," I said, grinning like it wasn't a big deal.

"Yeah, it's a different level of darkness out here. Perfect for owling and stargazing. That's why Dad and I love it." I could hear the happy memories in her voice.

I followed her across the big room. "This kind of thing must happen all the time—blackouts, I mean, not auroras."

"Not often." She opened the door that led to the garage and a blast of cold air greeted us. "But it happens. People who live here full-time have generators. But we don't come here often enough to need backup power or a landline."

"How often do you come up? Once a month? Twice a year?" The cold crept up my spine.

"Once every few months. It's where Dad feels closest to Mom." Jade bit her lip and opened up the breaker box.

"I'm sorry. It's hard, isn't it?" Oh, so crass. Like she'd want to confide in me. "If ever you want to, like, talk." I was so bad at this. I hated it when people did it to me.

"It was a long time ago. I was six."

I shouldn't have said anything. I changed the topic. "Are the fuses tripped?"

Jade flicked them off and on again. "Nope, they're fine. It's just a good old-fashioned solar flare power cut."

"Do you want to call Oliver?" I so didn't want to call Mum.

"My cell phone's out of charge."

Of course. That's why she'd gone for the charger. I pulled out mine. "No signal."

Back in the main room, the first flecks of snow attached themselves to the windowpanes, and the fire made little popping noises, filling the emptiness. We sat in front of it, staring at the flames. I waited for her to speak, but I guess she didn't have anything to say.

The silence thickened between us. A reminder that nothing was out there but smothering clouds and rummaging creatures. And far off in the distance was the faint rumble of a car engine.

"It's coming closer!" I rushed to the kitchen window, as if I would see anything that far away.

"It must be Dad. I knew he'd come back if he thought there was the slightest chance of danger." Jade shook her head but she smiled. She was actually relieved.

Who could blame her? No more pretending to get along. We could go back to being polite strangers.

A flurry of snow flew into my face as I cracked the front door open. The engine rumble filled the night. It had to be end-of-the-road close.

Jade pushed past me, flashlight in hand, throw wrapped tightly around her shoulders. She stood practically on her tiptoes watching for the Land Rover to appear.

The lights were blinding. At first, I thought it was going to zoom right by, but it swerved at the last minute, screeching the brakes as it slid into the driveway. It was a pickup truck. Red. Not our parents.

The driver beeped the horn four times, like they were picking someone up.

"Shit." Jade rushed back inside, pulling me with her.

I shook her hand from my arm. "We can't just hide," I hissed. "They must have seen us."

Jade crouched by the door.

The truck door creaked open.

I peered through the window. Stupid mistake. The headlights lit up my pale face like a lantern. I opened the door and stood half in half out. "Hello?" Oh so English. "Can I help you?"

A young white guy, with seriously sharp cheekbones, frowned at me through the windshield. Obviously, I was not who he was expecting. He jumped down from the truck.

"Oh no. I think we've come to the wrong place." He grinned. "Sorry to disturb you. We took a wrong turn."

"Hurry it up, AJ!" a guy called from the truck. I got a flash of his green beanie and shiny black jacket.

AJ stamped his black Timberland boots. "I thought this was our friend's cabin, and it obviously isn't. Didn't mean to scare you."

"Oh, we're not scared." I smiled brightly to prove it.

"We?" He tilted his head and looked past me.

Jade appeared at the door and gave a worried smile.

"Yeah, me and my…sister. Stepsister." It sounded so odd.

"Ahh, so you okay with the blackout, and that crazy sky stuff?" He pulled the black beanie off his head and shook out his dirty-blond hair.

I nodded. "Yeah, crazy. But we're fine. It's kinda cold so…" I started to close the door, ready to get back inside.

"Yeah, we're fine," said Jade, with a touch of ice.

25

AJ stepped closer. "I just want to make sure you're okay, since we're here. Do you need help with anything? You here alone?"

"Our parents are due back any second with takeout." Right, because there are so many places to get food in the middle of nowhere, during a blackout.

"Great." He zipped up his jacket. "We'll get going then. Have a good night."

"Thanks. Stay safe." I waved as they peeled out the driveway and beeped their goodbye. And sighed with relief as they disappeared back into the night.

"Stay safe?" Jade arched her brows. "Takeout?"

"I know, I know." I played with the flashlight button. "At least we know we're not the only ones out here." It did make me feel weirdly better.

"Yeah, and they know we're here alone." Jade rubbed her arms to keep warm.

"Look, they just took a wrong turn and wanted to be sure we were okay. That's a nice thing to do," I said.

"I hope you're right." Jade looked out into the dark. "At least they've gone. You should never have opened the door like that."

Yeah, like you weren't so excited thinking Oliver had come back for his precious daughter, I thought.

"At least we're fine as long as we have enough wood to keep this fire going." I laughed.

"I hope so," said Jade. "I guess Dad didn't expect it to be our only source of heat when he made it." She looked at the two small logs at the side of the fireplace.

"What about those?" I pointed to the basket of giant pine cones. Jade shook her head. "They're old and dusty and burn too fast. You know, sometimes Dad stacks firewood downstairs by the back door. I'll go and check."

"I'll come too." I still felt like I was being watched. I knew it was ridiculous. But the big windows in the house made it seem like we were in a goldfish bowl. Our flashlights would be easily visible in the dark night. Not that anyone would be wandering by, out here in the middle of nowhere.

We made our way down the stairs to the back door without saying a word. The cabin creaked around us.

"That's weird." Jade pointed to the empty hook next to the door. "Key's missing." She tried the door handle. The door swung open. "Shit, Uncle Marvin must have forgotten to lock it and gone off with the key. Dad will be furious."

We huddled outside around a small stack of wood. From the look on Jade's face, I guessed Uncle Marvin had depleted that supply too. We carried the three remaining logs back inside. Jade bolted the back door behind us.

"It's getting pretty chilly out there." I shook the snow from my hair.

"Yeah," Jade said, taking the stairs two at a time. "We should stay in the main room by the fire until the power comes back."

"Good idea." I hugged myself warm. It was amazing how fast the cabin cooled down once the central heating stopped working.

Back upstairs our flashlight beams made the world outside seem darker, a world of whispers, branches scraping against cabin walls, and snow dancing on glass.

"How far do you think this blackout goes?" I tapped my fingers on the wooden floor then stopped so Jade wouldn't think I was anxious, or restless, or worried, or anything like that at all.

"It's off-season. Most of the cabins out here are still empty so their lights won't be on anyway. Could be one mile or twenty." Jade's voice ricocheted across the cathedral ceiling.

"Great." Cold curled in under the windowsills. The fire gave a small amount of heat but highlighted the dark around us. Black, on black, on black—near shadows with darker shadows hiding behind them. "Should we add another log?"

Snow pattered against the window.

"Yeah, but we'll need them to last all night if the power…" Jade pursed her lips.

I got it. Saying it out loud made the possibility too real. I opened the glass doors to the fireplace and placed two giant Tahoe pine cones from the nearby basket onto the dying embers instead. They caught fast, blazing to almost nothing in seconds.

"Those aren't meant for fires," said Jade. "Use…"

I balanced a log on top of the flames as she spoke. "This?" I asked. The log fizzed and smoked. "Sorry, not that."

"No, not the damp logs." Jade coughed and fanned the smoke away. She coughed again. "Dry, never damp," she said between wheezes.

"You okay? Is it asthma?" I poked the damp log away from the flames. "I'm really sorry."

Jade nodded as she caught her breath. "I only get it around… smoke and cold air." She took a deep breath, slow in and out. "I'll be right back." She disappeared down the stairwell and came back two minutes later, clutching an inhaler. "See. I'll be fine." She took two puffs.

"You sure?"

"The miracle of modern science." She smiled to let me know she was fine, everything was okay, and having a stepsister who didn't even know how to make a safe fire was totally normal.

"Alright then. I'll fix this." I cracked the fireplace doors back open, and placed a dry log on top of the smoldering pine cones. The flames flickered, reluctantly at first, before running along the top of the log and bursting brightly as they fell onto the pine cones. We had fire again. I slammed the glass doors shut and grinned at Jade. "Crisis averted!"

"Yay," said Jade unenthusiastically. "I wonder if they have power in Reno."

"They'd call, right?" I checked my phone again. No signal. "Which would go to voice mail."

Jade frowned. "Yeah, and if I don't answer his calls or text him, Dad will freak out and drive back."

I shook my head. "That doesn't make sense. It would be dangerous to drive back in the pitch black, with no streetlights, and, anyway, they know we're together, two competent teens, right? We have fire, torches, food—why would they spoil their honeymoon to check on us when they know we're fine?" There was no way Mum would ruin her night worrying about me.

Jade continued like I hadn't spoken. "I just don't want him to be worried."

"He trusts you. Whatever happens, right? Smart scientific daughter and all that."

"True." Her shoulders relaxed.

"Hey, you're not wheezing anymore." My foot tapped restlessly against the floorboards.

Jade glanced down the stairs. "We should get more blankets to stay warm, so that we don't need to make a big fire and use all the logs too fast." Her shadow chased her flashlight beam down the stairwell.

The flames flickered and dwindled in the fireplace. A nagging seed of doubt sprouted in my gut. I avoided looking at the black expanse outside for fear of how big and empty it was, and how awful it would be if a face appeared at the window. I tried to shake the thought from my head, but it stayed in there, banging around the sides of my skull.

I could hear every movement Jade made, bounding down the stairs, creaking open the door, running across her room. Then nothing. What was she doing? I waited for her to come back up. There was nothing down there, just the wind making unfamiliar noises, rattling against the windows, blowing down the chimney. We'd go to sleep and wake up and that would be it, night done, and we could go home, and I could get on with the rest of my life. Except I couldn't. I swallowed hard. I didn't have a home. We'd left San Francisco. This was my new life. Forced time with Jade, playing besties in the weekend cabin, while Mum went off with Oliver. My head throbbed.

Jade emerged, carrying a pillow and a huge puffy quilt. She'd put on an extra sweater. This was probably the worst night she'd ever had, stuck in the dark and cold with me.

"Alright, Jade?" I asked my fellow prisoner.

"Yep." She laid her bedding down near the fire. "You should get more layers on in case the fire goes out while we're sleeping."

I hadn't even thought of that. I didn't have that many clothes with me.

"There's spare fleeces and Dad's old Morehouse College sweatshirts in the coat closet if you don't want to go downstairs again."

I nodded and walked to the coat closet. I threw on the first fleece I touched. It was a bit too big, but it was soft and warm. I gathered up all the artfully folded throws from the sofa to make a blanket fort. "Want to make s'mores or tell ghost stories or anything?"

"Let's not pretend this is a fun sleepover." Jade buried herself under her quilt.

"Alright then." That was one way to make the night go quicker. I huddled by the fire. The cabin grew extra rooms around us in the dark. The walls were higher, the corridors longer, the creaks louder. Swaddled in night, sounds became sharper: the crackle of fire, the dust of snow on the windowpanes, and the faint crunching of very careful, very quiet, footsteps.

4

11:15 p.m.

I FROZE, WAITING TO HEAR THAT SOUND AGAIN. IT
wasn't the wind or the snow: it was a slow, deliberate crunch, like a
boot trying to tread silently. I could hear Jade's even breathing. At
least she was asleep.

It could be my mother and Oliver, coming back early. Jade said
they might return. But Mum wouldn't worry about waking us.
She'd be fists pounding on the door, or car horn blaring to wake
me. And even if Oliver preferred a calmer entrance, he had a key, so
there would be no reason to creep around the back. I wondered if it
could be the guys from earlier, but the sound of their truck engine
would be pretty unmissable. Anyway, they'd just knock at the door.
No need to sneak around.

I shivered and checked my phone in case Mum had texted. Still
no signal. The wind dropped. My breathing, my heartbeat, the fire

popping, filled the hollow room with sharp, quick sounds. So much space, so much dark, so much nothing surrounding us.

We were so alone—no people walking, no familiar sounds of sirens, tires screeching, or late-night cheers. Here in the mountains, every sound was amplified and alien. Were bears nocturnal animals? Even if they were, I doubted they'd be trying to walk softy.

A chill crept across the back of my neck. I'd felt this dread before, years ago, curled up in the car, watching snow cover the windows, listening intently for Dad's footsteps, and waking alone in the frozen dawn. I dug my nails into my palms, willing myself back to the present. I was in the cabin. I was safe. No one was abandoning anyone.

I pulled out my journal and doodled a hedgehog next to my last poem. *Push me, push me, push me off. I'm sinking anyway.* My tortured-soul journal, according to my mother. Not that I'd ever let her read it.

The swing in the front yard grated, metal against metal, as the wind pushed it. Out the window trees swayed and the sky hung low, a hammock of dark clouds. Nothing to worry about.

Jade was probably right; if they had a power outage, Oliver would want to come back and Mum would convince him we could handle it. But if Oliver thought for one second Jade was in any danger, he'd be back straight away. So either Oliver didn't think there was any danger at all, or else it was so small he trusted we could handle it. Or at least that Jade could.

She obviously loved the mountains, being alone in the middle of nowhere, surrounded by nature, squirrels, deer, and bears with long, evil claws. I held myself as I listened for a footstep, as if I could hear anything above my heart thudding in the hollow space.

If someone was out there, they'd been standing still a long time. They could be frozen. Or it could have been nothing at all. I overthought things, turning everything dark into something deadly. Too many horror movies, Mum would say. Born from experience, I'd snap back.

I took a deep breath and focused on the wind gathering strength outside and waited for the sound of shingles flying off the roof, or trees crashing into the cabin. Calm yourself. I focused on the crackle of fire, Jade's steady breathing, and the tiny, soft tick of my watch.

A rattle came from the back door downstairs. A key in a lock.

My heart lurched. I seized the flashlight, swinging the beam to flood the stairs with light. The rattle stopped.

"What the actual?" Jade sat bolt upright. Not asleep then.

We crept in silent agreement, down the stairs, one step at a time, backs against the wall. I led the way, mouth dry, flashlight in hand, ready. Not ready. A chill raced down my spine. A branch scrapped against the window. That couldn't be all it was. Branches don't sound like rattling keys. We froze.

I could feel eyes on me, tracking my every move. I turned off my flashlight and faded into the darkness. If anyone was there, they'd have a hard time seeing me. I tightened my jaw. I'd got this.

"Do you think it's the guys from earlier?" Jade asked, eyes wide.

I shook my head. "Why would they come back?"

To my left, the long corridor stretched into infinite black; to my right, Jade's bedroom door swayed slightly where she'd left it ajar. I shut it. In the daylight, the ground floor would be flooded with sunshine, but at night, the only things down there were loneliness and nightmares.

A low whine came from outside—an animal right by the back door. I edged closer, peering out the window into dense black, heart thumping in my throat. A scrabble, then silence. I held my breath, waiting for the next sound. Shit, shit, shit. I so did not want to be down there with whatever it was. God, make it be nothing. I closed my eyes, took a deep breath, and opened them again. Nothing. It was nothing.

Jade crouched at the back door beside me. "Could be a porcupine," she whispered.

"Then why are you whispering?" I whispered back.

The cabin was solid wood, steel, and thick glass. It wasn't like anything was going to crash through the door. I placed my hands on the cold windowpane, as if I could feel the shape of the nothing that was out there.

Silence washed over us, stretching into the corners.

"Hear that?" Jade frowned.

I scrunched up my face. "No, I don't."

"There, I heard it again." Jade leaned her ear against the door. "Like a..."

"Snuffle, a definite snuffle." Only animals snuffled. "You were right, probably a porcupine." I was relieved.

A dog barked. Followed by a voice. *Shushhh!*

Someone was out there.

5
11:36 p.m.

THEN... NOTHING. WE LISTENED, NOT DARING TO MOVE in case we missed another sound. But after sitting still for at least ten minutes of silence, it seemed that no one was there.

The cold pushed through the windowpane. I stood, releasing the pins and needles that had gathered at my feet. "Whoever was there has gone."

"How can you be sure?" Jade asked.

"The dog would have barked again by now. Its owner probably called it away and they're long gone." Assuming there was only one owner and one dog. "They were probably just out for a walk." That made the most sense. Being out this late at night in the snow and the cold, trying to break into a cabin, made no sense at all. "There's no way they'd be this patient, and keep a dog that quiet for so long. Come on." I tapped her arm, but she stood rooted, listening.

"Okay," I whispered. "We'll go to my room and look out that

window. They won't expect us to do that, if anyone's still there."
And then we can finally go to sleep, wake up, and this nightmare
night will be over. We crept along to my room, at the end of the
long corridor. A single bed covered in thin vintage quilts and an
oval mirror that refracted the light weirdly, like seeing reality as a
sepia print. I held my hands together to stop them from trembling
and blew on them to keep them warm.

"They could be waiting for us go back upstairs," said Jade.

I peeked through the blinds. "No one's out there, just a lot of
blustery trees." And deep shadows where people could be hiding.

"It feels like we're being watched." Jade rubbed her goose-
bumped arms. "I'm freezing."

"Yeah, me too." The dark crept in around us.

A branch scraped the window. We both jumped then laughed
nervously.

I let out a deep breath. "We're just scaring each other."

Tap, tap, tap.

At the back door. Not a branch.

"Holy crap." Jade looked at me, wide-eyed.

The stairs were just past the back door, our only escape route. The
hallway seemed to grow longer with every step toward the staircase.

A shadow moved on the other side of the back door.

We flattened ourselves against the wall to stay out of sight. This
could not be happening.

"Hello?" He sounded young, unsure of himself, nervous, even.
The dog barked. It was a trick; it had to be. Pretend to be nervous,
make us feel sorry for him.

Jade grabbed my wrist. "Don't open the door."

"I know that," I hissed at her. "Do you think I'm stupid?" Obviously, yes.

"Can you help? I'm lost." He put his hand to the glass, peering like he could make us out in the pitch dark. "Hey, I know you're in there. I saw your flashlight. I'm just looking for some directions, and maybe some water for my dog?" He looked about my age, cold and worried. Still, before he saw the light, he'd been trying to break in.

"You can't come in." I banged on the window.

"What the hell?!" Jade shouted at me. "Now he knows we're here."

"He knew anyway," I snapped back.

"Hey, got a map?" He grinned. A small flashlight beamed from his right hand. Snow freckled his dark hair.

I smiled back, caught by surprise. Then I clenched my jaw. "No. Use Google Maps!" I yelled through the glass.

"No signal." He shrugged, eyes twinkling in his flashlight. He turned his beam on me. God, I couldn't stop blinking. The flashes felt like they were trapped in my retinas. I rubbed my eyes to get the flickers out.

Jade pushed in front of me. "No maps here, either." Like that would make him leave.

"Can I come in and warm up for a few minutes? It's only me and my dog. My dog's friendly." He rubbed his hands together and shifted his weight from one foot to the other.

I glanced down at my hands, which looked like plastic limbs, appendages stuck on the ends of my wrists. Not mine, not mine at all. "Jade?" Shit. I couldn't remember what I was going to ask. My head pounded. Not now, please not now. I struggled to calm my breathing.

"Lottie." Jade's voice was soft, worried. "You okay?"

I closed my eyes. I was going to be sick. "I'm fine." I so didn't need one of my infamous migraines to start right then. I swallowed, willing it away.

The dog whined, nose to the door. It sounded so sad and cold.

It *was* cold.

The guy tapped again. "It's snowing out here. If you're going to let us in, can you be quicker?"

Jade looked from the guy back to me. "He does sound freezing."

He could sit in the bloody jacuzzi for all I cared. Oh shit, of course, no electricity, no hot water. Not that I'd really make him do that. There was nowhere else nearby for him to go.

I unbolted the door and cracked it open. "We can't let you in, sorry. But I can tell you roughly where you are." Like that was so badass of me. I could feel Jade rolling her eyes.

I shone the flashlight on him. He was Asian—cute in a sparkling-eyed, skinny kind of way. Probably used to his charm and looks getting him exactly what he wanted. Disarming people with his grin. Like me. I clenched my jaw.

He shielded his face from the light. "Can you lower it, please?"

"She has no idea where we are, but I do." Jade to the rescue. "Where are you headed?"

"Okay, hold on." He took out his phone and tapped his map app. "It can't find my location. It's like we're in parallel non-magnetized world." He looked up expectantly, like everyone was always kind to him. Like we would be too.

"No," said Jade, her face pinched and serious. "It was solar flares. They knocked the cell signal out. You must have seen the auras— big green spirals in the sky?"

"Ah. That's what those were." Snow fluttered around his jet-black hair. "Can I step in a moment to get a better look?"

Jade looked at me. My head throbbed behind my right eye. I couldn't see her face properly. I hesitated, with my hand on the door frame, and in that second a massive bolt of white-and-black fur shoved past me and went bounding up the stairs.

"No!" Jade raced after the dog.

Then the guy was in the cabin. All six-foot-something of him, towering over me. I couldn't move, think, or speak. I just stared up at him, trying to stop his face from swirling.

"Oh shit." He glanced up the staircase. "I'm so, so, sorry. I'll get him." He ran up taking the stairs two at a time. "Otis, Otis, here boy."

What the hell just happened? Snow gust in, lowering the temperature from frigid to freezing. I slammed the door shut. Dog paws padded above my head, along with footsteps and laughter. Laughter? I clamped my mouth and ran for the bathroom.

The metal bowl spun across the floor. "He's probably thirsty," said Jade. "I'll get him some water." She filled the bowl to the brim. So much for letting him in for just a moment.

"Thanks," the guy said, bending down to ruffle the enormous dog's ears.

"Well, this is cozy." I couldn't keep the sarcasm out of my voice. I'd made my way upstairs, barely five minutes later, to find everyone in best-buds mode.

"You let him in." Jade bent down to cuddle the dog, which was hard because his tail was whacking everything around it. "Anyway, he can't be that bad, he's got a good dog. You can tell a lot about people from their dogs."

I swallowed. My mouth felt dank and tasted weirdly astringent. Focusing was still hard, but neither of them noticed, which was a relief, and also kind of annoying.

"Thanks for letting me in." The guy leaned against the kitchen counter, staring at me. His black puffer jacket was unzipped over his purple hoodie. He'd taken off his black beanie, freeing his messy black hair. Damp strands of it covered his right eye.

I blinked. Zigzags of flashing black and white arched across my vision. "Why are you even out here?" The zigzags grew in size, swirling in and out of my eyes.

"I got disoriented by the snow and lost all sense of direction." He turned to Jade. "I'm trying to get back to my aunt's place, Wolf Creek Way?"

Jade frowned. "Sounds like it's in a ski resort. Do you know which one?"

"NorthStar?" he said uncertainly, looking out the window. "Is that far?"

"A few miles." Jade patted the dog's enormous head. "I can draw you a map. It's easy once you get to the main road. Kind of far on foot." She looked down at his black Chelsea boots.

"Yeah, don't I know it. A map would be awesome. I got so turned around out there. Just taking my dog for a walk, and before I knew it, well, here I am." He ruffled his dog's fluffy head. "I'm Alex, by the way, and your new best friend is Otis."

Otis ran to the metal bowl, nudging it occasionally, as if to check if it had been magically refilled.

"A Saint Bernard, right?" Jade beamed at Alex.

"Yep, that's right." He grinned back.

"I'm Jade, and that's…"

"Jade, got any notepaper so Alex can be on his…" Shit. I pointed outside, having lost the word for *way*.

"That's Lottie." Jade said my name like it was a bad taste, then filled the bowl with more water for the dog.

Otis emptied it in seconds. Not a drop spilled. Then he jumped up and licked her face. Priorities.

Finally, Jade grabbed a notebook and drew a simple map. "Here we are, and here is the main road. You must have wandered off onto the fire road in the dark."

I swayed slightly, with my hand over my mouth. "You should…" I pointed to the front door.

"Guess you're right," said Alex, watching me carefully for any chance that I would let him stay. "Are you okay? You look kind of sick."

"Yep." A dull ache throbbed behind my left eye. I nodded my head, leaving a blur around the edges of everything.

Alex frowned. "You sure?" Half of his face was crystal clear: his left eyebrow, his cheekbone, the corner of his left eye; the other half of his face was a shadow.

I winced. It was gathering force. I couldn't surrender. I couldn't speak. I couldn't see. I hadn't had one this bad in over a year.

"Lottie, what's wrong?" Jade's words rang in my ears, shockingly loud and clear.

I whimpered, "Migraine."

Perfect triangles of black and white, etched with neon, yellow, green, and red, pranced across my eyes. I swallowed a wave of nausea, swayed toward the sofa, and sunk deep down into its cushions. My stomach rolled around my feet, and everything fell into slow motion. I panted to keep from puking. Squeezed my eyes tight to block the pain and let everything fade to black.

DAY TWO

October 26

6
12:45 a.m.

MY EYES WOULDN'T FOCUS. SNATCHES OF LIGHT sparked against darkness, tumbling, flickering. It was still dark, still night, still with a fire flicking in the corner.

"God, Lottie, are you okay?" Jade clasped my hand. "You were so out of it."

I swallowed down the bile before I could speak. "Need, pain… meds."

"Where are they?" Alex asked.

I clutched my head. "Don't know." Each word stabbed like a dagger in my temples.

"Bathroom cupboard," said Jade. "Downstairs."

Pain, pain pounded behind my squinting eyes. "Quickly."

"I'll get them." She ran downstairs.

Alex crouched next to me. "Can I help? You look like you might puke."

"I'm fine." I held on to the sofa for balance and pushed myself all the way up, swaying slightly as I stood.

"I'll get some water." Alex rushed to the kitchen and came back with a tepid glassful.

"Thanks." I couldn't see the edges of the glass to pick it up. Every thought hurt. The connections between my synapses were sparking electric shocks and zapping my brain.

Otis pushed his wet nose into my hand. I gave him a pat on the head.

"Here." Jade pushed a giant-sized bottle of ibuprofen into my hand. "From your mom's stock." Of course she'd have plenty of meds.

"How long was I out?" I whimpered.

"Thirty minutes," said Jade, checking her watch.

I shook out three red pills. They felt like stones going down. As long as they worked, I'd be fine, slow, but fine. If they didn't, I had about ten minutes before I wouldn't be able to think or even speak. I retched and swallowed back the bile. My head thudded. I needed to go back to sleep and lose myself in total silence and darkness.

But, there was Alex. Who hadn't killed us yet.

I peered at him. He was just a lost teen with a giant dog, who'd fetched me glass of water. Possibly. I squeezed my eyes together. It hurt to think.

"Come and sit by the fire. You'll feel better," said Alex and led me by the hand.

"Thank you." I felt pathetically grateful to be guided. I listened to the pop of the fire, and the plop of the snow, and pulled a blanket around me.

"We've been talking," Jade said, sending Alex a quick, sweet smile, "while you were sleeping. It's crazy cold out there and so late that it's stupid for Alex to try and find his way in the dark. I said he could stay until morning." She jutted out her chin, daring me to disagree.

"By morning there'll be enough light for me to find my way, even if the signal's still out," Alex added. "And I'll be out of your hair like I was never here." He smiled.

It's not like I had a choice. I nodded, which hurt like hell. "Promise you'll leave first thing, before Oliver and Mum get back, or we will all be dead." Wow, that was an exhausting sentence.

"I promise." Alex bowed his head solemnly.

"Good." Jade patted the floor. Otis bounded over and snuggled up against her, as if he'd known her his whole life. "No offense, Lottie, but you look terrible. You should sleep."

Alex poked at the failing fire. "She's right. Let the meds do their job and sleep it off."

Just what I needed as my face was falling off—the two of them uniting against me. "I'm fine," I mumbled. The word *risk* spiraled around my mind. There was something I was missing, something I'd forgotten. Something important, a reason I shouldn't trust Alex, and I couldn't find it. It was in there floating around my malfunctioning brain.

Risk.

Risk.

Risk, risk, risk.

The word lost all meaning and became a hissed warning instead.

"Hey, here's another blanket." Jade tucked it around me. "We can all sleep around the fire." She glanced at Alex, who grinned back at her.

I stifled a yawn. No way was I falling asleep with Alex roaming the cabin.

"Yeah, I'm wiped out too." Alex eyed the telescope case. "What's that?"

"Just an old telescope," said Jade, gathering her quilt around her like a nest.

Alex skimmed his thumb over the brass plaque. "Who's the science enthusiast?"

"Oliver," I said.

"Dad," Jade answered at the same time. "He uses it sometimes."

"Priceless," I murmured.

Jade glared at me, hard enough to make my whole face squint.

"You'll have to tell me about it in the morning," said Alex with a smile.

The dog nuzzled into Jade's side.

Alex curled up on the leather La-Z-Boy, using his jacket as a blanket. "Okay, everyone?" asked Alex. "Lights out." And he turned off his flashlight.

I stared into the tiny flickers of flame, watching until they became orange ribbons and fluttered across the floor, dancing in my visions, like auroras dancing across the skies. I dug my fingernails into my palms to keep myself from drifting away and watched the shadow that was Alex watching the shadow that was me.

7

4:02 a.m.

A CHILL CREPT ACROSS MY NECK. I SAT BOLT UPRIGHT.
Jade was snuggled next to Otis, both snoring softly. No Alex, just
a black backpack lying against the sofa. The front door swayed
slightly in the wind.

Bright, white light dazzled through the kitchen window. The
rumble of an engine purred from the driveway. Shit, Alex had gone
out there, propping the door open with a snow boot, leaving his
dog behind. Maybe he'd found a ride. Yes, in the middle of the night
standing in the snow. God, think, think, think.

I shook my fuzzy head and peered from the kitchen window. An
oversized red pickup truck with huge snow tires idled in the driveway. I knew that truck. AJ and his friend were back.

Clumps of snow, falling slow and steady, were spotlighted by the
headlights. Alex leaned into the driver's-side window and laughed,
loud, hollow, and fake. He glanced back at the cabin. I ducked

down, counting to twenty before daring to look again. Was Alex the friend they were looking to pick up earlier? He wouldn't be hanging off the door like that if he didn't know them. But his laugh sounded worried. Maybe it wasn't them. Maybe it was a different truck. I chanced another look.

Yep. Even from this far, it was definitely them. AJ's chiseled features were hard to miss—sharp jaw, high cheekbones, like a model. The other guy was easier to see this time. He looked a little younger than AJ, late teens or early twenties, with a round face, light brown skin, and dark curly hair. His beanie was pulled low over his ears and an oil-slick black puffer jacket was zipped up to his neck. I edged closer to the window, to listen better without being seen.

"We don't like to be kept waiting," I could hear AJ saying. "Isn't that right, Nico?"

So that was the other guy's name.

AJ flicked his cigarette butt at Alex and pointed at the kitchen. I squashed myself against the wall, not daring to poke my head around in case he'd see me. I was pretty sure I'd be better off if they didn't know I was watching.

"No problem," Alex said, voice slightly raised. "Fast asleep."

My heart rattled. He might not mean us. Or they might be checking if we are still okay. He might be asking for a ride to his aunt's and saying she'll be fast asleep. Or they could be asking Alex for directions. Again. In the middle of the night. Having been lost here earlier. It didn't add up. Those were a lot of people to be lost in one night.

"No, tomorrow." Alex swept his hair from his face. "I'll see to it when they've gone."

When they've gone. He meant us. Something was very wrong. That nagging doubt I'd had before I fell asleep, that's what I should've listened to.

"Time to find out who you are, Alex." I dragged his backpack over. As long as the truck was idling and I could hear the murmur of voices, I'd be safe. I tipped everything out—fleece, pack of boxer shorts, three striped socks, blue beanie. Why was he packed for an overnight stay if he was already staying at his aunt's? A wallet; *Taken*, a sci-fi paperback, much faded and dog-eared; two black, fine-tipped ink pens, a spiral sketch pad, and a toothbrush.

I flicked open the pad. It was full of tiny, detailed line drawings of insects, beetles mostly. I tore a page out, folded it carefully into four, and slipped it into my back pocket. Evidence that he'd been here, even if he disappeared on us later.

Funny, I didn't remember him arriving with a backpack.

He could've had it stashed in the cabin. He could have been staying here for days. That would explain why he was dressed so badly for snow, if he'd just slipped out, not expecting us to be there when he came back. No wonder he was so bloody frozen. If my head hadn't been so fuzzed, I'd never have let him in. I didn't let him in. He'd let his dog push his way in.

Otis woke and ran to the door. I stopped him and pulled the door shut. The last thing I needed was Alex dragging Otis back in and discovering what I was up to. I listened at the door for a few moments, just to be sure they were still talking, then refocused on Alex's backpack. The contents didn't scream psycho killer, but he was up to something. I nosed through Alex's wallet. No cash, no credit card, a driver's license in the name of Alex Youn, a Contra Costa library card, and a little black Moleskine notebook. I flicked the elastic band off, opened up the notebook, and scanned the first page: names, items, numbers. Dread crept into my veins. They were all ski resorts: Donner, Palisades, NorthStar. I frowned. NorthStar, 2345, Wolf Hollow Chase. That was the address that popped into his head when he was asking for directions. It could be his aunt's, or he could have faked his way in, using his dog to make us trust him. Well trust Jade, anyway. If it wasn't for my stupid migraine, I'd never have fallen for his act.

Alex must have been pretty freaked out if he had been staying here at the cabin and came back to find it suddenly occupied. If he'd seen the fire and our flashlights upstairs, that would explain why he tried creeping in downstairs. If he'd been waiting out there ever since we arrived, that feeling of being watched hadn't been my imagination.

So many ifs. I was torn between confronting Alex and hiding that I suspected anything. He'd tried to break into the cabin, and now he was in, he didn't want to leave. That was all I knew for sure.

"They won't know." Alex's voice grew louder. "Leave it to me." He made it sound like we were puppets in his hands.

I glanced at the knife rack in the kitchen. The steel glinted silver in the light. No, it wouldn't come to that. I peeked out the window again.

Alex extracted his forearm from AJ's grip, stepped back, and scratched his neck. He glanced at the cabin then back to the truck. He said something I couldn't catch that made Nico laugh. They had seemed so nice. Maybe they were just friends who happened to run into each other. In the middle of the night at someone else's cabin. Yeah, right.

AJ shoved Alex's shoulder, just hard enough to know he would give worse if he needed to. A warning. A pit of dread squirmed in my gut. I'd seen Mum on the receiving end of those types of warnings with past boyfriends, though thankfully not since Oliver. I didn't need to be around that kind of intimidation again.

Otis pattered back to Jade, flopping down like he'd been there forever.

That was it. A key rattled in the door before I went down there. Alex hadn't just arrived. He had the missing spare key. He'd been staying, thinking no one would use it off-season. Somehow, he'd blindsided us into thinking he was lost. And it had worked, big-time. Crap. No wonder Otis raced upstairs for the bowl. He knew where everything was already. No wonder Alex was so cold. He didn't expect to be locked out for hours before he could sneak back in. A shiver ran down my spine. Who the hell was he, and what was he doing here?

The truck door slammed. I rushed to stuff everything back and shoved his backpack across the floor. It hit the fireplace. A spark flew up, landing on it, leaving a tiny gray smudge.

Jade rolled over. "Where are you?" she asked sleepily.

Otis snuggled tighter into her side.

"Right here," I whispered. Jade could have meant Oliver or Alex. I'm pretty sure she didn't care where I was. Her eyes moved into deep REM. Not faking it this time.

Alex could have bound and gagged us in our sleep, but he didn't, so he wasn't here for us.

The truck wheels squealed as they spun away. I skidded back to the fireplace and curled myself into a tiny ball beneath the blankets.

The front door creaked as Alex entered. "Lottie?" he whispered.

I felt him hovering right there, over my head.

"I know you're awake." He poked me with his foot. "Doors don't close by themselves."

I played dead. Jade's first instinct was right: *We can't let him in.* Alex was here for a reason. I just needed to figure out what it was, before we got caught up in any kind of trouble.

8

6:05 a.m.

"WE'RE GOING TO NEED A BIGGER FIRE."

I woke with a start. The danger of pretending to be asleep was *actually* falling asleep. I looked at the world between my fingers. Alex crouched in front of me, staring through his long, straight bangs. Alex, the enemy.

"What?" I rubbed the sleep from my eyes and pulled my blanket tighter. A thick grayness filled the room, the dim before dawn.

"It's snowing harder. The power's still out, and so is the cell signal." Alex waited for me to say something. Snow splattered against the window, as if to prove his point.

My mouth felt like the inside of a snail's shell: slimy, with a touch of grit. Still the three of us. Still alive. TV still there. No new strangers. I checked my watch. "Why are you up at six?"

"It froze in here overnight." Alex rubbed his hands together.

That's what happens when you leave the front door open.

"And I wanted to restart the fire and maybe get some coffee going, before you both woke up freezing cold." He said it like we were in this fun camping adventure together.

I scrunched my nose up as Otis gave me an oversized lick on the face.

"He likes you," said Alex. "He has good instincts."

"Mmm." I wasn't so sure. Alex didn't even look tired. His T-shirt wasn't even creased. I wondered if he'd actually slept at all.

"I washed already. A splash of water and clean teeth is great for making you feel alive." He said it with a grin, in that annoying I-know-what-you-were-thinking way, only if he did, he'd be a lot less nice to me.

And, actually, my breath probably stunk of puke, so maybe he didn't mean it nicely at all.

I pushed Jade's arm gently to see if she was awake. She blinked like she'd forgotten I was there. Then frowned when she remembered. "Still alive then?"

"Apparently." I leaned back, so I wasn't scarily in her face. "It was just a migraine. Painful but not life threatening." I smiled, like it was nothing.

"Great, we all survived." She sat up, pulled back her hair, and rearranged it into a tight bun on top of her head. Going from the sleep of the dead to absolutely awake in seconds. "Is the power back?"

"Not yet." I tried the light switch, realizing I'd only taken Alex's word for it. But he was right, there wasn't any power, and the snow was still steadily falling.

Jade gave Otis a hug and Alex a grin. "Thanks for the loan. He kept me warm."

"Anytime." Alex turned to me and smiled. "Good to see you can talk now."

I shivered. "You're right. We need to warm this place up." It was freezing outside of my blanket cocoon.

"Dad will be back soon," Jade said. "We can go somewhere fun for breakfast, like Soto's. They have the best shakes and doughnuts."

"Shakes in the snow? Was that an invitation?" asked Alex.

"No," Jade and I said at the same time. Something else in common then.

"Anyway, if the power's out here, it will be out there too." I stared at the snow-covered windows.

Jade sighed. "You're right. Thanks for dashing my doughnut dreams." But she gave a tiny smile. "Hopefully it will be back soon and then we can go."

"Yep, hopefully." I tried not to sound too cynical.

I had about two hours max to get rid of Alex. Or the real danger would be explaining to Mum why there was a guy in the house. She'd expect the worst—of me, anyway—and I'd be grounded for a hundred years. "You should go while it's light, before the snow builds up even more," I told Alex. I didn't care what he was up to. I just wanted him to leave. "You promised you'd leave early."

"Soto's won't be open this early in the season, anyway. Not enough customers," said Alex, ignoring me completely.

"So wait, how do you know about Soto's if you don't know your way around here?" I frowned at him.

"Like I said, I got disoriented in the dark and the snow. I didn't say I'd never stayed at my aunt's before." He was right, but it still felt wrong.

"Mr. Soto will be there. He'll open up for us. He and Dad are friends." Jade grinned. "We're the only BIPOC in the hood." Then she looked at me and paused. "I didn't mean...I'm sure he'd welcome you too."

"It's strange, isn't it? This new situation." I smiled my best caring-sister smile.

"You could say that." Jade stared out the window.

Alright then. Even thinking of myself as a sister felt weird.

Alex prodded the fire with the poker. It had reduced to a mound of ash scattered over a few crusty logs. "I'll build this fire back up. As a thank-you for not throwing me out last night."

"And then you'll go." I stared at him, arms crossed, unmoving.

"Sure." He got on his hands and knees and poked at the ashes. "You got any more firewood?"

"Not much," said Jade, looking at me.

"Alright, I'm sorry. I wasted a log. I didn't know how to build a friggin' fire." There were only two dry logs left. I threw one on and struck a match. "It's all we've got, until our parents come back." It went out immediately.

"No, not like that. Here." Alex grabbed a newspaper, shredded the pages, and bundled them into a loose paper ball. "First you need kindling." He grinned at me. "Eagle Scout training."

I didn't grin back.

Jade went over to supervise. "You know there's a stack of

recycled paper waste for that, in the kitchen too." Now she remembers.

"This is fine to get it started." Alex struck a new match, setting the paper on fire before replacing the log on top.

"At least it's there if we need it," said Jade. She stayed mesmerized by Alex's fire-starting technique. "Oh, that's cool, a pyramid of paper. I normally crunch it up under the logs." Great, geeks bonding over fire building.

Otis snuffled around the closet. He could probably smell the dog treats Uncle Marvin left.

I pulled out the Tahoe guide from the bookshelf and passed it to Alex. "It's almost light. We can find you a real map and get you on your way." I could be amazingly helpful when I didn't have a migraine.

Alex placed it on the floor. "So, I've been thinking. About my aunt's, since it's snowing so hard, and I've proved that I'm trustworthy, and not a dangerous murderer." He raised his brows at me. "Maybe I could stay until your parents get back, and then catch a ride?"

"Well, I was thinking, it's best you go now." A gust of wind buffeted against the roof. "Unless you want to witness my mum killing me for letting you in?" I knew for sure Oliver wouldn't be blaming Jade.

Jade blew on her hands and rubbed them together. "I don't know. They wouldn't have wanted us to let Alex freeze out there. Dad would have helped him, if he was here."

Of course he would. What perfect dad wouldn't?

"I don't think they'll mind. Do you, Lottie? Not when they see how helpful he's been and how cute Otis is." Jade was all about the dog. "And how bad your migraine was."

Helpful how? "Yeah, and you're not the one who'll be blamed." I glared at Alex.

He just smiled. "They won't mind when they find out how you saved a lost kid and his dog from freezing to death in the snow. Like Jade said, they'll take you out for breakfast, right?" He patted the rug for Otis to come and sit next to him. "They can drop me off on the way." He was so bloody charming. Mum would eat it right up. And it wasn't like I had proof that he'd done anything. I could have gotten it wrong, jumped to conclusions from a lifetime of assuming the worst and being right. But the key…

I flicked my fingernails with my thumb. "I don't know."

He raised his brows, daring me to kick him out. "It's the perfect solution. You won't have a frozen dead boy and dog on your conscience. And I won't be lost."

"You wouldn't be on my conscience." I tried staring him down, but he wouldn't even look at me. I went into the kitchen.

Jade grabbed the dog treats from the closet. "Luckily my uncle left these behind. There you go, good boy." She fed a few to an eager Otis.

I raised my brows.

She shrugged.

"Alex is a stranger. Your dad will go mental if we let him stay."

"Not if I we explain what happened. Honestly, Lottie, let it go. We might have saved their lives—who's gonna be mad about that?" So much for sibling solidarity.

62

It must be nice to know that your parent had total trust in you. I checked my phone signal. Still dead. They would have definitely tried contacting us by now. They had to be on their way back. I checked my watch. It was Dad's old one and dangled from my wrist. I'd forgotten how early it was. Mum would still be sleeping.

Jade came to the fireplace clutching a saucepan full of water and three mugs preloaded with Swiss Miss. "I got one for you too," she said to Alex.

Great. I tried a different tactic. "Won't your aunt be worried," I asked, feigning innocence, "that you were missing all night?"

"She's not there yet, so she won't be worried." Alex placed the saucepan over the fire on a grid he'd created from the ornamental pokers. Trying to prove how clever he was.

"How convenient." I went downstairs under the pretense of changing into more layers. My head settled into a soft throb. I needed alone time. It was hard enough to think, post migraine, without having to try to outmaneuver Alex and Jade. I could force him to leave by telling him I knew he'd been staying, that I'd heard the key, that he probably didn't even have an aunt, that I knew he'd met with his friends last night. Or not friends. I had no proof though. Alex could say I was crazy, having migraine delusions, and Jade would tell me she knew they were trouble, as soon as she heard it was AJ and Nico. But were they, or had Alex double-crossed them too? So many questions throbbing around my head.

The wind whistled through the cracks in the windows. I could see my breath. I went into Mum and Oliver's room and rifled through their closet. I was unfolding Mum's pale pink Patagonia vest when I turned and noticed the radio at the side of their bed. A windup, solar-powered radio. Of course, Jade was right. There was an emergency radio. Oliver would be prepared. He'd never leave his kid in the back of a car with only a thin blanket and a sad smile the way some dads did. I shivered the memory away.

My fingers hovered over the dial. The click echoed in the silence. I waited, counted to a painfully slow ten, then turned it up, little by little. It crackled, playing in and out of tune, louder then softer, until I found it—the emergency alert channel.

9

7:05 a.m.

"SOLAR FLARES...SATELLITE FAILURE...POWER OUTAGE...
Northern California, Western Nevada, Southern Oregon...
shelter...repeat. Shelter in place...blizzard warning..." Shit,
blizzard warning. It crackled out of tune. I played with the dial,
trying to retune it. "Winds of fifty... increasing to..." I turned it up
to hear the words behind the static.

"Lottie? You okay? Need any help?" Alex called down.

I almost dropped the radio. "I'm fine." I turned it off and shoved
it under the bed. I shivered. But we were already sheltering in place.
It wasn't like we could do anything more. And maybe blizzards
happened all the time here. Maybe they were like earthquakes—
nothing to be alarmed about until the big one hits. What if I was
freaking out over nothing? I'd wait until I knew more. Until then I
wasn't about to throw Alex into a blizzard.

I put on Mum's vest. It was soft, thick, and the least she could do for me. I grabbed the king-sized quilt off their bed, trailing it behind me as I went back upstairs.

Jade and Alex were crouched by the fire, nursing mugs of lukewarm hot chocolate, as if nothing was wrong. As if the snow would stop, parents would return, and no one was trying to deceive anyone.

"Does it normally snow this much?" I tried to keep the worry from my voice.

"Not this early in the season," said Jade, "but I guess sometimes."

"Last year it was seventy degrees one day and snowing the next," said Alex.

"And how do you know that?" I asked.

"My aunt told me." Alex nodded at the snow-speckled window. "It gets crazy out here, now more than ever."

"Climate change is messing with everything," said Jade. "We shouldn't even be burning wood. Dad's going to convert it to a gas fireplace."

Alex stood and stretched. "Yeah, well it is kind of an emergency heating situation."

We all looked at the feeble fire. A gust of wind whirled down the chimney, sending sparks up the flue. A lot of snow was falling and it wasn't slowing down. I glanced at Alex.

"Nice vest." A smile hovered at the edges of his mouth.

I clenched my jaw, ignored his comment, and sat by the fire. Snow spattered harder against the window. Alex played with Otis, unconcerned, as if this amount of snow was not a problem at all. But the radio announcement sounded like they expected it to get a lot worse. Blizzard worse.

A gust of air blew the back door open, sending snow flying into the room. Jade shut it, making sure the lock clicked closed. "It's freezing out there."

"Yep." I rubbed my arms, like that would help. "We'll need gloves and coats at this rate."

"No problem," said Jade. "The closets are full of extra jackets and gloves and snow boots. Everyone forgets to bring a good pair of boots. We always let guests help themselves." She pretend-smiled at me. Like I needed a reminder that this was her place, not mine.

"Thanks." I pretend-smiled back. I couldn't imagine having all that for two people. How many friends did they have? I hugged myself, knowing better than to think this new life could ever be real.

The wind picked up, scraping branches across the cabin walls. Otis jumped up excitedly, paws on the windowsills. It was only just past seven. No way Mum would be up before nine, eight if there was an emergency, which meant she'd be a no-show for at least another hour. Oliver would probably ignore a stay-in-place order to get back to Jade. So, they'd be back before the blizzard even hit. And Oliver would know what to do. Jade didn't need to be stressed out until I knew for sure we were going to have to deal with the blizzard ourselves. I'd keep the radio to myself until they needed to know. Which hopefully was never.

One more hour. How did such a short time feel so long?

Gusts of snow spiraled around the cabin. It was going to get a lot worse. No one was going anywhere. Except those guys in their massive four-by-four, that looked like it could take a road trip across Siberia. What if they knew about the blizzard and came back here? We'd be like sitting ducks, nowhere to hide, no escape. They could just ransack the whole place. Not that I even knew what they wanted. Maybe they had just meant to pick up a friend. What if Alex was the friend they'd meant to collect?

I bit the hangnail on my thumb. "You can stay, until our parents get back."

"Thanks." Alex hugged Otis. "Hear that, buddy? Lottie doesn't want you to freeze your tail off."

"And neither do I," Jade added, ruffling Otis's fluffy head.

Alex glanced at the fire. "We should beef that up and play cards or something, until they get here."

"I guess we could play a game while we're waiting." Anything to kill the time and stop my angst from spiraling. I glanced out the kitchen window. The driveway was covered in thick snow, no sign of human life, just small animal tracks, birds or rabbits, no footprints.

"What are you looking for?" Alex spoke softly but there was an edge to his voice.

"Nothing." I smiled. "Just seeing if they can actually get up the driveway when they arrive."

Jade looked out on to the driveway. "It's not that bad. They'll be able to get here easily in the Land Rover."

If they ignored the blizzard warnings, Mum would want to stay in Reno as long as possible, but I doubted Oliver would stay in place if he thought for one second that anything had happened to Jade. Come on, come on. Come back so I don't have to deal with any of this.

"Let's play a board game," said Jade.

68

"Do you have any?" I asked.

Of course they did.

Jade slid open the polished walnut coffee table, revealing a treasure chest of board games I had no idea existed. Perfect for a happy family. I could imagine Oliver's saying for that—the family that plays together, stays together. Not now though, not when there was a shelter-in-place warning, and we were miles apart. I grabbed my journal and pen from the end table. Maybe writing a poem would ease my worries.

"See?" said Jade, bringing me back to reality. "Chess, Life, Monopoly, Carcassonne, Pandemic, Scrabble?"

"Can't spell," said Alex. He grinned at Jade but watched me closely. There was no twinkle in his eyes, just wariness. He knew I was hiding something.

"Scrabble it is then," said Jade.

We set up our flashlights around the edge until Alex pointed out we might want to save the batteries, so I lit the row of tealights that ran across the mantelpiece and sat them on the corners of the coffee table instead. The candles sent long, flickering shadows up the walls. It was now daylight, but the snow and the clouds cast a slate-gray dimness over everything.

I blew on my fingers, in between pulling out wooden tiles from the black velvet bag. I startled at every sound, thinking that behind each gust of wind, each plop of snow was a tire, or a footstep. That our parents had arrived, because getting back to us was way more important than obeying a blizzard warning. I tapped the tip of my pen against my journal.

"What's that?" Alex asked.

"Nothing." I shoved it under the sofa. Pain gathered behind my right eye, as I watched Alex slowly place his first word.

Sitting so close to the fireplace made the rest of the open-plan room seem enormous. The vaulted ceilings soared above, and the mounted deer head watched from the mantelpiece with its black beetle eyes. Black and white. Snow and silhouettes. Life and death.

"LAG," he said laying his tiles in the middle of the board. Yes, time was definitely lagging.

I placed my letters and hoped Jade was paying attention.

Alex nudged the board. "That's not a word."

"It is in Britain." I touched each tile as I read out the letters: "BLAGGARD. A smooth-tongued liar."

"Is that where you're from?" asked Alex, ignoring my definition.

"Ap-*par*-ent-ly," I answered, exaggerating my English accent.

Jade looked impatiently at Alex. "It's a word. I looked it up." She held the pocket dictionary out for Alex to see. She was ready for anything. The radio announcements wouldn't even freak her out. She'd probably had blizzard survival training from Oliver, the perfect dad. I wished I'd learned more from mine, the professional explorer, apart from how to survive being abandoned, not that I'd even figured that out. Perhaps I should tell Jade. But not Alex. Not until I knew what he was really doing here.

I narrowed my eyes. "If your aunt's cabin is so close, why do you need a ride there?" I spun the letter Y between my fingers.

"It's snowing hard, in case you haven't noticed."

Jade laid down the word *LIAR*, using the R in *BLAGGARD*.

70

"Come on, it's like you're both out to get me," said Alex. He added an S. "Hah, triple word score for *BLAGGARDS*."

"Not bad." I laid out *BLIZARD* and raised my brows at Jade.

"You need two Zs," Jade pointed out, totally not getting the hint. It wasn't just an incoming storm. It was an incoming *blizzard*.

"Yeah, cheat," said Alex. "I thought I was the only one who couldn't spell." He stood, stretching his legs. His eyes went from the telescope to the window, then back to the telescope.

I stared down at my letters. This wasn't going to work. "How did you find us?" I asked, trying to keep my tone light. "It's not like you were on a direct path to anywhere else, unless you got wildly lost."

"Well, those solar flares…"

"Auroras," said Jade. "The solar flares caused the auroras. You can't see solar flares without a telescope." She glanced at it, safely locked away in its case.

"Those auroras," continued Alex, "lit up your cabin like a beacon."

"But that was way before you knocked."

"It's your turn, Alex," said Jade, cutting in between us. "And I'll trade you this so you can spell *blizzard* correctly." She placed her blank tile on the board. Fixing another one of my mistakes.

Alex sat back down, facing me.

I heard his footsteps before the key rattled. He'd waited out there for us to go to bed. "Have you been here before?"

Alex shook his head. "Of course not. Why would you think that?" He placed the letters to make *FOOL*. He'd caught on to my game.

I shrugged, all innocent. "I just wondered," I said and handed him the bag of letter tiles.

The fire dwindled. There might be updates. The blizzard warning might be canceled. They might even know when the power would be back. And the sun would come out and the birds would start singing, and Mum and Oliver would arrive with doughnuts and lattes. Yeah, right.

I spun the flashlight in my hand.

Alex played with his jacket zipper, up, down, up, down, and glanced out the window again. That boy had no poker face at all. "We're going to have to make a better fire if your parents don't turn up soon." He added the last log. It was so dry it quickly dwindled into soft embers.

"Right," said Jade. "Time for more layers." She went to the hall closet and pulled out thick, warm ski jackets, throwing them at me and Alex. It was welcome protection against the dropping temperatures. "And snow boots," she said. "Pick your own."

We ransacked the pile like we were playing dress-up. Getting warm was all that mattered, yet Jade managed to look like she'd been styled, bright blue North Face puffer ski jacket, Timberland snow boots, and a #blackbirders beanie. I looked like I didn't know how to dress. Everything was either Oliver-sized or skinny-teen-sized. Mum obviously had catch-up ski-season shopping to do. Luckily, I had small feet and could wear Jade's cast-off dirty snow boots. Alex just looked like Alex in a cool teal Patagonia ski jacket and Oliver's brown Timberlands. Annoying.

I shivered even under my own long-sleeved, I PREFER BOYS

WITH BRAINS zombie T-shirt, my old fleece, Mum's vest, and a too-big forest-green ski jacket. We sat back down in a semicircle by the fireplace.

I shook the bag of letters, like any of us really cared about the game.

"Where are they, anyway?" Alex patted the rug, and Otis flopped down beside him.

"Reno, for their honeymoon." Jade flicked my shoelace. "Your turn."

As I picked up a tile, we heard a vehicle rumble outside. It sounded close, at the end of the road.

Jade rushed to the front door. I raced right behind her. Clearly, we were both dying for it to be Mum and Oliver.

But once we opened the door, I recognized the engine rumble all too well. The red pickup truck slowed down at the end of the driveway, saw us, and sped on by, flinging fresh snow in its wake.

Jade stood gazing after them. "That's so weird. Why would they come back?"

I shook my head. "Lost again?" Doubtful. I stepped back from the open door. "Don't let in the cold."

Jade shut the door behind us and rested her back on it, deep in thought.

"Did you see who it was?" Alex looked past us, like he could see through the door.

"It was too snowy," Jade said. She turned and raised her brows at me. So now we were secret-sharing stepsisters. I had to tell her about the radio, get her downstairs alone somehow.

Alex must have been expecting those guys. Why else would he ask? But what would they come back for? He had a notebook with addresses and numbers—maybe he was collecting information for them. But he wanted a ride out with our parents. Adult protection. And he'd only want that if he was afraid of AJ and Nico coming back for him.

And if Alex was worried, he must think they're dangerous. If they knew about the blizzard coming, maybe they'd come back to sit it out here. They could take anything and trash everything. They knew it was only us and Alex here. I thought back to the conversation I'd overheard. Alex said, *I'll see to it when they've gone.* What was *it*? Something they wanted from him, or something from the cabin? My stomach squirmed with anxiety. Until I figured the situation out, there was no way I was telling Alex about the radio. The further he stayed in the dark, the better.

He caught me watching him. I tilted my chin. *I'm so on to you.*

10
7:45 a.m.

JADE MADE HER WAY TO THE KITCHEN TO GET A GLASS of water, and Alex stared at the snow-spattered front window. This was going to get worse.

I opened up the fireplace's glass doors and threw the last three pine cones on top of the crumbling fire. At least they'd keep the fire burning brightly for a little while longer. The radio was calling to me. I needed to know exactly what was happening.

"I'm getting more ibuprofen. Back in a sec." I headed downstairs, taking care not to appear rushed. Maybe I'd misheard and there was no blizzard warning, or it had all been a radio play, like the *War of the Worlds* broadcast that had freaked everyone out in the 1930s. But if the blizzard was real, we needed to be ready for the possibility of AJ and Nico coming back. They'd think we were easy targets stuck here—just Alex and two scared girls. Well, we'd show them.

I clung to that little bit of bravado while I sat on the floor of the master bathroom, door locked, radio to my ear, ready to hear the worst.

"Emergency Alert System. The National Weather Service has issued a blizzard warning for the following counties: Placer County, El Dorado County, Douglas County, Washoe County, and Carson City." I had no idea if we were even in one of those counties.

"Blizzard warning effective from October 26, 600 hours to October 28, 1900 hours. Avoid travel. Shelter in place."

Crap. Three days. The radio crackled with static.

"Power outage…affecting the following counties…radio channels…snow…emergency supplies…"

That was it. Only static left, no matter how violently I twisted the tuning dial. My mother and Oliver wouldn't be coming. There wouldn't be power. We would be trapped with Alex and Otis. Snowed in at the cabin, running out of food and warmth, and what if AJ and Nico showed up? All bravado had slipped away.

"Lottie?" It was Alex, standing right outside the door.

"Can I get a second of privacy?" Of course he'd creep down to spy on me. I flushed the toilet to give myself more time and hid the radio in the wicker basket full of toilet rolls. I'd let them know about the blizzard soon as I found out what Alex was really doing here.

He waggled the door handle.

I flung the door open. "What the hell is your problem?"

"What were you doing?" He looked over my shoulder into the dark behind me.

"What do you think? It's a bathroom. And why are *you* following me down here?"

"I thought you might be sick again." He frowned. "What's wrong? You seem so angry."

"What's wrong? I know you weren't lost on your way back to your aunt's cabin. You had a key to this place and you're pretending to like us, pretending you're stuck here, pretending to be oh so nice with your cute dog and fire-making skills, and making sure we're in your debt so I don't throw you out. What are you even doing here?" My voice shook at the end.

He held up his palms. "Hold on, hold on. You've got it so wrong."

I leaned in and hissed, "Oh, really, got everything under control, have you? 'They won't know. Leave it to me'?"

The furrow grew between his eyes. He took a deep breath. "The thing is…"

"Before you deny everything, I saw you last night." I braced myself for his reaction.

Jade's footsteps crossed the floor above us, fast. We paused to follow them with our eyes.

"No shit, Sherlock. You're not exactly subtle with your Scrabble clues." He shook his head. "Seriously, a couple of guys get lost on the road, I go out to help them, and you think that means I'm some kind of what, criminal?"

I glared at him. "Who are they?"

"Honestly, I don't know. I went out to help. I didn't want them to wake you and Jade."

Lost once, okay. Twice, no way. "'They won't know. Leave it to me?' That doesn't sound like lost. That sounds like they expected to find you here."

He pulled himself taller, all angles and edges. "You're so paranoid. What's it like not to trust anyone?" His nose almost touched mine.

"Back the hell off." I inched toward the door.

He spun away from me. "If your parents don't get back soon, I'll take my chances and leave, so you don't have to have me here anymore." He brushed the hair from his eyes. "I only stayed to help you both, while you were so…out of it."

I sighed. "Okay, you did stay for that." I scratched my forehead; something was still off. "I don't get why you were so friendly to those guys if you didn't even know them."

"Better to be friendly and helpful, get them away as soon as possible, and make them think there were a bunch of us staying here, so they wouldn't come back." He gave a half smile. Like he knew he'd won me over.

It sounded believable, but I knew he was wrong. Shadows whispered through the dark, in the sighs of the trees, and the creaks of the floorboards, and the persistent splatter of snow, snow that wasn't going to stop anytime soon.

"How much longer are you going to wait for this ride?" They weren't coming back. My lungs didn't work properly. It was just me and Jade and him. "Like, what if you get snowed in with us?"

He shrugged. "Then I'm screwed." He gave another half smile. "There are worse people to get snowed in with."

"I don't know about that."

He looked stunned.

"Look, it's not like you're Mr. Innocent. You had a key and you've been staying here. You weren't lost." I raked my hands through my hair. "I want to trust you, but nothing you say makes sense."

"Lottie!" Jade shouted down the stairwell. "A little help!" Her footsteps darted across to the kitchen and back again.

"Hold on!" I glared at Alex. "I found your list."

"You've been sneaking through my backpack?"

"You've been sneaking through our cabin."

"I didn't know you'd be here." He tensed his jaw. "Okay, you're right. I was taking Otis for a quick walk, and when I got back, it was suddenly occupied."

"It's *our* cabin. You're the one who's not supposed to be here." I hugged myself.

"I was only staying a couple of days. I wasn't doing any harm. I never would have stayed once I knew you were here." He jutted his jaw.

"Lottie!" Jade yelled again.

"Coming!" I yelled back. "You tried to break in while we *were* here!" I poked him in the chest. "The things on the list? What are those?"

He leaned his forehead against the windowpane. "Look, the owners wouldn't notice stuff was missing for months. So many empty vacation cabins, so much space and stuff, totally unused. It's all insured anyway: TVs, game systems. Not that I'd do that, but plenty of others around here would. Like those guys, they could have been scouting out empty cabins."

Thin, gray light penetrated the space, making it feel even colder.

My temples pulsed. "So do you scout or steal?"

"Now!" Jade yelled down.

Jesus. "Just a minute!" My head was going to explode.

The wind thudded against the window, and cold curled in under the panes. Something thudded on the floor above us, rolling to a halt. A strong acrid smell wove its way downstairs. Jade must be burning whatever she could find to make a fire.

"I could have stolen anything and snuck off while you were sleeping. My bag could be packed full of telescopes, but it wasn't, was it? I'm not the bad guy here."

I glared at Alex as I tried to untangle my thoughts, reason against instinct.

A shrill beeping noise started up outside the door.

"What's that?" Alex said. "Smoke alarm?"

"Fire!" Jade screamed from upstairs.

Otis barked, high and sharp. I threw open the bedroom door. The stench of smoke was sickening.

"You get Otis. I'll find Jade!" A thick flume of smoke gathered at the top of the stairs. I didn't think. I raced toward it, taking the stairs two at a time, with Alex right behind me.

11

8:21 a.m.

"JADE!" I PULLED MY T-SHIRT OVER MY NOSE. MY YELLS came out as muffled yelps. I couldn't see through the thick smoke, could only hear her coughing her lungs up. Oh shit. The pine cones. Smoke poured out of the fireplace. I'd left the doors open. Shit, shit, shit. I fought my way to her, crawling across the floor, staying low beneath the acrid smoke, my eyebrows singeing with the heat. Don't die, don't die, don't you dare die on me.

I grabbed the fleece blanket and threw it on top of the flames breaking across the rug, dropping it just in time before the flames could reach my hands. Polyester and fire, not a good idea. The suede sofa ignited and became a blaze of bright orange. Flames raced up the curtains, dancing along the walls, across the books, and up the ceiling.

Jade banged on the french doors. She was on the deck outside, frantically waving the fire extinguisher at me.

"What the hell?" I grabbed my sleeve and used it to yank open the back-deck door. Smoke billowed out into the frosty air.

"I needed to get away from the smoke," she gasped.

I grabbed her arm and pointed to the front door—or where I thought the door should be. "Cover your mouth and nose." My words turned into coughs. My eyes watered like crazy.

Jade froze in the middle of the room, wide-eyed at the destruction. I dragged her along, shuffling blindly through the smoke as fast as I could. The fire belched like an angry dragon from the fireplace, setting the cushions alight.

I ducked as something fell from the ceiling, just missing my head. "Come on, come on. Too late for that now." I pried the fire extinguisher from her hands.

Focus on the exit, the door, stay low, don't breathe in the smoke, keep going, we can make it. We have to make it. Coughing made my eyes blurry with tears. I squinted in the smoke, trying to see a way out. A blast of cold signaled the way to the front door. I gripped Jade's hand, pulling her along until we reached the outside, and collapsed in the middle of the driveway. We gasped for breath. Snow clung to our faces.

We were alive. We'd made it. Mum would kill me, but for now I was alive. And Jade was okay. Thank God.

I put the fire extinguisher down by my feet. "You okay?" I asked in between panting.

She coughed too much to speak. All that came out was a wheeze. Smoke-damaged already. She gave me a nod. Good. Better than nothing.

I looked back at the cabin. Otis barked like crazy, refusing to leave the doorway. I tried to reassure him, pulling at his collar, and finally managing to drag him to Jade.

"Hold on to Otis. You see Alex?"

Jade shook her head. Otis stayed by her side, whimpering with his tail between his legs as she continued to cough her guts out.

"Alex! Alex!" I yelled, hoping to God he'd gone out the back. "Alex!" I waited for a moment, praying for an answer that didn't come. "Stay there. I'll be right back." I did my best to sound calm, while inside I was a nest of panicked wasps. I picked the extinguisher back up and stood at the door, blanching at the intense heat. I couldn't go back in. I didn't even know him. But I didn't want him to die. I had to try.

I pulled my fleece off and drew my T-shirt over my nose, taking one more second to steady myself. Get in, get out. I took a deep breath and then completely covered my face with my shirt. Find Alex. Don't die.

Fire up close is ferocious, like giant waves of eye-smarting orange, sucking up all the sounds and all the oxygen, and turning it into a furious never-ending roar. Flames licked the windows. Smoke whirled out of the front door. All around was the sound of crackling, popping, chewing fire. No sign of Alex.

"Alex!" Bad idea, the smoke made me cough, which let in more smoke. I had to get out, but I had to find him.

I pulled the pin off the fire extinguisher and squeezed the trigger. If I could control the fire, I might be able to stop the smoke and find Alex. The force blew me backwards. The sofa was black with smoke. I picked up the extinguisher again and gave it a feeble squirt while trying not to inhale the thick smoke. *I can't do this. I can't do this.* I have to try. Ten more seconds.

The rush of adrenaline made me dizzy and panicked. The ceiling was a vault of fire. Flames dropped into the kitchen and dining room as the burning plaster fell to the floor. Smoldering then running flickers of flame, reached like demons' fingers, for the cabinets and closets, jumping in between the steel appliances, and all so freaking fast. I'd spent too long staring, paralyzed. I'd die like this, crouched on the ground, breathless with blackened lungs. Not a valiant death, failing to save a stranger.

"Alex! Alex!" He had to be okay. "Alex!" My shout came out as a rasp.

"Here!" Alex yelled. He was by the bookshelves.

I crunched on glass to reach him. The telescope's display box had smashed to the floor.

"Otis and Jade are safe. Go!" My eyes streamed. I couldn't breathe. Everything was burning. Smoke billowed all around me. There was no time. No time to think, to run, to get out. I lost sight of him.

The cabin groaned and spat like an overweight monster.

"Lottie?" Alex called into the haze. "Lottie!"

I dropped on my stomach to the floor and crawled to his voice. My throat was on fire. My head, my eyes. I couldn't see, tears streamed, snot streamed. *Get a hold of yourself. You're not on fire,* Mum's voice said in my head. She was right. I scrabbled my way to the open door. "Alex?" It came out as choking coughs.

And then there was a hand, his hand, catching hold of mine. He hauled me over his shoulder, like a limp rag doll, and staggered out. He placed me gently under the pine tree where Otis and Jade waited.

Tears streamed down Jade's face, leaving sooty trails.

I'd done it this time. There'd be no forgiveness, no excuses. I wished I couldn't see the disaster unfolding, but I couldn't tear my eyes away. Don't screw this up, my mother had said. I'd screwed everything up. Royally. Jade would never give me another chance. I didn't care about Mum.

Billowing smoke mingled with the snow, sending ash everywhere. The fire ran along the garage roof, hopping from one side to the other, until the whole thing flickered with flames. So much for the fireproof door from the garage to the living room. I didn't bother wiping my tears away. I was way past hiding my shame.

The wooden frame of the cabin went up like tinder, all brittle and dry in a mighty flame of glory. The smoke was acrid, plastic mixed with iron, the sofa, the books, the pictures, the rugs, the cushions, gone. All those photos, memories of Jade's mum, whoosh, gone. Truly up in smoke. I was so stupid, thoughtless. If only Alex hadn't followed me downstairs. If only I hadn't gone to listen to that stupid radio. If only I'd run up as soon as Jade called. If only I hadn't thrown on the stupid pine cones. "Shit." I took another deep breath.

"That's one hell of a big blaze," said Alex. He looked dazed, shell-shocked. He'd saved me like a bloody hero, over-the-shoulder fireman's lift and everything, but why was he even still in there? "What the hell were you doing running back in?"

"Getting you," I said, not knowing where to look: his teared-up eyes, his floppy black fringe, or his smeared-soot cheekbones.

No smiles now. He pushed his hair back from his face and stared at the wreckage, shaking his head. "You went in for me? After all… that."

"I wasn't going to let you die." I choked on the smoke, and swallowed.

Jade sniffed. "It was Dad's favorite place." Her breath came out in shaky sobs. "Those pine cones exploded, fell onto the rug, and I tried to stop it, to get the fire extinguisher, but it spread so fast. And it was so smoky. I called for help. But I couldn't breathe."

"It wasn't your fault. It was mine." I squeezed her arm. "Thank God you're okay."

"Everything's destroyed." She murmured it like she couldn't quite believe it.

The wrath of Oliver would be nothing compared to Mum's. "I'm so sorry."

"It could have started a wildfire!" Jade looked at the ashes painting the snow gray. "It's a miracle none of the sparks made it to the trees." She sat on her heels and shook her head, taking it all in.

Mum always said I was like my dad. She was wrong. I was worse. It was my fault the fire started. Jade could have died. The whole forest could have gone up in flames. I'd failed Jade, just like Dad failed me.

The cabin crumbled. Ash mingled with the falling snow, making it thick and slushy. The stink was awful. We were lucky to be wearing ski stuff, so we didn't freeze to death. My heart dropped.

This snow wasn't going to stop, and the wind was supposed to get really strong, and no one was supposed to travel. And I was the only one who knew. I looked at their faces. Jade absentmindedly stroked Otis's head. I think she was in shock and didn't even know she was doing it. I tried to hug her, but she tensed. It felt stiff and forced. I folded my arms behind my back.

Otis turned his huge puppy eyes to Alex, who was transfixed, watching the cabin slowly burn. Our cabin. One night was all it took for me to ruin everything.

We stood not knowing what else to do but wait for the inevitable sound of the sirens. With flames crackling that intensely, and smoke billowing that high, someone would surely have alerted the emergency services. Even if all the power and cell phone signals were out for miles, anyone nearby would come to see what was causing it. But there was no one else for miles around. I let that reality sink in, as ash continued to stain the snow around us.

12
8:43 a.m.

JADE BENT OVER, COUGHING TOO HARD.

"Got your inhaler?" I asked.

She gave me a killer side-eye but pulled out her inhaler and took a puff and stuffed it back into her pocket. Which I took to mean she didn't completely hate me.

Alex frowned. "Don't you need two puffs?"

"No, I don't, and what's it to you anyway? Christ." Jade hugged herself tight against the wind. Coughed some more and took another puff. "Happy now?"

"My little sister, Izzy, has asthma." Alex's eyes twinkled, highlighting gold flecks I hadn't noticed before. "She's just turned ten. She hates taking her inhaler too."

"Okay, I'm sorry about that, but I'm not your sister." Jade stared at the cabin and shook her head. "It's all gone. I can't believe it." A tear trickled down her cheek. She angrily wiped it away.

The towering pine tree next to the cabin was reduced to a black skeleton. Embers rained down from the cabin's ceiling, as chunks of the wall burned up and left gaping holes. The wind rushed around the trees, sending sparks flying. Snow fell through the gaps in the ceiling, sizzling as it touched the flames. The whole place stank of smoke, ash, and disappointment. It looked like a war zone—black stains brushed the walls, and tiny sparks flickered on and off, like glow worms, as the fire continued its relentless dance of destruction.

There was nothing we could do. Not even call for help. Only watch as the cabin crackled, and moaned, disintegrating into ash and rubble right before our eyes.

When Mum and Oliver saw this, we'd be so dead. No, I'd be so dead. "What were you doing out there on the back deck? Why didn't you run out the front?" I asked.

"When the pine cone exploded, the rug caught fire, so I ran for the fire extinguisher, but by then the flames had spread, so I figured I'd make sure the telescope was safe because by then you'd both fucking be there to help me." Jade jutted her chin.

Alex and I exchanged a wary glance.

"I know. I'm so, so, sorry. It won't ever happen again." What a stupid thing to say. "At least you got your inhaler."

"Really, that's what you take from this?" Jade shivered under her puffer jacket.

My knees wobbled slightly.

"We all got out." Alex squeezed Jade's shoulder. "We're alive, no injuries. Could have been a lot worse."

"We could have died." My adrenaline left me shaking.

I twisted my soot-stained hair out of the way. Part of me wanted to get away from there as fast as possible, so I wouldn't have to face the parents; the other part wanted them to swoop in and take control. But they wouldn't, because this was the beginning of a blizzard warning and everyone except us was sheltering in place.

Jade suddenly darted toward the cabin. "The telescope, it's probably still there."

"Too late," said Alex. "The case smashed. There was glass all over the floor."

"I smashed it by accident when I was getting the telescope out." She ran down the side steps.

"Wait!" I raced after her. "Watch out for the..." A piece of burning wood clattered by her feet. "Where are you going?"

"Back deck!" Jade yelled. "That's where I left it."

"It's just a telescope." I finally reached her. "Nothing's worth that much money."

"I just want to see"—Jade paused—"if it's in one piece."

"Where is it?" asked Alex, catching up to us.

From the back, the cabin looked like a burnt-out shell; even the downstairs flickered with flames. The only thing left virtually intact was the scaffolding that held the upper deck up, and weirdly, the deck itself. And there, glinting through the deck's floor beams, was the telescope.

"There." Jade pointed at the bronze canister rolling across the floor.

"If it means that much to you, I'll see if I can get it." Alex shivered in his jacket.

"Seriously? It's insured and not worth getting injured for," I said.

"We'll tell the fire department to search for it when they get here. We should keep moving, before we freeze to death." Not that it would be worth surviving, if Mum knew what I'd just destroyed.

"It's priceless," said Jade. "It doesn't look totally ruined." She glanced at Alex.

Alex checked his phone. "No signal. No one's coming to help. It's all going to burn." He raked his hand through his hair. "I'm going for it." He grabbed hold of a supporting beam like he was going to climb up. The whole thing wobbled.

Otis barked with excitement.

"Leave it. It's not worth the risk." It would make things worse, if that was possible.

Jade watched Alex's efforts, biting her bottom lip so hard it started bleeding. "Just this one thing, if we can save this."

"You don't need things to remember people. The people you love stay with you in your heart," I said. No matter how much you'd like them not to. I thought of the photo I'd trashed before Mum and I left San Francisco. Dad's face crumpled in my fist. Love and hate forever battling in my heart. It was amazing it still worked with all those scars.

"It's not Dad's. He'll get fired for bringing it here." Jade's teeth chattered as she spoke.

"Oh." So much for sisterly comfort.

Jade turned to Alex. "Can you reach it? I can try. I'm lighter."

Alex shook his head. "That beam will collapse." They both stood on tiptoes looking at it. There was no way to safely reach it.

"At least it's not going anywhere," Alex pointed out. "It'll just get covered in snow."

The snow fell faster. Jade stamped her feet. I hugged myself. Otis went for a pee against the pine tree. There was nothing else to say. The smells, the textures, the things, paintings chosen together on road trips, their photographs, the story of their life as a family, gone.

"I'm sorry about everything, but we can't stay here. The storm's only going to get worse." Blizzard-worse. The radio's warning spiraled around my brain.

"You don't know that. You don't know anything about Tahoe." Jade pulled her hood tighter.

"Trust me, I do." More than I wanted to. "We've got to find shelter fast."

"True," said Alex, "unless your parents get back really soon."

"They're not coming back. There's a blizzard warning and a shelter-in-place alert." I just blurted it out. My heart sunk at their stunned faces. "I heard it on the radio. I didn't want to freak you out. After all this."

"On the radio?" Jade's mouth dropped open. "You had the radio I was looking for? What else are you hiding?"

"That's what you were keeping from us in the bathroom," said Alex. "When were you going to tell us?"

"I just did." I wasn't the only one keeping secrets. "If the cabin hadn't burnt down, we'd all be safe inside and it wouldn't have changed anything."

"It would have changed everything!" Jade frowned. "I can't believe you, pretending our parents would be back soon."

"Yeah, you should have told us," Alex agreed. "We could have been gathering more fuel for the fire, instead of waiting for people that you knew weren't coming!"

"Well, you were going to steal shit and run off with those guys anyway!" It was all out in the open.

"I was not!"

Otis barked and jumped up at Alex. The wind howled around the ruins.

"It's too cold to fight," said Jade. "We should stay in the garage. It might be okay. It's got a fire door."

We all looked over at it. The door may have held but the roof was ruined. Snow blew in through the gaps in the beams and landed on the out-of-power Tesla. That car had been wrecked fast.

Alex shook his head. "It's too dangerous. The whole place could collapse on us."

"Are there any cabins close by? Neighbors?" I knew the answer but asked anyway.

Jade shook her head. "We should head for the nearest fire station to get warm. And tell them to save the telescope."

"They must have seen the smoke from it if they're that close. So if they didn't, maybe the station is on the other side of the mountain. I mean, they've got to have a bunch of fire stations out here with all those seasonal wildfires, right?" I asked.

"Or the station could be ten miles away," said Alex pointedly. "They get help from outside when it's peak fire season."

"There's one a short car ride away. Dad used to take me when I was little. They gave me a red plastic fire hat." Jade walked to the end of the driveway. "It's this way." Obviously, she'd know.

Otis trotted at her side as if he'd been there before.

"We'll get there fast enough for them to come back and save the telescope," said Alex, running to catch up. "Before anyone else comes and finds it," he murmured, making eye contact with me. "Either way you get shelter and safety, so win-win, right?"

"And don't feel like you have to talk on the way." Jade set off in front, leaving a stream of icy air in her wake.

This was so far from win-win, but there was nothing else we could do. I sighed and pulled my hood tight, taking one last look at the smoldering cabin before stepping out into the bleak, snowy horizon.

13
9:51 a.m.

THE SNOW WAS FALLING FASTER. SHAKING IT OFF MY hood didn't cut it anymore. I pulled the drawstrings tight, not caring that I looked like a demented goblin.

Wind would blow straight through the new holes in the roof and back wall of the cabin. The settling snow would turn to puddles and dampness and then mold. The smell would linger for weeks. It would take months and thousands and thousands of dollars to fix the place back up and all because I threw a stupid pine cone on the fire. This was so messed up. My heart pounded in my ears. Mum was right. I was a total screwup. Guilt burrowed its way into my chest, heavy and sullen. I stumbled along faster.

"Where's Alex?" I suddenly realized it was just Jade and me.

"There," said Jade pointing in front of us. "Checking the direction. It's harder to tell when it's this snowy."

"Hey," said Alex, as we caught up to him. "North is this way. Jade, you said the fire station's near NorthStar, right?"

She huddled in her jacket and nodded, while stamping her feet up and down.

"Okay, so you're right. We're super close." He said it like it was a big adventure, not a giant catastrophe, though I guess guys who break into cabins looking for stuff to steal live every day on the edge.

Alex walked between me and Jade, while Otis ran ahead, stopping at every other tree and barking as if to hurry us. The farther we got from the cabin, the more he treated us like sheep, herding us along. Nobody spoke. Jade coughed every now and then and pretended it was nothing. Alex kept starting to say something and then not, and I focused ahead so I didn't have to meet anyone's eyes.

The light was tinged with yellowish pink, like a dull bruise. It was so quiet, just our crumping footsteps, the cracks of branches, and my occasional swearing, as we slipped and stumbled our way along, getting our boots stuck in snowdrifts, or sinking to our hips in hidden snow traps. No birds, no scurrying chipmunks, no planes, no cars, no people. No life. Just snow falling, falling, falling.

We trudged in silence, lost in our own thoughts, heads bent against the wind. Just step, crunch, and freeze when we thought we'd heard something. I looked up at the blanket of clouds. My forehead ached. The ibuprofen had long worn off.

The telescope had to be ruined already. We just needed to get somewhere warm, anywhere. I looked out for any other cabins, while shaking the flurries from my face. It was getting harder to see as the wind kicked up. Powder that was softly resting on the ground was blown into spirals of ice. It was like walking through a snow globe.

My ears tingled. The ends of my fingers were numb. I rubbed them together, blowing on them. It worked for seconds. "How far, Jade?"

She huffed. "I don't know. Walking in snow takes longer."

"I know that." I had no clue where we were, but I had an excuse: it was my first time there. "You know Tahoe so well, but you can't find your way to the firehouse?"

"There's a blizzard warning and you didn't think to tell us?" Touché. Jade's #blackbirders beanie was flecked with snow. She kept shaking her head from the cold and knocking her puffer jacket hood down. Not that I cared.

"It can't be much longer," Alex said unconvincingly. "See those trees?"

I nodded.

"We follow the road beyond them, until it goes right for Truckee. The firehouse has got to be there." At least he knew where we were going or was good enough at lying to convince me. I was too tired and cold to bother answering.

Alex smiled at Jade. "We'll warm up once we're there."

Jade gave a small smile back. It must be nice to be in the Best Friends' Club.

I trudged along silently, watching Alex and Jade bounce against each other as they walked. I walked slower, watching the distance grow between us. I could slip off. Find my own shelter. They wouldn't even notice, wouldn't even care. They'd be fine together, and I'd be fine alone. No one to disappoint.

I looked up. They'd stopped, waiting for me to catch up.

"You finally made it." Jade kicked a snow pile. An explosion of crystal shimmers fell at her feet. "Thought you were in a rush?"

I didn't bother to reply. Each breath was a little harder than the last, even though we were heading downhill. I hadn't expected it to be so hilly, which was stupid of me, seeing as we were in the mountains.

The cold was biting, ragged, numbing. Thank God for the pines, blocking the full force of the wind, pointing boldly to the clouds. We passed a row of them, then it was back to whiteness and gusts of snow blowing into our faces. White clouds, white snow, white sticks...

"A pole!" I said, scampering over and grabbing at the red painted end, which was sticking out of a pile of snow. A lot had come down already. And the blizzard hadn't even started yet.

"This must be a main road. The poles show the snowplow where the road is. They only do that with main routes. We're on the right track," said Alex, as if we might not have been the whole time.

"Let's stop for a second." I panted by a tree, blinking away the stars that appeared before me. "Water." I held out my hand.

Jade shook her head. "You finished it back there, remember?"

I grabbed a handful of snow and sucked on it. It cut my lips and stuck to my cracked skin. It took ages to get a little water from it. The hot cocoa breakfast was so long ago. No wonder I felt dizzy.

"You shouldn't do that. It lowers your body temperature," said Alex.

"Yes, well, it's this or die of dehydration." I bit a little more just to spite him.

"You have to eat a tiny bit at a time." Jade picked up a chunk and nibbled it. "Like this."

"When did you two suddenly become the experts?" I asked.

"I didn't *suddenly* become one. It comes with loving nature and being outside," Jade said. "You can learn a lot from people who share interests."

"Right, I guess I never had any." I felt like a bitch as soon as I said it, but doubled down. "And don't remind me, *you're* a frigging Eagle Scout," I said to Alex.

He nodded, knowing better than to speak right then.

As well as being a liar, and a charming manipulator. Though I suppose he did save me from a burning fire. "What blessed company I have." I pulled my jacket tighter. "I was a Girl Guide once."

"Girl Guide?" Alex asked.

"That's the Brit version of being a Girl Scout," I explained.

"I can't imagine that," said Alex. "Tell me something, Girl Guide."

"I only went to two meetings."

"Ha." He laughed. "Bet they kicked you out."

"Something like that." Mum had signed me up so she could go out on dates while I went to the meeting. She went on two dates, I was a Girl Guide for two hours, and for both of us the experiences were disasters. Then we moved again. So that was the end of that. I hung my head and carried on, crunching softly on the snow.

14
10:17 a.m.

"IT'S *REALLY* COLD," SAID JADE, SHAKING SNOW OUT OF her eyelashes.

"We've got to almost be there. No one dies walking through snow in Tahoe," I said.

Alex gave me a horrified look. Apparently, they did.

"You really don't know this area, do you?" Jade didn't wait for an answer before pushing past me.

It wasn't like we were hiking off trail or venturing into the backcountry. Dad had rescued hundreds of climbers doing crazy stuff like that.

I slipped and almost fell. Otis nudged me from behind. At least he had my back. Visions of that fire-filled room swirled in my head. My journal was in that burning mess. All my stupid thoughts and scribbles of unreadable poems. Better burnt than lost. At least no one would ever read it.

We moved in slow motion, like moon walkers, our big, puffy hands gripped together. The ski jackets we'd been wearing saved us. We'd never have survived without them. The snow slowed to lighter flurries and the wind dropped.

Otis barked and stopped in front of me, almost making me trip, so he could shake the tonnage of snow from his fur.

Jade wheezed gently as she rubbed the ice from Otis's coat.

"Do you want to stop for a minute and get that asthma under control?"

"I don't have asthma."

"What's with the weird zombie breath then?" I asked.

"Fine, but it's mild." She paused and took a deep breath.

"Better?" I asked.

"Yes." It was not.

"Jade, take your inhaler. Honestly, you'll feel better." Alex knocked her hood playfully, making it fall down again.

She crossed her arms. "I'll take it when I need it, okay?"

"Like when you're wheezing, like, now?" Alex asked her gently.

Jade pinched her mouth, took her inhaler out of her pocket, and showed it to Alex.

"Oh shit," Alex's face fell.

"Yep," said Jade, digging her hands deep into her jacket pockets.

"Look!" Alex pointed to the road. It took a sharp turn to the right. "They might have a spare."

There it was, a large, square, brick building, with a giant red number 52 poking out of the snow. I grinned at Alex. His joy was infectious. Even Jade cracked a smile.

"Made it." Alex punched the air and then my shoulder. "See, see. I knew it was here!"

Otis ran up to the metal doors, barking as if to say, let us in. Let us in!

The giant doors were shut. I rattled them and rang the doorbell. It chimed like a church bell—sharp and unnatural in this snowy wilderness of a landscape.

"Hello! Hello!" Alex shouted.

"Oh shit." Jade pointed at the scrap of paper stuck on one of the doors. "It's decommissioned. They've relocated. This notice is from last year."

I slammed my back against the brick and squeezed my eyes to hold back the tears. "Why would they do that? I thought they needed all the help fighting fires they could get."

"They do. They probably moved it somewhere more useful than way out here," said Jade.

I rattled the doors again. "We could still shelter here if we could get in. They might even have some supplies left."

"Yeah," said Alex, "and the door might magically open by itself." He shook his head. "Meanwhile, we're freezing, and the cold's making Jade's asthma worse. We need to find somewhere else."

"We could double back and follow our footsteps before they get covered in fresh snow and wait at the cabin—what's left of it. At least Mum and Oliver will find us easily."

"We can't go back." Alex looked panicked. He gave Jade a nervous smile. "You don't have a spare hidden away, do you?"

She shook her head and bit her lip.

"What's going on?" I stamped my feet while I waited for an answer.

"Show her."

Jade rolled her eyes. "He's making such a thing of it. There's eight left. If I go easy, it'll be fine." She pulled out the inhaler and showed me the counter.

"Oh shit." My heart sunk.

"Exactly," said Alex.

"It's okay. Eight puffs will last days. It would have been nice if they were open for business though." Jade looked reluctantly up at the firehouse, then shivered. "Now where are we going before the blizzard hits?" She was not going to let that go.

I gave the doors a kick in futile frustration.

"Maybe there's a fire crew at the cabin," said Jade. She shrunk into her jacket.

"I don't think so," said Alex. "We'd have heard the sirens."

The only sounds were the soft plops of falling snow. We all looked up and stared at the empty windows.

"We'll freeze to death out here." Alex rubbed his hands together. "We should see if there are any cabins nearby with fireplaces and food. Maybe even a landline."

"We could try the road, hitch a ride to Reno," said Jade.

"Hitch a ride or break into a cabin. Hitch a ride it is then." I smiled at Jade. Peace offering.

"And break into a cabin on the way." Alex was more stubborn than I'd realized.

"Deal," said Jade.

"Okay, let's go!" I wrapped my scarf tighter and pulled my hood in closer.

And off we trudged.

I stopped still. "If there's a shelter-in-place warning, that means stay inside, right?"

Jade frowned and Alex nodded.

"Then there aren't going to be cars on the road. There isn't going to be anyone to flag down." I blinked back tears of frustration. A bit of hope goes a long way until it's dashed by reality.

15
10:45 a.m.

WE WALKED IN CIRCLES, WHICH SEEMED IMPOSSIBLE since we were walking downhill. But these were the same trees Jade had stopped to cough at before. Or I was going insane, and everything looked the same. Gray sky, white snow, black trees, no houses, no roads, no landmarks. There was no way to even tell where the sun was with clouds this thick. And the constant snow turning from feathers, to clusters, to marshmallows. I was hungry. And cold. My back was clammy. I needed water and to stop walking endlessly, getting nowhere.

"Seriously, is this a blizzard yet?"

"Nope," said Jade. "And we need to find shelter before then, or we won't be able to see anything. Too bad you didn't save the radio instead of hiding it and then accusing everyone else of having ulterior motives."

Alex rubbed his hands and blew on them. "Come on, team. You're tired and cranky. Hey, look here." He pulled a chocolate almond Protein Puck bar from his pocket, broke it in half, and threw one of the halves at Jade. "This will help."

"Thanks!" Jade ate it in three bites.

"Where's mine?" I held out my hands.

Alex grinned. "Only for emergencies."

I caught the half he threw to me. The chocolate melted in my mouth, bittersweet flavor bursting around my tongue. Bliss. I licked my lips, not wanting to waste any of it. "Where did that come from?"

"It's amazing what you can find lying around," Alex said, and he went to bump into me accidentally on purpose, but I stepped out of the way. He'd have to do more than throw me a stolen protein bar to win me over.

Thick snow blew into my face as the wind picked up again, sending ice slivers down my neck. "My kingdom for a thicker scarf," I said, shivering.

"You should have grabbed more ski stuff from the closet." Jade stopped to let us catch up, but I had a feeling it was also to see if Alex had any more treasures in his pockets.

"At least we're already wearing jackets and ski boots. We'd be dead already if it wasn't for that." I ran a little to keep warm, and to stop the wind from buffeting me away from them.

Alex skidded to a halt so abruptly that I almost smacked into him. "Shush." He tilted his chin.

Gentle flumps fell as snow slipped in between the branches.

I huddled in my jacket. Standing still meant shivering in place. If we did this much longer, we'd be totally frozen. I stomped my feet. "There's nothing."

"Listen." Alex took off his beanie, letting the snow cover his silky black hair with white sprinkles.

There it was, very faint, the sound of a vehicle. We galloped, bumping along across the dips and gullies until we slowed to what looked like the edge of a road. Otis's tail wagged. Alex clutched his leash.

I stared at the snow-drifted road. No one had driven along it for a while. There was a single car parked crookedly along the road across from us, abandoned and half covered in snow. But we could hear another car in the distance, coming closer.

I turned to Jade. "Here's hoping!"

"Yep." Jade breathed heavily. "Let's get the hell out of here." And, finally, for the first time since before the fire, she flashed me a small smile.

"Listen," said Alex, "here it comes!"

The low sound of an engine rumbled toward us. Jade and I rushed after it, scrabbling down the bank onto the slippery main road. A silver SUV hit the curve in the road too fast, skidded past us, and smashed into the parked car. We just caught sight of a pale kid's face, staring at us from the rear window, before the SUV reversed and accelerated off again.

"Bloody hell, so much for neighborly help!" I rushed over to the smashed car. No wonder it was abandoned; it probably skidded at the same spot.

"They saw us," said Jade, following me. "They saw us and sped away!"

"Wankers." I blew on my hands. "We can stay in here." I wrenched the driver's-side door open, shut it fast, and swallowed.

The steering wheel was slick with blood. It had pooled onto the floor and sprayed across the driver's seat and onto the passenger's side. Whoever had been in there must have hit their head on the steering wheel. The bag had inflated and everything. But it was the shoe that got me, left lying upside down on the floor, a black, patent-leather dress shoe, ringed with blood. I held my palm to my mouth. I knew snow and storms could be dangerous, but it never hit me before what that really meant.

I pulled my head out and took a deep breath. "Actually, be ready to wave the next person down."

"There won't be a next person for ages." Jade frowned. "What's wrong with the car?"

I shook my head, worried I'd lose it if I spoke. Whoever was here had gone. No bloody footsteps, so they must have been taken away to the hospital. With that much blood loss, they had to have severe injuries. Or paramedics removed their dead body. The hair rose on the back of my neck. We weren't staying in the car. The cloying scents of iron and rust filled my nose and throat.

I stepped back from the open door, feeling faint for a second, then okay, then not. Jade looked inside. I could hear her gag. Then she took a deep breath and seemed to pull herself together.

"This car's no good!" Jade shouted over to Alex, who was waiting under the shelter of a pine tree with Otis.

"We'll find another."

"There aren't any others!" yelled Alex, coming closer. "What's wrong with that car? It's a Lexus."

"Trust me, you don't want to know," said Jade.

"Seriously, what's wrong?" Alex handed Otis's leash to Jade and bent to look inside. "Oh shit." His eyes went wide as he shut the car door.

"Yeah," said Jade. "So, we keep looking."

Alex nodded. "But if this gets much worse…"

We'd catch hypothermia. "Alright, we walk down this road and find another unoccupied car, or wave down a car, and if that doesn't happen in the next five minutes, we double back and deal with the horror car," I said. I doubted there would be another car breaking the shelter-in-place order, but I clung to that hope.

"Deal," said Alex and Jade together. Even Otis barked.

"Great, onward!" I pretended to be optimistic. Still, the stink of blood would be better than death.

16

11:15 a.m.

A FINE WHITE FOG HUNG ACROSS THE ROAD. A SPIRAL of snow spun into view then merged back into the frozen mist.

It was too cold to talk or think about anything but finding shelter, without losing sight of each other. No one except us was stupid enough to be out in this storm.

"Lottie, stay with us." Alex tugged my arm. "You look like you're having another migraine."

I shook my head. "I'm fine." Not fine. Freaking out about that car. I hugged myself and stumbled along. That could have been me the night my dad left me in our car. That's how I could have ended up if Mum hadn't got worried in time. No pools of blood, but a small, iced body under a quilt, unseen in the back of a car. Left for good.

At a bend in the road Otis barked and ran ahead. We followed him and saw the tail end of a car peeking out of a snow mound. The mound was a scarlet Mini Cooper, under a thick layer of snow.

"Who'd drive that up here?" Alex asked. "No wonder it got stuck. It's shelter, at least, and we can put the heater on."

"Oh yeah, that's way better." Jade ran up to it, "I love Mini Coopers!"

We started brushing off the snow. A soggy, yellow abandoned-car notice clung to the windshield. I peered inside, fearing the worst.

"Probably from before this storm started," said Alex, brushing off more of the snow from the windows.

Jade reached for the door handle.

"Let me look first." I pushed past her and cracked open the door. "Empty. Thank God."

Jade frowned. "Don't feel like you have to watch out for me or anything." Jade clambered into the back seat. "I'm not the one who starts fires." She muttered it under her breath.

I pretended not to hear.

"Hurry up and get in!" I yelled at Alex. So I don't murder my stepsister.

Sitting inside the car was five-star luxury compared to the frozen bleakness outside. Alex used a little tool on his key ring to unscrew the panel under the steering wheel. He pulled out a plastic plug with colored wires running through it.

"Let's get some heat. Hotwiring 101. You can learn anything on YouTube."

Jade and I watched as Alex twisted the ends of the brown and red wires together, flinching as they sparked. The dashboard lit up and static came from the radio. We had power!

"Wahoo! That was awesome." Jade gave Alex a fist bump.

"Pretty cool, if a little shady," I agreed.

The heater pumped out burnt dust at first and then blissful warmth, enough for us to take off our ski jackets and warm our hands from solid blocks to movable fingers. The relentless splat of snow gave way to sideways blasts. Every time the wind picked up again, I figured this was it, full-on blizzard, but then it died back again and left me braced for the next bout. How much worse would peak blizzard be? I was frozen to the bone, sitting in a car that smelled of old socks and fake pine, but the relief of not having snow slapping your face, not bending your head against the wind, not having streaming eyes, was overwhelming. I closed my eyes and said a silent prayer to a god I didn't believe in.

I rubbed the tender tips of my fingers together. "We could try driving this out of here. Go to Reno and meet up with Mum and Oliver."

"Can you drive?" Jade asked.

"Well…not really." I looked down at my lap and thought about the last driver's test, where I ran a red light.

"Didn't think so." Jade stared out the iced windows. "Me neither. I just got my permit."

We glanced at Alex, but he shook his head. "No point with the roads like this. We'll only skid around and get stuck somewhere else." Alex hooked up the ignition anyway. But the wheels spun on the ice. "See, no chains either."

At least we were safe, and almost cozy, with the constant spatter of snow and the swaying of the car, as the wind gusted around us.

Inside, we'd thawed out enough to not be shivering. And despite Jade insisting we keep the driver's-side window open a crack so we wouldn't die from carbon monoxide poisoning, we could still wriggle our fingers and toes. My clothes stuck to me as the cold, dry snow thawed to a layer of damp.

"So," I said, "how did you learn to draw so well?"

Alex narrowed his eyes. "You looked in my sketchbook?"

"You looked in our whole cabin."

"Only to get Otis," said Jade, conveniently forgetting the reality of what had actually happened. Or perhaps that's how she really saw him. Fun Alex and his friendly dog. That would explain a lot.

Alex glanced back at me, waiting for me to say more.

"Your drawings were quite good," I said, "if a little bizarre." They were stunning, but I wasn't going to tell him that.

"I have some I can show you," said Alex, and he pulled out a fistful of paper from his pockets. He passed delicate sketches of shiny black insects to Jade in the back seat.

"They're awesome," said Jade, holding each one up. "A dung beetle, elephant, scarab, oriental cockroach, fancy. Did you draw these from life?" Jade smiled. "Not from our place, I hope." So, she did get that he'd been staying there.

"Ha." Alex laughed. "No, you keep a clean place. I'm sorry about all that stuff before."

"The staying-in-our-cabin-and-breaking-in-when-you-thought-we-were-asleep stuff?" I asked.

"Yeah, that." Alex scratched Otis behind his ears, causing the dog's tail to thump against the car seat.

"Okay," said Jade.

"That's it?" I stared at her. "You forgive him just like that?"

"Well, the shit has kind of hit the fan since then." Her face cracked into a huge grin.

I didn't know if it was the relief of finally being warm, the knowing we were okay and it would all be over soon, or just craziness, but within seconds we were all laughing so hard tears rolled down our cheeks.

"Oh shit," said Jade, "we needed that." She wiped her eyes on her sleeve.

I smiled at her.

"I'm still mad at *you*," she said, but she gave a small smile back. "Here." She passed the drawings back to Alex. "You should keep them safe."

"Yeah, they just come crawling onto my sketch pad." He looked down at his hands. "Beetles are my current obsession." He smiled to himself, then tried to mask the joy, bringing himself back to reality.

"They're beautiful," I said. "If I was that good, I'd have given up on school long ago." My eyes rested on his just a little too long. I blushed and turned away.

"It's just a hobby." He flicked back his hair like it was nothing. "It takes more than talent to be an artist."

"But you can try," said Jade. "I want to be a doctor, like my mom."

"You do?" I had no clue. But then I didn't know anything about her.

"Yep, that's why I'm in all the AP classes. It takes more than luck and talent to get into the right med school." She bit her lip like she might have said too much.

"I can see you doing that. I bet your mum would be proud." I wish I knew what I wanted to do. Survive. Stay somewhere for more than one year. Belong.

I looked at Alex. His head was against the window like he was sleeping, but he was watching me. He raised his brows.

I subtly shook my head. *You are not forgiven.* And with that the car spluttered and died. The heater had finally drained the gas.

17

1:15 p.m.

I JOLTED AWAKE. DROOL SEEPED FROM THE CORNER of my mouth.

I'd been deep in one of my reoccurring dreams. Leaning out of a bedroom window, staring across the freeway at a tiny, bright, Caribbean-blue house. Like a child's picture, square with a triangle roof, one window, only it had become real, and it was surrounded by a sea of gray concrete, stuck in the wrong place, in the wrong country, maybe even the wrong time, and I had no idea how to get home, and suddenly there I was awake with two people I didn't know, stuck on a frozen highway somewhere in Tahoe.

Alex raised his eyebrows and smiled. "Nope, you're still in the nightmare."

Too right. I shivered. It was freezing. I could see my breath. I wiped the condensation off the window to see out into the swirling white.

We'd decided to stay in place. Being inside a heated-up car, even if it was slowly cooling down, had to be better than being out there, with the snow pelting from all directions. We had a thick layer of snow as insulation, even if some of it had made its way in.

Behind me on the back seat Jade had managed to fall asleep with Otis dozing in a heap over her.

I whispered to Alex, "How long have you been staying in the cabin?"

Alex blew his hair from his eyes. "It wasn't planned. I *was* lost, took the wrong path, and stumbled on it. It wasn't on the scouting list, too remote. But it was easy to open, and Otis was hungry, and I was cold. I'd have left it in the same state as I found it."

"How long?" I locked eyes with him. "No bullshit."

"I'd been there a day. I wasn't going to stay once you arrived." He curled around to face me. "It was a crap base, too far from anywhere."

"You'd been watching, hoping to sneak in while we slept." I frowned.

"Only to get my backpack."

"You had a key with you. You took it so you could let you yourself back in. You probably still have it." I held my hand out. "I'm not stupid."

Jade stirred and muttered something about nightingales.

"I'm telling you how it is," Alex whispered. He pulled the key from his pocket and placed it in my palm. "It was unlocked. I locked it and brought the key with me when I took Otis for a walk. That's why I had to unlock it to get back inside. It's lucky I was there to keep those guys in the red truck away or they could have just walked in and taken everything." He flicked the hair from his eyes. "I mean, it was odd that they were 'lost' in the early hours. They could have been checking out empty places to see what they could steal." He nodded to me like he was our savior for providing free security.

"It's not lucky that you broke in. And you left the back door unlocked. That's why it was bolted when you came back." I glowered out the window. "You said those guys in the truck were lost. Now you're saying they were casing the place." There was no way I was letting him know I'd spoken to them before he'd arrived on the scene, not when he still wasn't coming clean. "What about that list in your notebook?"

"I risked my life to save you!"

"I only went back in to find *you*!" I owed him nothing.

He sighed when he saw my glare. "I know you saw those lists, but I swear I wasn't planning anything with your house. Once I knew there were people there, I wasn't going to come in again. I honestly just needed my backpack."

He was so easy to believe. "Look, whatever you were doing… just because the house was there, doesn't make it right," I said.

"No. I guess not." Alex grimaced. "Sometimes people get into situations they don't realize they're in until it's too late."

The wind buffeted against the Mini, making the whole chassis shudder. Jade stirred, flopping her hand onto Otis's ear.

"So, you are mixed up in something?"

Alex wiped a peephole on the condensed window. "Sometimes it's not that simple."

We could hear a car engine in the distance.

Jade sat bolt upright, suddenly awake. "Another car!"

We scrambled and got out of the Mini to wave the driver down.

As the engine got louder a shape emerged from the fog of snow—bright lights, big tires, red double cab, pickup truck.

"It's AJ and Nico!" I called out.

"Hide!" Alex yelled. "They're bad news."

I glanced back at the Mini, but it was too far away. They'd spot me before I could make it back there for sure.

"Over here!" shouted Jade from her crouched position behind some trees.

I raced to her. Otis ran barking into the road. Alex pulled him back and joined us behind the trees.

"Stay still." Alex kept his hand on my shoulder, just to be sure. Like I was going to put us all at risk.

The tires screeched on the icy road. What were they even doing out here? I ran through it in my head: they were lost (they were not); Alex had been staying at the cabin; they were picking up a friend. There was something about the way they'd acted with Alex, gripping his arm, the cruel laughter, the cigarette flicked at him. A sense of power, of ownership.

The truck came to a skidding halt.

Nico jumped down to the Mini, yanking the door open so hard the whole car swayed. He rifled through the glove compartment, then the car-door pockets. "Good stuff in here! Idiot left his backpack!" Not friendly, not friendly at all. He threw Alex's backpack over his shoulder.

"Any sign of life?!" AJ yelled.

Nico took a quick glance around. "Nah, too cold for anyone to be out here. They must have got a ride."

Jade gave me a warning look. Don't move. Not that I would. We were both petrified.

AJ slammed on the accelerator and off they went, skidding down the icy road.

18

2:25 p.m.

"WE CAN'T STAY ON THE ROAD. WE DON'T WANT THEM to see us," Alex said.

"Why are they looking for you?" I glanced up in time to catch a snowflake in the eye.

"What makes you think they're looking for me?" Alex stomped his feet up and down and hugged himself. The wind slapped his hair into his eyes.

Jade shivered beside him.

"They must know you. Nico said *he* left his bag. Not *there's a bag*," I pointed out. They'd find his wallet and where he lived and everything.

"Um, because it's a big black backpack, they figured it was a guy's." He shrugged. "Anyone would assume that, wouldn't they?" Alex tightened Otis's leash around his hand. He glanced at my worried face. "It's okay, they won't know who I am." He tapped his jacket pocket. "Moved my wallet after the last invasion of my privacy." He grinned like I might grin back. I didn't. "Wait." He frowned. "How do you know their names?"

"AJ and Nico," said Jade before I could deny anything. "We met them already."

I shrugged. "They were at the cabin earlier, looking for a friend, but they were lost, except I guess they weren't."

"So, who are they?" Jade crossed her arms.

"You met them already?" Alex glared at me. "Why didn't you say?"

"You don't need to pretend you don't know them. Jade knows you met them last night."

"What?" Jade turned to Alex then back to me. "No, I don't. What the hell? So we're all keeping secrets, are we?" She shivered and shrunk further into her jacket.

"Yes, they were there last night asking for directions." Alex was sticking to that lie. "They've met you two already, so they know there were three of us in the house. And they've probably seen the state of the cabin. Not a stretch for them to be looking for us."

His argument felt wrong. A curl of distrust wriggled in my belly.

"But why bother looking for us?" asked Jade.

"I agree. It makes no sense." I shivered. "But right now we need to find shelter before we freeze to death."

We were still huddled behind the trees off the side of the road. We weren't going to last there for long, that was for sure.

"We should go back to the cabin. Mom and Dad might be there by now." Jade looked longingly at the horizon.

God, I hoped not. "No one's driving anywhere in this, unless they've got a giant pickup with massive snow tires," I said. Like those guys. They'd probably been gearing up for this kind of thing all their lives, seeing themselves as rugged survivors. I shuddered. To think I'd thought they were nice. "Where do you and Oliver go when you're up here? A supermarket, petrol station, restaurant, anything. It can't be all dead up here."

"There's a Safeway," said Alex, "but that's back in Truckee, which is pretty far."

No help at all. "What about that doughnut place?"

"Soto's. Yes, of course. Mr. Soto will help us. Can't be more than a couple of miles away." Jade's face fell. "That's where we'd have been anyway, if everything hadn't gotten so messed up."

"What do you mean 'messed up'?" Alex nudged her. "You met me and Otis!"

Otis barked and wagged his tail.

Jade rubbed his head. "I guess there's a tiny silver lining." She grinned at Alex.

And he grinned back. Great.

"Perfect. Food, warmth, maybe even a landline. Yay, it's a plan." I rubbed my hands together with fake glee. "I'll leave a note, in case someone comes along, so they can let Mum and Oliver know we're alive. And where we're headed." Because surely, Oliver had to be worried about Jade by now.

I was so impressed with my message idea that I didn't realize how stupid it was until I looked back. The snow rapidly covered my SOS, LOTTIE JADE ALEX with an arrow and SOTO'S, carefully made from twigs that I had stuck across the rear windshield. Only the twigs would be around when the sun finally came back. I just hoped we would be too.

We walked in silence. My cold cloud breath puffed around my thoughts.

Silhouettes danced against the sharp mountain ridges and the vast slate sky. My toes tingled with cold. The snow fell steadily, ice-mush dropping straight down, but at least the wind had lessened. I stopped every few seconds to wipe the snow from my eyelashes. I needed a bigger hat, or a balaclava. It only took a few moments for me to fall behind.

"I didn't think you'd wait again," I said, once I'd reached them.

"Of course we would," said Jade. "You would for us, right?"

Dad didn't wait or come back. He left me there, an eight-year-old, freezing in the car, waiting, waiting, waiting for someone who'd forgotten how to love.

I nodded. "Always." Or maybe I was just like Dad, and when push came to shove—as Mum would say—I'd be out of there, free to do my own thing, instead of everyone else's.

The two-lane road finally came to a fork in the road. A sign pointed to Truckee, eleven miles to the left, or Soto's Shakes & Supplies, two miles to the right.

"Right turn," said Jade, "for Soto's. OMG, those malt shakes."

"They're the best." Alex pulled his hood up like it was all settled and we'd chosen our adventure. "Chocolate with a cherry on top."

"Jesus, I can't believe you're craving ice cream when it's this bloody cold." I stamped my feet in a desperate attempt to keep the circulation flowing.

"Any time's a good time for ice cream," said Jade, then she coughed a wheezy cough.

"Your asthma's back." I stopped stomping to hear her breathe.

"I'll be okay. Jeez." She tried staring Alex and me down, but she took two puffs then spun the orange canister in her hand. "Happy now?"

We both nodded. But I couldn't help counting down, six puffs left.

Alex whistled for Otis, who'd run off to sniff out a squirrel.

We turned right and the wind turned with us, straight into our faces. Ghost trees loomed out of the whiteness, iced and silent as we passed. Witnesses to the death march. Needles of pain pricked under my fingernails—blue ice ran in my veins, making my limbs heavy and numb.

Otis bumped up against me, tongue out, face covered in snow. Poor thing. He hadn't wanted this either. I knelt and knocked the ice off his ears and nose. He licked me gratefully, wet nose against my iced one.

"We'll follow this road for a couple of miles. It's not far." At least Jade knew where we were going or was good enough at lying to convince me. "We can call Dad as soon as we get there." Yep, that was her highest priority too. Take us away from this nightmare.

I linked my arm with Alex's on one side and Jade's on the other. She could hardly refuse. A huddle of three lost people would stay warmer than a huddle of one. Assuming they didn't stay lost for too long.

19

3:15 p.m.

WHEN YOU CAN'T SEE WHERE YOU'VE BEEN, OR WHERE you're going, time becomes elastic, meaningless. We were not there, but we'd be there sometime in the future; in between was misty-white, sharp, and icy. Nothing was real, except the cold, the biting, ragged, numbing cold. Two sure things: one, Jade didn't have a clue where she was going, and two, Alex was too cold to care.

"I thought you knew Tahoe like a native." I was too cold to be kind.

"We might have walked past it and not seen it because everything's so white." Jade tripped over her boots and just caught herself. She was knackered too.

Alex stamped his feet and rubbed his hands together. "I'm so cold. I can't wait to see Mr. Soto and get warm. Hot chocolate first, then milkshake." He was so positive, like a constantly jumpy puppy. Cute but annoying.

On four hours' sleep and with a migraine head, I could barely smile. I always forgot migraines left me grumpy. What we needed was a distraction. Something to focus on that wasn't walking, or feeling so bloody cold, or wondering how much farther we had until we got to the mythical Soto's.

"Whoever has the best 'I haven't been this cold since' story wins the first shake at Mr. Soto's," I said. Because we had to make it there. I didn't even like ice cream.

"Scotland," said Jade. "The Highlands in winter. Freezing snow and wind and the rental car wouldn't start. Dad made me walk forever."

My stomach tensed, fearful of where this might be going.

"And it was muddy and steep, and my boots kept slipping. I saw the northern lights then too, up by Inverness." Her face lit up. "And it was magical. That's how I knew what they were." Way to bring us back to reality.

I tutted. "Pretty good, but I bet you ended up in a nice cozy pub."

Her face fell. "With me and Dad by the fire staring at a roast dinner, beef, huge potatoes, and those Yorkshire pudding things."

Good times. Happy, normal family times. The kind of times I never had.

Jade continued, "Mom always wanted to see the northern lights. It was our first vacation since she'd passed." Jade took a deep breath, "We were too sad to eat."

"God, I'm sorry. I shouldn't have started this silly game." I didn't know what to say; everything was wrong.

Jade sniffed and shook her head. "It's okay. You had no idea. It's just, Dad and I only have each other. What if we don't make it?"

"Oh, come on." Alex squeezed her shoulder. "There's no way I'm going to let that happen, Eagle Scouts' promise!"

I brushed the tear from my eye, shaking my head as if it were just snow. "Yeah, we're definitely getting out of here. No way I'm not going to live, only for my mum to kill me!" I smiled, and Jade smiled back. A small, sad smile, but still it was there.

"So," Alex started, "listen to this sad story. I got lost once when we first moved here. I can't believe I'm sharing this. I skipped school to go snowboarding and we went way up on the lifts, and they were all expert boarders and I had no clue, but I was all like, yeah, I go backcountry all the time. I hung behind and let them all go first, so I could copy what to do."

Yep, that sounded like him.

"And then I strapped up and pushed off and managed to balance all the way to the bottom of this ninety-degree drop, until I bashed into this woman, who was like this total beginner skier, and we got tangled up and stuck. And she managed to get herself back up and limped away. No one came to help, or report me missing. They just skied past me full speed. And I lay there not able to move for three hours."

"No way!" said Jade. "Someone must have seen you lying there."

Alex shook his head. "Nope, nobody stopped to help."

"At least there were people around you the whole time. I bet they'd have stopped if they realized you were badly injured." I hugged myself as I walked. "Better than being all alone. Or missing the people you love." I glanced at Jade.

"There are studies where they found if there's twenty people around and you need help, everyone thinks someone else will help or call for help. But if there's just one or two people, they will help, because they feel more personal connection, more responsibility." Jade brushed the snow from the tip of Alex's nose. She was back on form.

"That's not always true. Sometimes one person can look you right in the eye and walk away." Too much. I stared at my feet, so they couldn't see my face.

"That's bad." Alex glanced anxiously at me.

I smiled weakly. "Here's my story. Once I got locked out and had to sleep in the shed, until Mum got home at four in the morning. Jade wins!"

"Come on, after ours?" said Alex. "Yours doesn't even qualify." He gave me a teasing grin. "Don't downplay your trauma."

I took a deep breath. "Okay then, you asked for it." Why was I sharing this? Oh yes, because the game was my stupid idea. "One time, Dad and I were hiking on Mount Snowdon, and it was slow going, climbing over barbed wire, and padlocked gates. It was snowing, softly, not hard like this. But I was only wearing my flowery anorak, and I couldn't stop crying because I was so cold, and my teeth chattered, and I couldn't feel my knees. Dad told me to go back to the car if I was going to give up and wait for him. I watched his back get smaller and smaller and smaller. And I was just a little kid." I closed my eyes. "And I was freezing and tired and scared, so I curled up into a ball and fell asleep. And when I woke up there was a deer outside, a pure-white, albino deer. And it stared right at me with huge brown eyes. And I wasn't tired, or cold, or sad. Then a raven called out and the deer leapt away."

"What happened?" asked Jade. "Where was your dad?"

"I don't know. He never came back."

"I'm sorry," Jade whispered.

We walked on for a few moments in awkward silence.

I tripped and went sprawling into the snow. My knee was killing me, but I jumped up and brushed the snow off.

"Hey"—Jade ran over to help—"are you okay?"

I nodded. No fuss. "Let's just keep going."

"Yeah," said Alex. "You get the first shake." He gave me a tiny fist bump. "Not for your story, but for the pain of your fall."

I gave a fake smile. "I'm not hurt." That story was my pain. I'd learned to think of it in fragments, tiny pieces of the truth. Bit by bit it didn't seem so bad. It was only when I put them all together that the picture became clear. And the worst thing was, it had no ending. I bit my cracked lips. They'd be coated in a layer of dried blood by the time we got to shelter.

Jade narrowed her eyes at me. "You sure you're okay? You look so sad."

Wow, she'd noticed. "I'm fine, just cold and tired."

Otis and Alex wandered slowly ahead. Jade stayed by my side, keeping pace with me, slowing as the snowdrifts grew, and speeding up on the smooth flats.

I couldn't feel my feet, my fingers, or my nose. Walking felt like

I was balancing on ice blocks, no ankles, no feet—slow torture, wading through snow, sometimes sinking waist deep, and still the snow was falling, falling, falling.

Alex fell back to keep pace with us. Otis struggled beside him, as if he'd forgotten which paws to move to walk. One always got left behind, stuck frozen to the snow. His tail sagged between his legs. He stopped and looked at Alex with big sad eyes, as if to say 'Why are you doing this to me, why?' Then he nudged Alex like a giant sheepdog that had lost all his sheep but one.

My teeth chattered. We'd given up on talking. I hugged myself, tucking my hands into my armpits, which was not a great idea for balance when tripping over rocks and half-covered shrubs and occasionally my own boots.

And with that thought, I went flying into the top of a brick wall. The rest was buried under five feet of snow, leaving a curb of brick for me to catch my stupid, too big snow boots on. I sat in the snow, clutching my grazed shin.

"Lottie, you found it!" Jade ran to me, pulling me gently up on my feet. "Look!"

A carved wooden sign, SOTO'S SHAKES & SUPPLIES, painted in bright tangerine, peeked from a snow-covered roof ahead. The store stood alone, slightly back from the road. Its front door slammed open and shut with the wind.

20
3:55 p.m.

THE BUILDING WAS LONG AND LOW, A HOBBIT DEN built into the snow mound, with two small ice-covered windows in the front and a veranda around the outside, with steel grating laid on top of the wooden floor. If it wasn't for the sign, we might not have found the shop in this white-on-white world. I slipped on the thick-crusted ice, just managing to grip on to a veranda post.

"For the ski boots," Alex said, pointing to the grating. "Stops you from slipping."

I came to a halt and twisted around the post. But I grinned back at him. We'd found it. No more snow in the face, no more storm. We were safe.

The shack roof had a wedge of snow on it, at least eight inches thick. It hung over the side, like a person precariously close to the edge of an abyss, leaning over just a little bit too far.

Otis beat us to the door. He barked and whined on the covered porch, running up to the banging door and away again, like he was worried it might bite him.

"He's freaked out by something." Alex glanced around.

"Come on, sweetie." Jade cuddled Otis to calm him down. "Come and meet Mr. Soto. He'll have treats inside." But Otis wasn't having any of it.

Alex took a dog treat from his pocket. "Here, Otis, come inside." He opened the door, tantalizing Otis from the threshold.

Otis took the treat but stayed outside, barking and pacing.

"Guess Eagle Scouts don't cover dog training," I said with a grin. I gave Otis a pat on the head. He wagged his tail but still wouldn't go inside. He acted like he was guarding us from whatever frightening thing was headed our way from the woods.

The parking lot was a meadow of snow, flanked by a row of tall pine trees that marked the edge of the woods. There was nothing there. Nothing to worry about. The clouds hung thick and heavy. But the snow softened.

"Screw this, I'm going in." I held the wooden door open. "Looks like someone broke in." The screen mesh had a hole ripped in it. Glass crunched under my feet as I entered. "Surely Mr. Soto would have cleaned it up, if he was here?"

"Mr. Soto?" Jade pushed past me, eyeing the long icicles hanging by the door as we entered the store.

"It doesn't look like he's here." Jade sucked her breath in.

The whole place was dim and dank. It smelled of burnt coffee and stale cinnamon rolls. Snow covered the windows, giving off an opaque glow. I'd expected a restaurant, but it was more of a mini market with a countertop and an area with stools where they served shakes. A newspaper rustled on the stand, by the register. There was another smell too, musty, dank, and something more primal that I couldn't place. Icy shivers prickled my neck.

I whispered, halfway in the front doorway. "Hello?" My voice echoed through the store and came back to me. "No one's here."

The front door banged. Gusts of snow dust entered with the wind.

"Mr. Soto?" Jade called out. "Mr. Soto?" The worry in her voice echoed back. "He could be using the bathroom out back." She obviously knew all the ins and outs of the place. "Or he could be upstairs in his apartment."

"Would he leave the store door smashed up like that?" Alex passed Jade a Snickers bar. "Mr. Soto won't mind. It's an emergency, and he knows you, and we'll pay for it."

"Oh yeah, got money, do you?" I helped myself to one too.

"Of course we'll pay," Jade mumbled while biting into the bar. She helped herself to another then wrote down on a piece of scrap paper by the cash register *Alex, Jade, and Lottie owe four Snickers bars.* "Just keeping track." She pulled open a drawer and took out an orange inhaler. "He still keeps it in the same place. Thank God. Okay," she said, seeing my face. "I was running a little low; it's not a big deal."

"Until it is," said Alex.

"I've got a spare now, so you can both stop nagging!" And she slipped it into her pocket. "I'll replace it when all this is over." Jade's eyes drifted to the back of the store. "Did you hear that?" She froze for a moment. "Like a snuffle?"

"Nope. It's nothing." My stomach grumbled. I was hungry, but beneath that was an itch of fear. The store was full of shadows and whispers, if you listened hard enough. I knew it was only the wind, and the snow, and the wooden beams creaking. "Where's the entrance to the flat? Maybe Mr. Soto's watching TV or something and that's what you heard."

"There's no power," said Alex, like I was an idiot who hadn't noticed.

"You have to go out back to get to his apartment door." Jade leaned forward. "There's definitely something there." She pointed to the darkest corner of the store.

"Alright, we'll check it out," I whispered. I didn't expect there to be anything. The space was too small for us not to have heard an animal scrabble to hide as we came in. And a person would have stood out a mile away.

"Creep up quietly," Jade whispered back. "It could be a trapped animal." She turned on the flashlight she'd helped herself to.

Alex took a stick of jerky out to Otis, letting the door bang behind him for added drama.

"Here." Jade passed me a red Maglite, weighty enough to knock someone out.

I tested it on the newspaper rack—knocking the magazines and sending the papers flying. So much for staying quiet, but it was pretty clear I'd been scared about nothing. I picked up the newspaper lying at my feet and checked the headline: PREPARA-TIONS UNDERWAY FOR FIRST SNOW OF THE SEASON—TAHOE SKI SEASON COULD START EARLY!

I turned it over. You could get a lift pass for eighty dollars, early season special—*very* early considering the resorts didn't officially open for another six weeks.

I checked the date: Friday, October 25. The last papers delivered. Before the auroras and the power outage. For the first time in my life there was no 24/7 news. We'd stepped back in time. All we knew was what we'd seen, what we'd experienced, and what we could find out from others—if there were any others around here.

"Lottie." Jade jabbed my arm. "Come on." She put her finger to her lips. "Don't scare it."

Right, don't worry about our safety, but I nodded anyway.

There were three aisles running the length of the store, with shelves high enough not to be able to see over. We crept along the one closest to the back wall, accidentally rustling packets and boxes as we went. It was hardly a stealth mission. The back wall was lined with defrosting freezers full of pizza, and fridges full of beer.

A big gust of wind swept into the store, making the front door bang even more. We'd need to barricade ourselves in to keep the wind out if we stayed the night. I reached the end of the aisle and made my way between the two middle ones.

"Lottie? Jade?" It was Alex. "Otis still won't come in. Find me some more dog food, will you?" He came inside to rummage through packets of energy bars.

"Sure." I shone the flashlight beam along the shelves. Bread and other baked goods, pastries, and cookies. I broke into a packet of Oreos. We'd be so dead if Mr. Soto came in right then. "Does he eat cheesy biscuits?"

136

"He eats anything, but I'd prefer if you found him some proper food." Wouldn't we all.

I gripped my flashlight again, flashing the beam up to the broken dirty-white tiles that made up the ceiling. "Jade?" I called softly. I hadn't heard her for a while.

Tiny little patters clicked ahead of me. I cringed. There, a dark, furry outline. I gasped and dropped the flashlight. It froze in front of me. I took a deep breath to steady myself. "It's just a little mouse!"

"Give it a pathway out. It's probably terrified." Jade jumped to the side as it sped past.

Alex opened the door wide and watched as the mouse fled past Otis and vanished into the snow.

"Wow, Otis didn't even try to chase it. What's going on? Scared of a mouse, bud?" Alex scratched Otis's ears, but Otis still wouldn't come past the threshold.

"It was a vole, not a mouse," Jade said, munching her way through a packet of Lay's.

"Alex, drag Otis in. It's too cold to leave the door open." I shivered. "Alright, let's find Mr. Soto."

21
4:15 p.m.

"IT STILL SMELLS FUNNY IN HERE." JADE WRINKLED HER nose.

It was pretty musty smelling. "It's just damp and cold and maybe some of the food's starting to turn, with the freezers being off." I said.

"They've only been off just over a day. It would take forever for them to defrost. The ice cream isn't even melted," said Jade. "It's weird that Mr. Soto isn't here checking on everything."

"Well, where do you think Mr. Soto is?" I asked Jade, like she was the expert on him.

"He has to be around. There's no one else to watch the store." Apparently, she was.

There was a door at the back of the store. I'd thought it was the bathroom, and maybe he was in there. But no such luck. It was just a storage room. I closed the door, but the latch didn't work, so I left it as closed as I could, sticking a couple of cans of tomato soup in front of it. Whatever was in there (probably nothing) could possibly come out.

"Well, at least we've got somewhere to stay, anyway." I sat down too hard on one of the counter stools and stared up at the posters of shakes and malts and ice-cream floats in fifties-style glory hung along the wall. Not a bad place to be holed up in, if it weren't for the missing person, the weird smell, and the broken, creaking door.

"Yeah, we should wait the storm out here for sure. I know he won't mind. Wherever he is." Jade's voice tapered off into a worried frown at the end.

A gust of snow pushed its way through the cracks in the front door. Alex came in shaking snow from his hair and slammed it behind him. "We'll cover that up once I get my stupid dog inside."

"How about trying these?" Jade passed Alex a cold hot dog.

Otis refused to budge but ate it in one gulp from the veranda.

Alex grabbed a fleece blanket from the rack. "I'll throw this over him and hope he comes to his senses before he freezes his tail off out there."

Jade and I put on all the warm clothing we could find: scarves, beanies, and thin thermal gloves to wear under our ski gloves. I stuffed a handful of energy bars into my pockets. Jade found a half balaclava—the benefits of being close to a ski resort. I felt like a giant marshmallow, but at least I was dry and almost warm.

"But we *can* use more of these." I threw Jade a hand warmer.

"I love those!" Jade snapped it in half, making an instant chemical heat. "But don't get your hands too hot, too fast because of chilblains."

"Chilblains?" I frowned. "What the hell are those?"

Alex raised his brows at me as he stepped back inside. "It's what happens when you warm up cold fingers and toes too fast. Your fingers and toes blow up like sausages and get sores, and I'm not even joking."

"Okay, no popping fingers!" I threw a hand warmer at him.

He grinned and pocketed it. "We should check Mr. Soto's apartment, see if he's there. The entrance is around back."

"Let's hope he's there," said Jade, twisting on her stool.

"One thing first." I beamed my Maglite behind the counter. There had to be a phone here somewhere. "Ah, here we go." Attached to the wall was a seventies-style, avocado-green plastic phone, long cord and everything. But no ringtone. I twirled the cord round my finger. "It's dead." I looked at Alex.

He shrugged. "Makes sense. With this much snow, phone lines could easily be down."

"Yeah, it happens," Jade added. "Then it takes forever for them to come out and fix them all." She sucked the air between her teeth. "I hope Mr. Soto is just sheltering in place."

"We'll get going and check. Also, with all this stuff we're wearing we owe him like five hundred dollars," I added.

"Don't worry, Dad will cover that," said Jade, blissfully unaware that I hadn't spent that much on clothing ever.

Otis was quivering from the cold out there, even under the blanket. "Jade, why don't you stay by the door and see if you can coax him in?" I hugged Otis before I went by. "Since you're the animal expert and everything."

"Great idea. He adores you," said Alex, making it doubly hard for Jade to refuse.

She rolled her eyes but wrapped Otis in yet another blanket and cuddled up next to him. "Come on, silly, come on in." He nudged a little closer to her.

Steel clouds bumped overhead, but the snow had finally slowed to a light flurry. They'd get the roads open soon. Then there'd be Mum and Oliver and burnt cabins to explain. Part of me wanted the roads to be shut down forever. Alex and I walked the length of the veranda, stepping off the end to get around to the back.

"Ah, here's the bathroom!" I didn't realize how badly I needed it until it was there in front of me.

"Hey," Alex called after me as I bolted in, "don't sit down on the…"

"Got it." I'd been so close to sitting down on that porcelain bowl. That would have been all kinds of uncomfortable.

There was one bath stall, a small unisex deal, unlocked, luckily. It had one of those weird plastic mirrors that distorted your reflection. What was the point of them, to see that you made a reflection? I couldn't see the color of my eyes, or even that I had eyes, just vague circles and a red nose.

"Hurry, I want to go too," said Alex.

"You can go anywhere."

"It's a bit cold out here!"

A loud clang came from the front of the store. It could be Jade, but it sounded like something bigger. I waited a moment, listening. Nope, Jade was fine. She could totally look after herself. We just needed to find Mr. Soto.

The entrance leading to Mr. Soto's apartment was next to the bathroom door. We jammed ourselves against it, until it sighed open a fraction, enough to show the flight of stairs that led up to his second-floor apartment. We shoved into the door with our backs, pushing it open enough to squeeze through.

"Mr. Soto?" Alex shouted up but there was no answer. He ran up the steep stairs and knocked on the front door, then rattled it. "Door's locked. He must have gone somewhere."

"Would he leave the store broken into like that?" A dull sense of dread twisted in my gut.

Alex yanked his beanie down further over his ears. "We looked for him. He's not here. He could have gone for some tools or wood to fix up the door. At least we can stay in the store tonight." He pulled the door tightly shut.

"Yes, let's get back inside. I'm freezing already." I turned to go and noticed something smooth and brown poking up out of the snow—only five feet from the apartment's entrance—a shoe. My stomach lurched. I brushed the snow to reveal an ankle and then a leg. I'd found Mr. Soto.

22
5:03 p.m.

"OH SHIT." ALEX REACHED FOR MY HANDS, AND WE stood like that holding each other.

I tried swallowing the bile, but I couldn't hold it down. I puked in the snow.

"Did you find him?" Jade called from the front of the store.

"Em, kind of. Stay there." I glanced at Alex. His face was as panic stricken as mine. "We have to cover him. We can't leave him out here like this." Everything inside of me trembled.

"It might be a crime scene." He stood staring at the shoe.

"What do we do? Who do we report it to? How do we report it?" Silver spots spun before my eyes. Not another migraine. I bent over so I wouldn't faint. I puked again—all the Snickers bar. I'd rather faint.

Alex pulled the hair from my face. "Hey, you're having a panic attack. Breathe slowly." He put his arms around me, guiding me up.

I nodded and rested my head on his chest, focusing on the faint apple scent of his purple hoodie that he *still* wore under his ski jacket. And I closed my eyes and breathed it all in. But then I opened them and there was Mr. Soto. I clamped my hands over my mouth.

"First time?" he asked, as if he were a cop or something.

I nodded.

Jade walked over from the front of the store. "What are you doing?" She took one look at me resting against Alex. "Oops, spoiled a moment, sorry," she said in a not-sorry way. Then she glanced at Mr. Soto and her mouth fell open. "Shit, is that him?"

Alex pushed more snow over him. "He's already hidden, mostly. We just need to cover his shoes up."

"Are you *sure* it's him?" Jade asked, knowing the answer.

Alex leaned down to where Mr. Soto's head should be and brushed the snow away. Mr. Soto's face was purple. His cracked lips had crystallized, taking on a white sheen. He must have been there a while. A line of blood spread out from his forehead and had congealed into a frozen mass below his ear.

"Okay." Jade's voice came out cracked and high. "How, how"— she swallowed—"how did he die?" She knelt down next to him. "Oh, poor Mr. Soto. To lie there, dead, right outside your house. Where was he going? Was he…?"

The unsaid word hung in the air between us—*murdered.*

"You know," said Alex, looking at the door, "I wonder if it was simpler than we think. If he was about to close the bottom door and the ice and snow fell down from there."

144

I couldn't tell if he meant it or was just trying to make Jade feel better. I looked up at the missing patch. "How? He'd need to slam the door to jolt the snow, and then he'd have fallen right by the door. Maybe he slipped on the ice and couldn't get up, so he crawled over to there, to be nearer to the parking lot, and froze to death waiting for help." I clasped my hands over my mouth. "That's so awful. Can we close his eyes? I don't want to see them." I'd never forget his glazed, brown eyes. I shivered. The wind kicked up. Snow fell, thick and fast. We needed to get inside and get warm again.

"Yes, let's close his eyes." Jade leaned over and gently closed them. "Rest in peace, dear, sweet man." A tear trickled down her face.

We covered Mr. Soto's face up with snow, marking the spot by placing a twig of pine upright by his head, like some kind of macabre X marks the spot. I threw up a little more in my mouth. It was easier not seeing him. Easier but still awful.

"We'll let the authorities know, as soon as the power's back, and stay here for the night, keep warm, out of the wind. At least we have food and sleeping bags." Alex was trying to convince himself, but it wasn't like there were any other options.

Jade wiped her tears. "I'm glad it was us who found him. He'd want us to stay."

"That's lucky, as we don't have much of an option," Alex pointed out.

I didn't want to stay. Every moan, every creak would make me think Mr. Soto was watching, angry at us for being in his store while he was dead outside. But there was nowhere else to go. Alex was

145

right. Here we had shelter, warm clothing, food, and drink. And it was unlikely whoever came before would brave the storm to come out again. Once the roads were clear, people were bound to check in on Mr. Soto, even if it was only to top off their supplies. This was the only place to wait out the storm.

The front door blew back open, and Otis howled and ran over to us. It was getting colder by the second.

"He wouldn't come with me, and he wouldn't go in." Jade rubbed his head.

He looked up at her mournfully as if to say sorry.

"There was a weird noise when you left. I thought it was Otis, but it was from the back of the store, and Otis was right there by the door," Jade said.

I entered the store. "I think I heard it," I said as Jade and Alex came in behind me. My flashlight dimmed. I tapped it against the carpet-tiled floor. "We should barricade the door, but it just feels wrong leaving Otis out there."

"I've never known him to act like this. I don't know what his problem is." Alex frowned. He looked the most worried I'd ever seen him, much worse than when the cabin went up in flames, and even more than when AJ and Nico showed up and took his backpack. And it hit me then how much he really loved that sweet, stupid dog.

A rustle came from outside, followed by a thud. Otis was still out there, growling guttural and low at the front door. Maybe not so sweet.

"What the hell was that?" Jade whispered.

"It's just the wind and the snow whipping through the trees." I thought of Mr. Soto out there frozen under the mound of snow. I shuddered and zipped my jacket up. My flashlight gave out completely.

The three of us crouched under the counter, listening. The storage door creaked. That smell, that pungent dankness, thickened around us. A whimper. Chills ran up my spine.

A lone can of tomato soup rolled across the floor, stopping in front of us. Alex and I exchanged a what-the-hell look. A clatter erupted farther down by the cereal boxes. Something was knocking over piles of stuff in what sounded like random chaos.

Soft paw patters ran around at the back of the store in the dark.

"It's got to be a raccoon or something," said Jade.

"I'll take a look." He beamed his flashlight into the middle aisle. "Stay there."

"Why, because you're such a man?" Jade darted out after him.

"Bloody hell." I rushed after them—I didn't need looking after either—and smacked straight into a display of Doritos. They crackled and fell like a supersized intruder alarm.

There was a rumbling moan, not like a raccoon at all. Every single one of my hairs stood on end. I held my breath, waiting for the next sound. "Jade," I hissed, "is that you?" I crept around the edge of a display, clinging to the shelves of food, doughnuts, and ramen noodles. Two cans of dog food sat on a bottom shelf, by the hand sanitizer. I reached to grab one.

A fog of musk hung in the air—wet dog mixed with skunk. A sniffle came from behind. Toes clenched, I spun around. Two shiny black eyes stared up in surprise. It sniffed—breathing me in. I backed away, scrambling on the floor, tripping over my own legs, back to the safety of the shake counter.

Alex and Jade slid up right behind me.

I pointed frantically at the aisle. "Bear!"

23

5:33 p.m.

WE CROUCHED UNDER THE SHAKE COUNTER, TAKING turns to pop up our heads and scan for the cub. All the time the light was fading, as more snow clouds gathered, and the wind kicked up from a tiny whirl into more of a howl. And snow began to fall, soft and steady again.

"The thing is, where there's a bear cub…" said Alex.

"…there's a mama," Jade finished. "We'll have to be really careful not to scare it."

"Yeah, the last thing we need is an angry mama bear," Alex whispered.

"Why are they even here? I thought bears hibernated in the winter," I said.

"They can get food all year in Tahoe, as long as humans leave it lying around, which most of them do, also…" Jade paused.

"Climate change," Alex finished. "There was hardly any snowpack last year."

"Yep, that," said Jade and fist-bumped Alex.

I sighed and peeked at the bear. It was sweet, snuffling around, gnawing on a bright yellow packet of cookies, until you saw its claws, like a sheaf of knives.

"We could sneak out and wait for it to leave, then get back in and bolt the door," I suggested.

"Why would it leave? It's warm in here with a ton of food. It's more likely its mom will join it," said Jade.

"And then she'll find us and be really mad," said Alex. Like I needed it laid out.

"That's it. We'll run out loudly and see if it follows, then run back in and shut the door on it." I grinned. I was that sure of my plan. It was only a cub, after all.

"That's a stupid plan," said Jade.

"Worth a try," said Alex. "Better than sitting here waiting to see if it gets mad at us."

Jade nodded and gripped her flashlight tighter. So easily persuaded by her bestie.

I eased my way from behind the shake counter, after almost knocking over the chocolate sprinkle toppings with my new layer of clothing girth, and peered into the gloom. The aisle closest to us was empty, except for a Mountain Dew can, which had finished spilling its contents and sat at the edge of a green-fizz pool. I pointed to Jade and Alex. And mimed with my fingers, *One, two, three, we run out the front door.* I mouthed, *One...two...three...*

"Run!" I shouted, to get the bear to notice us and chase us, only not too fast, and not to hurt us. Just enough to get it out of the store.

But Otis had other plans. Once we'd raced out, he blocked the door, growling at the entrance, and baring his teeth like the overprotective, giant dog he was. The bear cub ran a little way forward then backed away and looked anxiously out the window at Otis. Then it started to cry, at least I think that's what it did. It was a cross between a deep, loud honk and a guttural protest call. It wasn't happy, that was for sure.

"Otis, out of the way." Alex tried pulling Otis from the doorway, but he wouldn't budge.

"He's so stupid," I said. Idiot dog. Snow darts spat down my neck.

"That's why he wouldn't come inside. He's smart, not stupid. If a dog won't go in, you don't go in," said Jade, the animal expert, who ignored her own advice.

"But then you wouldn't have got your double layer of clothes, your new torch, or your stomach full of Snickers!"

"Shut up, Lottie." Alex held a stick of turkey jerky in the air. Otis backed away from the door to give the jerky a suspicious sniff. The bear cub stood on its hind legs against the door, crashing it open, just as Otis snapped down on his meaty snack.

Jade threw a doughnut away from the door into the snow, while Alex led Otis back into the store to stop him from chasing the bear. The cub crossed the veranda, scarfed down the doughnut, and took a tentative step toward Jade for more.

"Give it to him!" I shouted. On its hind legs the cub was way too big to argue with.

"Oh my God." Jade threw the whole box out into the snow. The cub tore after it.

I backed into the store with Jade. Otis and Alex were already in there.

"The store is ours!" I watched the cub tear the Doughboys Donuts box apart.

Alex was running around filling a backpack with energy bars, Gatorade, and ramen noodles. "We've got to get out of here before its mom comes."

"Why?" I asked. I spotted the rack of backpacks and grabbed one, stuffing it with water bottles and energy bars. "The cub's out. We should stay."

Otis went mental, trapped inside the store, growling through the window as the cub sat outside.

"Not with an angry cub, its mother nearby, and this huge food source. You saw how strong the cub is. Do you really think that old wooden door can withstand its mother's weight?" Alex shook his head and zipped up his bag. "Fully grown bears are enormous!"

"What about Mr. Soto's apartment? We could stay there." Jade looked expectantly at Alex.

My heart sunk. Mr. Soto, poor Mr. Soto. I'd never get those dead eyes out of my head. Keep it down, keep it down. I swallowed, but the bile stayed in my throat, hovering.

I locked eyes with Alex.

He shrugged. "Could try it. It's dry, and the bears won't follow us up those stairs."

"We can't." It came out sharper than I'd meant it to. "It's locked. We don't have a key."

"What about the bathroom?" asked Jade. "There's nothing for a bear in there."

"That would be gross." I screwed up my nose.

"You'd rather freeze?" Jade arched her brow.

"We could at least look for the key first," said Alex, ever the peacekeeper. "Unless you have any other ideas?"

The way the wind was whipping up the snow, there was no knowing if the body was covered by a snowdrift or if it had been blown it bare. I dug my nails into my palms. The pain helped me focus. Stop thinking of the eyes; think about the key, and the flat, and getting somewhere safe where we could wait this whole mess out.

"I do have one idea." I looked at Alex. "That might solve everything."

24

5:57 p.m.

I'D INTENDED TO GO ALONE, BUT ALEX INSISTED ON joining me for safety reasons. Jade didn't want to see Mr. Soto again, and I couldn't say I blamed her. Otis stayed by Jade's side while she finished packing supplies into borrowed backpacks.

Icy dust from the snowdrifts blew along with the wind. The pines whispered behind me, bracing themselves for the next onslaught. Alex and I had our puffer jackets on, with hoods tied tight and zippers all the way up to our chins, and still I shivered. At least the snow had softened; gentle flakes spun around us.

From the end of the veranda the body was clear. A distinct mound in the snow, pants showing dark blue against the white powder layered in the creases. I hadn't even noticed his pants before. The wind must have blown the snow off. At least his face was still covered. I swallowed and took a deep breath. The pine branch was still in place, sticking up from the snow lump, perpendicular to Mr. Soto's face.

I brushed off the snow and tried to figure how I was going to get into Mr. Soto's pockets. I tried his jacket first. The left side was easy, as it was completely flat. The right took a little more digging, a break for a bile puke, and more trying to pull the fabric of his pocket apart. Don't think about it, don't think about it. I squeezed my eyes shut for a second, blocking out everything but the key. I was rummaging around a dead man's pockets. I hoped this was the lowest I'd ever get. "Don't judge me," I said to the watching blue jay. "You steal eggs."

The lump in the pocket was a wallet. I left it. Next, his pant pockets. I hoped it was a quick death, there one minute, splat the next. For a second, I imagined it was Mum under there. My stomach flipped. What if she wasn't safe with Oliver in Reno? What if they'd come back and found the cabin all burnt out, and thought we were in there, dead? What if they were relieved? I pushed the thought away. Shit like that was not going to help. Oliver would never feel that way about Jade.

"Do you want me to do it?" Alex asked. I shook my head.

"Hey, you can do this," said Alex, and he reached over and gave my arm a squeeze, and a glow of warmth shot through my heart.

"Okay." I took my gloves off to search. My fingertips were dead already. I felt my way toward his front pant pockets. Alex's gold-flecked eyes watched me as I worked. The fabric had to be cut open with his penknife. No key.

I sat back on my heels. "What if he didn't have one? Or it fell out of his pockets when he fell?"

"If we can't find the key, we'll break the door down, and if we can't do that, we'll stay in the hallway. The power has to be back on soon." Alex smiled. "Then we'll call for help. We'll make it work out."

"Hope so." I blew on my hands in a futile effort to warm them.

"It'll be okay. We'll find bear-proof shelter"—Alex swept his hair off his face—"then I could go for a beer."

"I'd kill for a double latte." Just the thought made me salivate. "And thank you for helping me, you know." Rob a dead man.

We pushed the body onto the side to get to his back pockets. He was as stiff as a block of concrete. Wedged into his left pocket, covered in fuzz, were three keys on a pink plastic Soto's Shakes & Supplies key chain. Finally.

"Sorry, Mr. Soto." I felt like I should say something else, but what do you say? Sorry you're dead and now I'm robbing you? "We'll leave money for everything we've taken, or at least our addresses."

"He's dead, Lottie. He doesn't care." Alex stomped his feet and blew into his hands. "Come on, I'm freezing."

I didn't want to leave the body lying there. But there wasn't much else we could do, and the police might want us not to touch it, which was a bit late, but still. God, I was already thinking of it as a body instead of a person. Soulless, that's what I was.

We covered the face again. I shuddered to think of Mr. Soto's frozen face.

"Alright, let's hope these are the right keys!"

Forcing the entry door open was easier once we knew it could be done after the first time.

"If it's been done before, it can be done again. That's what my dad used to say, though I think he got it from an old movie," I said.

Alex squeezed into the hallway, moving aside to let me in. "I'm not sure that's always true." He scrunched his nose up. "Maybe in real life luck has more to do with it."

"For sure, but my dad loved all those old man-against-nature types of movies." Too bad he learned nothing from them. *The Grey, The Revenant, Touching the Void*, where there's no way out but through. He was supposed to get through it, not disappear and never come back. It's amazing how fast anger could appear like a vat of lava in my gut.

"You okay?" asked the boy who seemed to notice everything about me.

"Fine." I gave a fake smile and willed my flush of anger to chill.

We walked up the stairs to Mr. Soto's front door.

The second key fit as smooth as glass into the flat's lock. The door glided open. The scent of lilies rose to meet us. This was going to work. Alex and I raised eyebrows at each other across the dim, still room. I pulled up the blinds, letting in the view of mountains, dark swaying pines, and snow, snow, snow. I hated ski country.

Otis barked, wild and fierce.

Alex gripped my arm. "He's in full guard-dog mode. Something's wrong."

We bolted back down the hall. I tripped over the first stair and tumbled down the rest. Alex barely managed not to fall on top of me. Otis's frantic barking came from everywhere until it didn't, and for two seconds everything was silent.

Jade screamed my name, and I couldn't breathe.

An engine revved.

We're coming! I tried to shout, but it stuck in my throat, caught up with the panic and fear in there.

"Otis!" Alex yelled, as we bolted through the entry door.

Chunks of snow fell from the roof behind us, and an ice shard shattered as Alex pulled me into the cold slap of air.

"No!" Jade's scream echoed in the frozen void.

I charged along the veranda, boots skidding, heart racing, lungs aching, and came screeching to a halt when I saw the red truck idling in front of Soto's. Its taillights highlighted the snow spiraling in the exhaust fumes.

Jade stood in the doorway. "Otis! They've got Otis!"

I froze—a deer in the path of an oncoming car, all legs, no balance, couldn't breathe, couldn't think.

Alex rushed past me. "What the hell?" He stopped short as AJ leaned out of the truck window, poised for action.

"What you doing here?" Alex stepped forward, then froze.

Otis whimpered. He was a lump wrapped in a burlap sack in the back of the truck, bound too tight to even bark.

AJ nodded at me. "It's just Alex that we've come to see. Stay calm and everyone will be okay." He glanced at Alex. "You see, he made a promise and didn't deliver. On the one hand, being old friends, I don't want to hurt him. But I've made promises too, which leaves me in a bit of a bind."

"A promise?" I looked from Alex to AJ. They both stayed fixed on each other, like two scorpions ready to strike.

AJ jumped down from the truck, chunky black boots smashing into the crusted ground, and sauntered over to Alex. "I expected more from you." He sounded like a disappointed parent. The kind who doesn't yell, but slices through your soul with disapproval. "After everything we've been through. We're like family. Haven't we always had your back?" He closed his eyes, like it actually pained him to say it. "You've forced us to do this. We're taking the one thing we know you care about, until you deliver on your promise."

My heart pounded against my chest. Stay calm. Don't rile them up. "Leave him alone," I blurted out. I couldn't stop it.

AJ smiled, all charm and cheekbones. "Maybe I've misunderstood the nature of your new entanglement?" He caught my eye and smiled sadly. "Don't get yourself mixed up with him. He's not what he seems."

It was like he'd read our history in one glance. I shook it off and glared at him.

"Ah, so she knows already. Alex?" AJ tilted his head slightly.

Nico rolled his eyes. "Let's go, man."

"No, no." Alex's words tumbled out and hit the ground running. "They know nothing. They have no clue about any of this."

AJ smiled. "Let's hope so, for all your sakes. You know what to do." AJ said it like it was just a business transaction. He winked at me and climbed back into the truck.

Nico spat out the window into the snow.

AJ crunched the truck into gear and the wheels spun out, leaving a dirty gray trail of spewed-up slush. Alex sprinted after them, without a backward glance, and disappeared into the cold embrace of snow.

25

6:27 p.m.

"OH SHIT, LOTTIE." JADE WIPED HER STREAMING EYES.
"It was so fast. I couldn't stop them. They wrapped him in a sack
and took him. We have to get him back."

"Did they touch you?" I blinked back angry tears.

Jade shook her head. "No, they were all about Alex and Otis."
She breathed heavy and hard. "They had a gun."

"What?" I hugged her tightly. "It's not your fault." Poor Otis. He
was lovely and patient, plodding through the snow and herding us
along. Alex put his own dog in this situation. Even if he caught up
with them, they had a gun. He had nothing.

I flicked the snow from Jade's hood. "Alex went after them. He'll
come back once he's got Otis. We've got no idea where they're
driving to. The flat's unlocked. We'll stay here until the power
comes back, then call for help."

Jade pulled away. "You don't care about Otis and Alex at all."

She looked at me like I was a bad taste. "You don't care about anyone."

"This is all Alex's fault. They probably took Otis as ransom for stuff Alex was supposed to steal for them. Maybe even from your cabin. We're not going to risk our lives saving someone who already put us in danger!" All the air sucked out of my lungs. What if they'd taken her instead?

Jade crossed her arms. "Alex stayed when you were out of it. He'd never do anything to hurt us."

"You don't get it. He's not our friend. No matter how much you want him to be." I bit my lip. "I know you *like* like him, but he's just using you."

Jade actually laughed. "Oh my God, get over yourself. For your information, not that you're entitled to it, I don't go for boys in that way. So, you can relax about that."

"Oh, I didn't realize." It sounded exactly that stupid to me as soon as I said it.

"Why would you? It's not like you know anything about me. And it doesn't help that I'm not wearing my rainbow #gayasf T-shirt either. And yes, that is real, and no, I'm not answering any of your questions."

"Okay." I nodded. "Fair enough."

Jade hugged herself against the cold. "Alex could have taken the Einstein telescope and left before the fire, but he didn't. Even when he knew how much it was worth."

The telescope. That was it—the stray glances, the casual interest, the wanting to help rescue it; so sweet, so kind, so selfish. "Oh my

God, Jade, you're a genius. That's what he was after, the telescope. He must have told them about it that night."

"Well, it's ruined now. I'm going after those guys. You do what you like." Jade clenched her jaw.

Maybe I should just let her go, like Dad did to me. Nope, I couldn't do that. "You're so freaking stubborn." I never wanted a new family, but there it was. Jade might be irritating, but she was my stepsister, and there was no way I was going to let her run into danger alone.

The wind pushed the broken front door open, wide enough to rustle the last paper on the stand. The snow swirled against the window. I went inside, grabbed the backpack I had started to fill with supplies, and held out the one that Alex had packed.

Jade grabbed it and headed to the parking lot, following the tire tracks in the snow. "You coming or what?" she yelled over her shoulder.

"Yep." I slammed the door behind me.

The snow fell soft and heavy, throwing a white blanket on the world. We'd be okay with our borrowed backpacks stuffed with food and extra gloves, hats, hand warmers, flashlights. Basically, we'd raided the store. Our survival demanded it. At least that's what I told myself.

A movement caught my eye. There, darting between the trees, was a huge golden-brown shape against the snow. It stopped to let a smaller, darker brown shape catch up to it, saw me watching, and stood on its hind legs, all six feet of her—the mama bear. "Oh my God." My whisper floated like snow in the air.

Jade inched her way toward me. "Don't run. Back away slowly, back away, back away."

We backed out, away from the building, away from the food and shelter, never taking our eyes off her.

The mama dropped to all fours and pushed the cub along to the store entrance. It honked in protest. Her fur rippled in the breeze. She let out a low, guttural growl that punched my chest. She lifted her nose, sniffing us out.

"Don't run, don't run, don't puke, don't run." Jade murmured it like a mantra to me, until we'd made it far enough away from Soto's Shakes & Supplies for the bear to lose interest in us. Then Jade grinned at me and yelled "Run!" and we fled headlong into the white horizon.

26

7:01 p.m.

I SHOOK THE SOFTLY FALLING SNOW FROM MY FACE.
The trees blurred into a white smudge. I couldn't believe we'd
chosen to be out in the snow again.

"This way." Jade pointed out the truck's tracks with her flashlight. The boot prints alongside them were disappearing fast as the
wind blew fresh snow across them. The dark had fallen, and it was
rapidly shifting into a freezing, bleak night.

I paused for a second to get my breath. The snowdrifts had a
layer of ice underneath them, from the brief time it had stopped
snowing, so every step was a slip-and-slide. It was a frozen death
ride of ice. We should have turned and followed our footsteps back
to the apartment before the snow rubbed them out.

Jade walked right into me.

"You okay?" I asked.

She nodded. "You couldn't have stopped me. So don't beat yourself up."

Jesus, so much for gratitude. "I want the truth from Alex, and there's no way I was letting you go alone." So there.

Jade narrowed her eyes, but it was too cold to stand there staring at each other, so we trudged on.

The truck's deep tracks were saving us. Alex's boot prints became rivets in the snow, and the wind blew snow-mist across them. I tripped over a huge lump of snow, climbed out of a hollow, and staggered after Jade, into the wind and the stinging snow.

My limbs were turning numb despite my newly acquired layers. I should have grabbed more from the store instead of worrying about taking too much stuff. "Hey, got any extra Twizzlers?" A shot of sugar always made things seem better.

Jade pulled two from her pocket. "Emergency supply."

I stuffed them into my mouth. "Sorry."

"What for?"

"Everything!" I yelled over the storm.

Jade shook her head, freeing her hat momentarily from snow. "I'm sorry too, for forcing you to rescue Otis."

"It's okay. It's the right thing to do." I stared into the bleakness. "But we're not out of the woods yet."

Jade smiled. "Not out of the woods."

Hurray, she'd smiled. So, not all bad. There was no sign of Alex, or the truck, just tracks that were getting fainter and fainter. Hopefully they were still ahead of us. Though the idea of ahead was no longer clear. I linked hold of her arm, so we could help each other walk without being blown over.

If we lost direction, we'd end up wandering in circles. People do that when they can't see where they're going. They think they're following the tracks but they're following their own footprints round and round. The dominant foot leads, turning slightly more that way, right, right, right, or left, left, left, until you've made a lovely big circle. Dad taught me that. Don't spend your life walking in circles. Don't repeat your mistakes. I should have paid more attention.

I watched Jade from the corner of my eye. She was letting me in little by little, I could feel it. And now we could both die out here.

"Can you hear anything?!" I shouted right into Jade's ear to compete with the wind.

She shook her head. We stumbled along. These tracks could go on for miles. Snow slapped against my face, my eyes streamed, and wind shrieked from the treetops, like warnings from past ghostly spirits. I looked up at them waving the branches, frantically clasped in shrouds of icy white.

The Donner Party died out here. I'd watched the Ken Burns special with Mum. They'd traveled in this same area, over one hundred and fifty years ago, in a snowstorm with hardly any food, making their way to the Promised Land and ending up stranded at Donner Lake, though I guess it was called something different then. They'd camped in shitty shelters and waited and waited. Dropping dead like flies, waiting for help that never came, and wondering if they should eat the dead. At least we weren't in that predicament.

Yet. Never expect anyone else to come and save you. Better to die trying to save yourself.

There'd be no one else to save us but us. No one to save Otis but us. Alex might even need saving by the time we found him. *If* we found him. I doubted it though. That boy always landed on his feet. We could get there and find it was all part of a plan. Just making it look bad, so Alex could run after them, show them where the telescope was, and they'd all go home, thinking Jade and I were still at Mr. Soto's. Waiting for Alex, who was never coming back.

My brain went into manic overload spiraling down the worst possible scenarios. I pulled my scarf tighter around my mouth and nose, and willed my feet to keep moving. The wind howled through my bones. Angry trees threw snow at us as we passed.

"What's that?" I pointed my flashlight at a dark shape ahead.

Jade shrugged and stumbled toward me.

Wood smoke hung in the air, thick and pungent; someone nearby had a fireplace. And suddenly there it was—a train caboose, planted out there in the middle of a snow meadow. Still on its black wheels as if it had just rolled right in and come to a stop in the snow. Metal-ridged steps went up to a little platform and down the other side for easy access. It was painted bloodred with a sign, SNOWSHOE AREA, at the front. There were two windows, and a little metal chimney, and parked up right outside was a big, fat, red pickup truck.

27

7:33 p.m.

VOICES. SOMEONE WAS TRYING TO TALK BUT KEPT getting shut down. No dog sounds. I raised my brows at Jade. We crept up closer, huddling below the window, the wind smothering any noise our footsteps made.

"He did try to bite me." A chair scraped on the floor. "Take us to where you've hidden it, or he'll freeze to death out there, even with that nice coat. Do people still make dog-hair coats?" Too bad Nico didn't actually get bitten.

"Don't be ridiculous. Otis was just doing his job, following orders, protecting his master. Like you're supposed to, Alex. When our animals turn on us, they have to be disciplined. You turned on us, Alex?" There was a small hovering silence. "No? 'Cause it looks like it from here." AJ's smooth voice resonated off the metal walls.

"It burned up with everything else." Alex's voice was a little shaky.

There was a thud, grunt, and a bark. Otis was there inside. Alive. Thank God.

"But," said AJ, "you told us about it. All the other stuff, the TVs and the Celestron telescopes were a given, but Einstein's telescope got your attention. It was *your* idea. *Your* promise." He sucked the air through his teeth. "I just don't see you letting anything happen to it."

So it *was* all Alex's fault. I leaned in closer. The metal wall almost touched my cheek.

"It's the girl's." I could barely hear Alex. "I can't do that to her." Nothing to do with letting me down then.

"It did survive! I knew it!" Nico sounded so pleased with himself. "Don't be an idiot. Just give it up and you can walk away."

"He's right. You owe us big-time—once, for not getting Einstein's telescope after you bragged you would, and then for lying to our faces right now." AJ was all calm menace. "Don't try to be a hero. Tell us where it is, or we'll go back and ask your friends. I bet they would gladly give it up. I'm sure they wouldn't want the dog to be hurt, or anyone else."

"No, no, no, no." Alex crumbled fast. "Leave them out of it." So we were friends.

Jade whispered in my ear, "We have to save them."

Really, when it was obviously Alex's fault? I looked at Jade's anxious face and nodded. Jade was doing it because it was the right thing. I was doing it for her.

"I'll tell you where it is." Alex sounded so resigned. But he'd put himself in this trap. No one made him break into the cabin. "As long as you promise not to hurt anyone else."

Nico laughed. "Yeah, like we owe you anything."

Jade and I looked at each other with complete understanding. We had to act fast. I raced to the truck and opened the driver's-side door. Of course they'd leave it unlocked with the key still in the ignition. Who would steal from them in the middle of a snowstorm? I was surprised a gun wasn't lying across the passenger seat. Jade ran to the passenger side and jumped in, slamming the door behind her. We sat motionless, as if we'd be mistaken for shadows if they'd heard us and came out.

"Alright," I said as soon as it was obvious no one was coming, "we need to create a diversion, so Alex has a chance of getting out with Otis. We need to divide them."

"Divide and conquer." Jade nodded. "That could work. But they have a gun, and we don't, and I don't want to try to get one," she added quickly.

"Oh God, me neither." Jade was right. "We could take the truck, go and get help."

"There's no time, and no one around." Jade took her hat off and shook out her hair. "And we can't drive."

"I never said I couldn't drive, just not legally."

Jade took her gloves off and blew on her fingers. "What if we, I mean you, drive it a little way off, then honk the horn? So they have to exit the caboose to see what's happening, and while they're checking on the truck, I'll sneak in and rescue Alex and Otis?" She looked up at me hopefully.

I sucked between my teeth. "That could work. Except for the part about me being stuck in the truck. What if you stay here, off to the side, out of sight? I'll drive the truck away a bit, but still in view, and honk the horn until they come out. Then I'll jump down and hide. Meanwhile, you signal to Alex that it's us, and he'll make a run for it with Otis. We'll go into the woods so they can't chase us in the truck."

"Yes! Let's get them." There was fire in her eyes; we were a team. We'd got this.

I waited for Jade to get into place, turned the key, and revved the engine. Wind rocked the truck, and snow lashed down sideways. They wouldn't hear the truck in this storm. I revved again, like I was going to ride right through them. I turned the high beam on.

A figure appeared at the window.

I threw the truck into reverse.

Jade gave me a thumbs-up from her hiding place. She mouthed, *Drive!*

I floored the gas and shot off backward, headed downhill, and skidded sideways, straight for a tree. I swerved the truck around, kicked it back into first, and stalled. I'd bloody stalled. I glanced at the caboose. The door was still closed.

Was I far enough away to give Alex a chance? I turned the ignition off, put the gears in neutral, turned it on again, crunched the gears into first, then accelerated slowly into second, and got a good five hundred feet away before I hit the horn.

As soon as I did that the wheels lost traction, skidding into a full spin—pines, tracks, snow, caboose, open door, AJ with a flashlight. The truck spun out, just missing a tree. And then the sound kicked in—yells, barks, and the crunch of gears—as I tried to gain control, and then came the horrible stench of hot metal. I slammed the brakes over and over. The stop was sudden. My head smashed onto the wheel.

"Hey," AJ said as he pulled me out of the truck, "you saved us the effort of coming to find you. Couldn't have timed it better. Your boy needs you."

My head was fuzzed. I wiped the blood that was seeping into my eye from my forehead and looked for Jade.

"Ah, you're not alone." AJ followed my gaze to the bright blue lump, frozen at the side of the caboose. "Who's that?"

I tightened my lips and yanked my arm away, almost falling on my newly rubber legs. I couldn't swallow, couldn't catch my breath, could only take short, sharp pants of air that were getting faster and faster until I was spinning in flashes of silver stars. "Run, Jade, run!" My shout came out like a whimper.

"Oh, it's the princess. Stop panicking." AJ held me tighter. "Stop, or you're going to pass out and I'll have to drag you back to the caboose unconscious, and no one wants that." I staggered back with him, leaning heavily on his shoulder.

Jade darted out as soon as we got close. Her whole body shivered with cold, and her lips were cracked and blue. There was no way she could have survived, running off by herself. None of us could.

I mouthed *sorry* to her, and she gave me a tearful nod. Warm blood trickled down my face. We were all screwed.

28

8:10 p.m.

INSIDE THE CABOOSE WAS A SMALL WHITE FORMICA table and two orange plastic chairs, which sat next to a wood-burning stove and one dirty white chair shoved under the table. At the front of the caboose was a countertop with a sink and a shelf of chipped mugs, and old cereal boxes lined up on the cabinets. On the other side wall was a long, thin bed, and at the end an open cupboard with a few dank-looking blankets. AJ gestured for Jade and me to sit on the bed.

"So nice of you to join us," said AJ, taking off his hat and sweeping his curly blond hair with his fingers. He sat in one of the orange chairs, feet resting on the table and cracked open a can of beer. "Alex fell into the door. He's always been so clumsy."

Alex was hunched over in the other orange chair. He gave a pathetic smile, making the cut in his lips bleed. His plan evidently didn't turn out that well either.

Otis barked once but stayed under the bed as far as he could get. He let Jade pet his nose and whisper to him, darting away whenever Nico's boots got near, which was often. Nico paced up and down the metal shelter, fingers to his lips, as if he were thinking things through.

"Otis's fine. No harm done." AJ took a swig from his beer. "Drop those backpacks. Make yourselves at home, take your hats off. I'm sorry Alex dragged you into this." AJ tapped the white chair by the table. "Sit down, Nico. You're unsettling our friends."

He sat. Eyes darting from Alex, to AJ, to the door.

"Right, let's see what's here." AJ rummaged through each backpack, face curled in disappointment as he pulled out the water bottles and energy bars. "Well, it's not in there."

We watched him from the bed, which was hard and narrow, more slats than mattress. No sheets, just a dirty yellow blanket. I took off my gloves and hat and shook out my matted hair. Jade took her hat off too. She swept her hair back up into a tight bun. I felt my sweaty hair sticking to the sides of my face.

Otis jumped up next to Jade like she was his trusty owner. She hugged him like she wasn't ever going to let go.

"He likes your new friend more than you, Alex." AJ grinned. "So much for the devoted guard dog."

Jade stiffened. Nico poked the fire and AJ watched each of us in turn, a silent assessment. I grabbed hold of Jade's arm to let her know we were in this together.

"We're all friends here. Isn't that nice? So now you've met the friend we were looking for. Seems he wasn't that far away." AJ sighed. "I guess you didn't know at the time, or you knew and hid him anyway."

Alex's foot gave an involuntary kick. "They know nothing."

"That's not true, is it? They've met you, met us, know you broke a promise. That's plenty. You got them all caught up in this." He turned to me. "Look at you, bad-ass girl of action, stealing my truck. Where'd you learn to drive like that? Stick shift, three-point turns, steering into the skid? Would have been impressive if you hadn't crashed." AJ smiled.

I turned my face away, clenching my lips together, sealing my unease inside. He sounded so friendly, but the glint in his eyes as he watched me was like a fox stalking a rabbit.

"England," I said, pushing myself as far away from AJ as I could without making it too obvious. "No one drives automatics there."

"*Eng*-land," AJ repeated in an exaggerated English accent. His Adam's apple glided up and down.

The musty wood smoke filled the room. I couldn't breathe. My lungs were going to crack and explode. Jade made a tiny, suppressed cough that had a wheeze at the end.

"Watch it, girl. You're hyperventilating, and we don't want any more accidents, do we?"

My whole body tensed. I glanced at Jade. She shook her head. *I'm fine.*

"There's no need to make this hard." AJ rubbed his hands together. "I'm sorry Alex got you caught up in this. Unfortunately, he's created a food chain. Alex, the tiny minnow, promised many things to two big carp, which we promised to a bigger fish—let's call that one a shark. And now it's circling around, waiting, and we have to deliver, or be eaten, and none of us wants that, do we?" He was so calm, so sure, my skin tingled with apprehension. "It's such a shame about the fire, but at least one thing survived, one high-value item that should help us all survive this ordeal." He smiled, but his blue eyes were cold and calculating.

"What…" Alex widened his eyes.

I carried on: "…do you want us to do, exactly?"

The fire pumped out enough heat to make the windows run with condensation. The wind buffeted us so hard that it felt like the caboose would set off again.

"Funny you should ask," said AJ. "Persuade Alex to deliver the promised item. He didn't show up when he said he would, so we searched for it, but that cabin is a disaster. We assumed he got held up somehow, but, in fact, he'd run off with you two. So, I can only conclude you have a powerful hold over him. And it would be terrible if you all ended up missing in the blizzard. Terrible, but tragedies happen out here in the wilderness. People can be so unprepared."

I glared at Alex. He'd set this whole thing up and we'd risked our lives racing into the storm to save him. My head was killing me. My eye had swollen almost shut. And it was all his fault.

"You should put some ice on that cut." Nico opened the door, scooped up some snow into a red plastic cup, and poured it onto my lap. "Oops."

"Oh, so fucking funny." God, I'd done it now. I waited, not daring to breathe. The air sucked out of the room; even the wood burner stopped crackling.

But AJ cracked up. "Trapped like a fucking rabbit in a noose and you don't give a crap. Put it there!" He raised his hand to high-five me, like I'd want to touch any part of him. "I can see why you like her." He grinned at Alex, like they were best friends.

Alex pushed himself up, gripping the sides of the chair.

It was too warm, too close, too tight in there. Jade started coughing again, struggling to catch her breath. She glared at AJ as she pulled out her inhaler.

"Go ahead. You're going to be fine." AJ watched Jade take two puffs. "We're not going to hurt you. What do you think we are, monsters?"

Yep, Jade was so right. How could I have misjudged them so badly? If only I'd never opened the stupid front door. Nope, Alex would still have tried to break in. We were screwed either way.

Alex looked terrified, pale in the face, with a light sheen of sweat above his lip. He'd got us into this mess; he'd better get us out of it.

AJ sat too close to me on the bed. I pulled my thighs tightly together, so they wouldn't touch his.

"Back to business. Alex owes us the goods. Setting fire to the cabin was drastic, but he's made his reluctance known." AJ dropped his voice, as if he were sharing a secret. "I've built a spotless reputation for reliability and trust. I have never disappointed. Alex has put my honor on the line. If everyone wants to get home, I need to get my hands on that item." His eyes pierced mine.

I shrunk back. "I have no idea what you're talking about. And Alex isn't our friend. We just came for the dog."

"I appreciate your honesty, but you've forced yourself into this mess, adding to my problems." AJ's smile made my skin crawl.

"I'll tell you where it is. Just leave him alone." I should have known what Alex was after. He'd shown way too much interest from the start. I bet that's why he was still in the cabin, even after Otis was safely out. "It's on the upper back balcony. It's probably not even that badly damaged." I didn't give a crap anymore. I just wanted to get me and Jade out of there.

"You should go"—Jade tilted her chin—"before the fire crew arrives." She was right there with me.

"Good point. You must be the smart one of this trio." He winked at her.

Jade clenched her jaw.

AJ didn't notice. "So, who's coming with?" He grinned at Nico. "What d'you think? Should we all go along, or should we just bring Alex?"

For a second, I really thought he was letting us go.

"We zoom in, grab it, and zoom back." Nico grinned. "No one's going to come looking for you in this crazy weather. They probably don't even know you're missing!"

Sour acid rose from my stomach. I was so going to kill him.

"True." AJ frowned. He opened up a duffel bag and pulled out a handful of plastic zip ties. "I'm not going to hurt you. But no one goes anywhere until the telescope is delivered. The last thing we need is your little gang running around and claiming it was stolen before then."

"If you hurt us, my dad will kill you." Jade said it like it was a fact, like she wasn't even scared for herself, only for them. "He has millions of followers, and they'll all be after you."

AJ ignored her and fastened our hands behind our backs with the plastic ties, then our crossed-over ankles, while Nico put his oil-slick puffer jacket back on and readjusted his green beanie.

"You'd better pray the truck starts, or you're going to be in real trouble," said Nico as he opened the door of the caboose to let AJ out. "Don't get any stupid ideas. If we come back and you're not here, we'll find you. Besides"—he grinned—"out there with visibility this low, you don't want to end up wounded in a hunting accident. You know, wrong place, wrong time." And he winked at me.

I collapsed with relief when the door reverberated behind him.

29

8:40 p.m.

THE TRUCK RUMBLED OFF IN THE DISTANCE. I PRAYED that AJ and Nico would get into an accident and never come back. My wrists chafed each other. The ties had no give. If I could get to something sharp—not the plastic knife that lay on the table—the ties would probably snap.

"Why the hell did you do this to us?" I glared at Alex, who was the only reason we were there at all, but his downcast eyes and worried brow made me think he hadn't expected this either. "Pretending to be lost, pretending to be our friend, and telling those guys about the telescope. I bet you thought it was piece of junk before Jade mentioned it was priceless. You set this whole mess in motion!"

"I didn't mean to get you involved. That's why I didn't tell you the truth about those guys. If you didn't know anything, they wouldn't go after you."

"And that turned out well, didn't it?" I stared at the snow-covered window. I couldn't look at his lying face anymore.

Jade bumped herself closer to the wood stove. "I'm the one who told him. None of this would have happened if I hadn't mentioned it."

"I told him it was priceless that first night, so it's not your fault. None of this would have happened if Alex hadn't broken into the cabin." I flicked the hair off my face. It was too hot in there.

Alex's jaw tensed. "Some of us only get to choose between bad and worse. We don't get the happily-ever-after ending."

"Everyone has a choice. You just chose badly." Like Dad. Like me.

"It wasn't the original plan. They sent me to case your cabin, so I knew it was empty and full of high-end stuff." Alex twisted himself around in his chair to get a better look at his fastened wrists. "It didn't used to be like this. It started with packages left outside vacation homes, then it moved on to mountain bikes locked insecurely—stupid, as they're worth thousands. But then you had TVs and telescopes lying around. I figured you'd get the insurance on them. Then you showed me Einstein's telescope and told me it was priceless, and I knew that was my ticket to freedom. With a prize that big, I could hand it over and leave. Debt paid."

Jade looked furious. "*And Dad would get fired*," she said, emphasizing each word.

"But"—Alex actually looked flustered—"I didn't know that."

"No, you didn't. You tricked yourself into magically thinking that it was a victimless crime, and here we are." The wrath of Jade was something fierce. I backed away a little.

"Jesus, I should have just handed it over that night." Alex shook his head.

"What?" Jade and I said together.

"It would have been better for all of us. Then you wouldn't be tied up in all this." He wouldn't meet my eyes. He knew that was bullshit.

"No," said Jade. "It would only be better for you. We would have lost everything."

"Yeah, well, it's not like your dad can't afford to replace it." Alex glared at Jade.

"Priceless means irreplaceable." Jade glared back. The caboose was going to explode.

"Face it, Alex, this is on you. You promised them that telescope and didn't deliver. It was crazy of them to take Otis from Soto's as collateral. Great friends." I rubbed my wrists against each other, and looked at that plastic knife again, trying to think of any way to get my hands free. "They're freaking nuts. There was no need to take Otis."

Otis whimpered in agreement.

Jade wriggled to get her hands free. "Otis warned us about the bear, and the truck, and you both ignored him. It's your fault he was taken."

"We didn't hear him barking." I was too busy falling down the stairs.

"Like when you didn't hear me shouting 'fire'?" So, not forgiven then.

"They wanted you both too," said Alex.

My gut churned. "Why?"

"Leverage. They like to play with people, mess with their heads.

Nothing would have happened, probably." He scooted his chair closer to me. "I'm sorry."

"*Probably?* They've got a bloody gun." I leaned forward. "Why did you even stay with us? You could have left at any time."

"I was trying to keep those guys busy. They only knew we were at Soto's because of your message on the Mini." Alex frowned. "I ran after them so you'd have time to escape."

"No, you ran after them to get Otis back." That stupid message, it was all my fault they'd followed us. "Escape how? There's nowhere safe to go!" I was boiling up, no air, too much fire. I never imagined I'd get sweaty so soon after almost freezing to death. "They've never been friends. They don't give a shit about you. And neither do I." I wriggled to my feet, trying to see if my pathetic attempt at stretching the ties would work. It didn't.

Alex smiled sadly. "It's more like they don't give a shit because they think I've been disloyal and have new friends. They think we're a team."

"We will never be a team," said Jade. "You screwed us over."

"You tell him, Jade." I knocked the plastic knife off the table, swinging both my feet at once, almost throwing myself onto the floor in the process.

"I didn't know you then. I'd never do that now." Alex pushed the knife toward me with his feet. "That's not going to help."

"No, but it's something." I shook my head. "I don't know who you are. But I know better than to trust anything you say."

He started to speak, saw my face, and stared at his knees instead.

The wind battered against the caboose, shaking it back and

forth. The roof dripped with moisture from the heat given off by the stove, as it hit the freezing metal. Otis whined. Too bad he wasn't trained to bite through plastic.

We sat silently, listening to the wind howling and the snow throwing itself at the caboose. It was wild out there, but it would be wilder in here if they came back.

I looked at the door. The wind was too loud to hear if they returned, and snow splattered everywhere, a constant erratic beat. "We can't just wait for them trussed up like this."

"We've got to escape," Jade said quickly. "We can't fight them."

There was nothing I could do. Plastic ties are a bitch. Sweat trickled down my back. If only I could get this jacket off and the ties. The cabin rocked from side to side as the wind howled through our bones. That had to be the blizzard.

Alex scooted his chair forward, using his crossed feet to pull himself along. He turned to Jade. "Can you pull this off with your hands?"

"That are fastened behind my back?" said Jade.

"How the hell did you get stuck with those guys? It's not like they own you."

"You know how it goes: the ties that bind." He smiled.

I frowned.

"I've known AJ since second grade," said Alex. "He used to be nice, stuck up for me, had a mob family everyone was scared of."

"A mob family? Is that even a real thing?" I let Otis lick my nose.

"Yeah, I mean, back in the day they were. But now it's like a point of pride trying to keep up the family name, you know, when the power's faded. It's kind of sad, really. His dad died in jail. That's why you don't want to mess with him—he'll do anything to avoid doing time."

My heart did pang a tiny bit for him losing his dad, but still. "Maybe a life of crime is a stupid idea then."

"It's not always that easy." Alex sighed. "Anyway, by high school everything changed. I heard AJ was working for his uncle. They were just rumors, and he was still fine with me. But it turns out he was the wrong person to do a small favor for—one always leads to another." He looked down at his bound ankles. "I didn't realize how crazy everything would get until it was too late."

I shook my head. "You'll have to make your part in this mess way clearer than that if you want me to have any sympathy for you."

"No." He bit his lip. "The less you know the better."

"I wish the mama bear had gotten them," said Jade, still wriggling herself around.

"Wait, what? It was there?" Alex's eyes glinted.

"Yeah, we were glad we didn't get too close. Talk about huge." I shuddered. At least we had a fighting chance stuck in the caboose. One swipe from her and we'd be history.

"Yeah, she was so cool." Jade's eyes shone with the memory.

Wind gusted down the chimney, forcing the doors of the stove open. Jade coughed in the spewing smoke. Her eyes teared from holding in a wheeze. She couldn't get to her inhaler with her hands tied behind her back. I dropped to my knees, so my hands were in front of her. "Which pocket is it?"

"There's no way you can reach it." She coughed again, bending forward, head close to the wood stove. "Oh, wow," she said suddenly. "I just figured something out. Thank you, Lottie!" And she crouched into a ball, letting herself fall onto her bum, then swung her hands under her feet, bringing them out in front of her. Then she placed her wrists on the metal flue of the stove and laughed.

"Oh my God, genius!" I meant it too. It was so obvious once I saw it.

I copied Jade's moves, and Alex scooted himself over so he could do the same. The plastic stank when it melted, but that was a small price to pay for freedom. Our ankle ties were simple to force off once Alex had access to his penknife. Otis ran around, jumping on and off the bed. At least AJ and Nico had left him free the whole time.

"Do you think they found it?" asked Jade.

Alex nodded. "If it was still there, then yes. They need it badly, or they'll be in trouble."

"We were only in trouble because of you." Jade took two puffs on her inhaler and waited for Alex's answer.

He bit his lip. "I know I was stupid, and awful. I'm sorry. Can you forgive me?"

Jade gave him a curt nod. "But you put Otis in danger again and we're through."

Alex nodded solemnly. "Deal." He turned to me. "And you?"

He'd been an idiot. But so had I. "No second chances. Don't you dare let us down again."

"Never." He looked so serious and sincere, I almost believed him.

I collected the melted ties and threw them into the dustbin.

The tiny caboose swayed in the lashing winds. Snow pounded on the windows.

"What do we do now?" I asked. It was crazy to leave, crazy to stay.

"It's wild to go out in this if we don't have to. They probably won't even come back tonight. And now that we're free we can ambush them when they come in." Alex hugged Otis, who responded by putting his paws on his shoulders and giving him a big doggie kiss. True love.

"I don't think ambushing someone with a gun is a good idea. Let's make a run for it. What do you think, Jade?" I asked.

"Yep, let's leave while we can." She coughed again from the smoke. "Anywhere has to be better than this."

"Okay," said Alex. "Go it is."

It took seconds for us to throw on our jackets, grab the backpacks, and charge out of the caboose. We rushed headlong into the churning snow, whipping wind, and two blinding beams of light.

30
9:07 p.m.

WHEELS SPUN ON THE ICE AS THE TRUCK SKIDDED TO A stop right outside. We had to break free now or we'd be trapped again. We ran blindly for the trees–anywhere the truck couldn't chase us, anywhere we could hide from the lights. Jade slipped. I grabbed her hand and pulled her along with me.

A bullet whizzed past my ear and hit a tree. Shots in the dark. Shit. Nico was serious about the hunting accident.

"Zigzag!" Jade yelled and tore her hand away.

Alex whistled. I heard Otis panting, close by. There, in the headlights, a black-and-white dog against the snowy tree trunks. AJ steered the truck, highlighting Nico's dark shadow of a shape, rifle poised to hunt us down.

"Get out of the light!" I shouted to Alex, and fell, dropping down into the snow. Was I hit? No. Not yet. I'd lost sight of Jade. If I couldn't see her, neither could they. I hid behind a tree to catch my breath before the next bolt. The snow was knee-deep and fell thick and fast. It was hard to wade through. I slipped in furrows up to my waist at times, and always, always, I stared ahead, on the lookout for Jade. Please still be there.

"You can't get anywhere!" AJ shouted over the wind. "The roads are closed. No one's coming to rescue you. Call it fate, or luck"—the gun clicked—"that we were forced to turn back in time to catch you!"

A shot rang out, hazy through the slush. I wondered if it'd get deflected, if a big enough clump of snow could stop a bullet. A branch fell off above me. I ran from trunk to trunk. The wind roared in the treetops and slapped my face with slush-snow. I panted. My heart pounded in my throat. My hands were numb.

Headlights whooshed over me. AJ and Nico were in the truck again. I zigzagged, uphill, scrabbling, knees falling, sliding backwards and rolling behind banks of snow, running sideways, away from the caboose, away from the road, away from Jade, away from Alex, away from the truck. I hid inside a cracked tree trunk, stomping my feet and blowing into my gloves.

I could stay here, on my own, wait for the sounds of everyone to die down and then head off, alone. That's what I'd wanted this whole time. No one to betray me, no one to be stuck with, an easy life.

AJ and Nico couldn't stay out there forever. They'd get bored and cold and figure we'd freeze to death anyway, and they'd look for us in the morning. Our stiff bodies covered in crystal ice. It was doubtful we'd survive out there together. I was certain I wouldn't die alone.

Something was coming toward me through the trees—a bear, a

shadow. I became one with the trunk, pushing myself as far against it as I could, swaying with it, breathing in time with the wind gusts, a frosted tree spirit.

"Lottie?"

"Jade!" My heart leapt. I barely held it together. "You okay?" A very pushy black nose nuzzled my hip. "Thank God." My legs gave way with relief.

"He's a search-and-rescue dog," said Jade. "He found you. It's his job." I laughed and wiped the tears streaming across my cheeks.

Alex crashed toward us, a shadow in the frozen wood. He paused to catch his breath. "I caught up with Jade after you two got separated. She figured Otis would be smart enough to find you." He gave Otis a big hug. "And he did."

"God, that was close." I stood against the tree for support. Jade and Alex had come back for me. And I'd nearly gone it alone. Trust and gratitude, two emotions I was totally unused to. So, I did the English thing and pushed down the overwhelming feelings and kept my composure. "Have they given up?" I asked.

"For now," said Alex. "Once the worst of the storm's over, they'll come looking again. They can't let us go until they've delivered. We need to get away from here."

We had to shout to hear each other and huddle together or we'd get lost for sure. The snow slapped our faces, trying to find a way under our skin. Our numbed, rubber, frozen skin. There was no point using flashlights. They'd only give our location away and highlight exactly how much snow and wind was raging around us.

"There's got to be cabins around here." I covered my nose with both hands and breathed. "Let's break into the first place we see, even if it's a shed."

"Or a tent," said Jade.

"Yep, that too." I tripped into her. "A mountaineering tent." And just like that I saw Dad's face. Before he left, his smiling, ocean-eyed, weathered old face. I had loved him so much. He was everything. My superhero, my heart. That he crushed. I bit my lip hard and focused on the taste of blood.

"You okay?" Alex linked my arm with his. "You seem sad."

"Oh, like I'm supposed to be happy trudging to my death in the snow?" But I did smile.

"Point taken." He nudged me and grinned back.

We trudged deeper into the forest. Alex held me on one side and Jade on the other. Otis ran back and forth checking his that flock was all together. There was an unspoken rule: when one stopped, we all stopped. There was no way we'd find a straggler in this.

All the world was ice and snow. Even staggering that close together, we could barely make out each other's faces. Alex used his phone compass to get the direction. We figured northeast to be vaguely heading toward Truckee and civilization. Searching for landmarks was hopeless when everything looked the same— miles and miles of furious storm. Everything was frigid and howling and thrashing things in the trees, and hearts pounding, and breaths panting, and doubts growing. I stopped to yank my hood back on, pulling the drawstrings tighter. What were we doing? Walking, walking, just walking into white death. Like soldiers in a battle, marching with no meaning or purpose, just marching because those were our orders. Survive.

Alex shouted something against the wind. He looked like a frozen scarecrow. Otis waited beside him, head low, big ears dripping with snow, big mournful puppy-dog eyes.

"What?" I had to yell right next to him.

He pointed back to the caboose. "We should go back. It's crazy out here."

I shook my head. "No way." There was nothing to stop AJ and Nico from dumping our bodies in the snow. No one would find us until spring. It was a stupid conversation. Visibility was zero. I could hardly see my own hands.

"No, we'll die out here!" he yelled. "I'll take them to the telescope in the morning. It's not too late to save ourselves."

I shook my head. "We passed the point of sanity when they started shooting at us. You can't trust them!"

"Staying out here is suicidal," he pleaded, eyes watering, earnest, but wrong.

I pulled my scarf around my face again, leaving a narrow slit for my eyes. I could hardly see anyway. "Help and hope is out here. All that's back there is cruelty with a gun."

Jade's hood was frozen solid over her beanie. She hugged herself as she walked. "There's no way I'm going back. We'll make a shelter in a tree if we have to."

I smiled at her with gratitude. Jade smiled back. Then her left foot disappeared, and she gasped in agony.

31

9:33p.m.

HER FOOT WAS TOTALLY STUCK.

"It's probably a fox hole. Hold on." I grabbed her left calf. Slush dripped down the back of my neck. So, so, cold. I shuddered.

I pulled. Jade winced.

"Can you wriggle it at all?"

"I don't know. I can't feel anything." Her lips were blue.

Great. I tried again, lifting her leg a half inch, but her snow boot was caught.

"Lean on me. See if it will come out now." I held her around the waist, so all her weight was on me. "Come on. One, two, three, pull."

"You could dig the hole bigger with a stick," said Alex, selecting one from the ground.

"Frozen ice, frozen mud. We'd be here forever," I said, puffing.

Jade's face crumpled. "Don't leave me."

"Why would you even say that?" Alex asked, eyes wide.

"Not you, her." She wiped a tear from her eye. "Don't say you never wanted to."

"Jeez, you are some messed-up sisters." said Alex as he scraped the stick around the edges of the hole, enlarging the space everywhere except where Jade's foot was actually stuck.

"Stepsisters." It just slipped out, proving his point. "I promise I will never leave you. Okay, satisfied?"

She nodded, wincing in pain.

"Ah, come on, we've got this." I grabbed her calf again, yanking tightly with both hands, digging my heels into the snow to brace myself. I heaved. Her foot came out with a pop, leaving her boot in the fox hole.

Jade collapsed. I tugged her boot back on and tried helping her up. But she was deadweight.

She leaned against me and glanced at her foot. "Is it still…?"

"There? Yes, it's totally fine, just a little swollen." I glanced at Alex's stick.

He passed it to Jade. "Use this to take the weight off your foot. It's probably just a sprain. But this will make it easier to walk." He gripped under Jade's arms, helping her up.

Jade managed a wobbly one-legged stand. She hobbled two steps, then the makeshift cane slipped out from under her. Alex tried to give her a piggyback ride but stopped at the first stagger. The last thing Jade needed was for Alex to slip, drop her, and cause more pain. The slow pace we were going was painful enough.

"We should go back. It's not far. She can rest it," said Alex.

I gave Alex my iciest glare, cold enough to freeze the air between us. "Yes, at gunpoint. We're witnesses to all that mayhem. Do you really think they'd let us go again?"

"No. Way. In. Hell," said Jade. That was final.

"We've got this." I squeezed her arm. She knew it was a blatant lie, but she nodded.

Flurries of powder came at us in gusts, mixed up with the steadily swirling snow. Our footsteps crunched on the iced ground. My breath fuzzed against the wool. My nose itched. I knew if I scratched it, a layer of frozen skin would come off under my nails.

"Any water?" I asked licking my chapped lips.

"Here, finish mine. I'll check the direction." Alex passed me a brand-new steel bottle, a Soto's Shakes & Supplies special.

Ice-cold water slid down my throat. I took three more slugs and handed it to Jade. She gave some to Otis and got it all back immediately in licks. Otis had obviously learned a few survival tricks since this started, snuffling aggressively all over my jacket and finding half an energy bar. I fed it to him.

"Stop," said Alex. He brushed some snow off a tree trunk and inspected the mossy bark. "We're still headed north. We should hit the road to Truckee soon."

"Eagle Scouts?" I asked.

Alex shouted back, "One of my forced life skills!"

Alex and I waded with one arm out for balance and the other practically carrying Jade. I imagined my nose was slowly frosting over and kept twitching it to stop it from freezing solid. Until I couldn't twitch it anymore. My body was shutting down, giving up the fight, drawing blood away from my extremities, preserving the limited warmth and energy for my vital parts. My heart would give up last.

Mum was wrong. She always said my heart was stone-cold ice. But for the first time in a long while, I could feel the fire inside, which was ironic, considering I was about to freeze to death.

32

9:51 p.m.

MY EYES KEPT CLOSING. I COULDN'T TELL IF IT WAS PITCH black outside, or if they were shut sometimes. I couldn't feel the lids anyway. My eyelashes were frozen stiff. The wind hurt too much to do more than squint into the dark. Jade hobbled along at my side and Otis bobbed up and down, over the snowdrifts, in out of view, as the snow began to fall heavier again. Jade shivered under her thick jacket. Even Otis, with his thick fur coat, was frozen to the bone. Weighed down in snow, each step tentative, as he padded through the icy landscape.

I felt for him, though I couldn't feel my ears. My toes burned. Every step felt like a stab with a sharp pencil, right under the toenails. I'd probably lose them all, black toes, black nose. "We should stop and make some kind of shelter," I said. "Even if it's just under a tree." I don't think they heard me. I didn't dare stop to yell, for fear I'd lose sight of them. Walking was more of a stagger and sway.

The wind roared through the trees and the snow pelted down. I had the horrible feeling we were going in circles. Everything looked the same, not that I could see much at all, just a thin curtain of white snow with dark shapes surrounding us. Were they even Jade's and Alex's shapes? My stomach lurched. Yes, yes, they had to be.

Dad must have felt like this, shivering with cold, ice veins pumping ice blood, not being able to see anything but whirling white. He must have gotten lost and disorientated, trying and failing to get back to me, like he'd promised. And leaving nothing—no sign, no broken fence, no dying wishes—just vanishing into the snow. It was like he was still out there somewhere, wandering in an infinite white horizon. Because there was no way he'd disappeared like that on purpose.

I closed my eyes and let the wind sweep my tears away. Hold still, beating heart, hold still.

We shuffled past a flat meadow of snow that Alex swore was a frozen lake, hit a snowbank, and fell onto a sheet of thick ice. The snow pierced our layers, leaving frozen slivers to work their way under our skin.

Jade swayed against a pine. I seriously thought she was going to puke. The purple circles under her eyes had deepened. She sat on a pile of snow. "Leave me here." Her words came out in gasps. "I'm just slowing you down."

"Nope." I tugged her up by her arms. "No one gets left behind. I'll bloody carry you if I have to." I put my arm over her shoulders, so she could rest against me. She was not going to flop into the snow and die. I wouldn't allow it.

Alex took her other arm, and between us we staggered on the path to nowhere.

"Hey, look!" said Alex, pointing to where Otis was racing ahead.

A pale, yellow light shone from a building ahead. It looked like a clapboard church. But it sounded like a country-and-western concert.

33
10:11p.m.

A FILIGREE IRON CROSS PEEKED ABOVE THE TOP OF the snow-tipped church, white icing upon white clapboard. With its pitched roof and perfectly scrolled edging, it looked like a child's drawing of a church.

One pair of footprints led up the gray-slushed path to the entrance. Boot prints at least three sizes bigger than Alex's. We stood in front of the towering oak door.

Hallelujah, country-style blared from inside. "My worst nightmare," I said.

"Which part," Jade asked, staring up at the cross with me. "Church or country music?"

"Both, in equal parts. But I'll put up with anything to get out of this storm."

Jade and I exchanged a grin.

"Shelter, water, warmth, all that good stuff, maybe even food. We've made it." I could feel my whole body thawing already.

"Hell, yeah!" Alex grinned and Otis barked in agreement.

The iron door knocker was hand-shaped, like it was the hand of God, or something. "The music's too loud. They can't hear us." I gave up knocking and pushed the heavy door open.

A man stood at the podium with his back to us, singing wildly, waving his arms exuberantly along. "Hallelujah! Hallelujah!" He was an older guy, dressed in dark gray pants, a worn brown bomber jacket, and a gray baseball cap. Definitely not a vicar.

"Hello?!" I shouted.

"Ahh!" He strode over. "Welcome!" He had to shout over the music. "I've been expecting you!" He held out his hand for me to shake. It was dry, warm, and calloused.

"You were expecting *us*?" I looked up at his craggy, salt-worn face. His eyes were bloodshot, and his nose was lined with tidy red spider veins—a drinker's nose. "Expecting us how?"

"Lost strangers on a stormy night. Come on in. That's it, just you three and a dog? I thought there'd be more of you. No one else following?"

"No, not that we know of," said Alex, glancing uneasily behind us.

I certainly hoped not. I also looked behind me to make sure. As sure as I could be in a whiteout blizzard.

"This is great. You found the place, on a night like this too." The guy scratched behind his ear.

"Yes, it's been awful." I took off my hat and ran my hands through my long, straggly hair. "It's such a relief to find somewhere warm like this in the middle of this never-ending storm." I'd gone from freezing to death, to English polite, as instinct and upbringing demanded. A defense tactic until I'd figured out where we were, and what we'd walked into.

"A miracle, isn't it?" the guy answered. "Oh, sorry, you can't hear me!" He clicked a remote. The music fell silent, leaving the moan of the wind, the patter of snow, and the soft mechanical hum of a generator to fill in the spaces the sound left behind.

"You have a generator." I lapsed into stunned silence. Maybe it was normal to be prepared for catastrophe; that's what the Bible predicted, after all. The brilliance of the interior lighting hurt after so long in the dark. I was dizzy with the lights and the sudden warmth. "I'm sorry…" I sat down hard on the nearest pew. "We're just exhausted."

Jade sat beside me and pulled her sock delicately over her swollen ankle and foot. "It's broken," she said forlornly. It was super puffy and so very purple.

"Can you wiggle it?" asked the old guy.

She moved it very slightly.

"Ahh, there you go. Not broken. But you can rest up here." The guy smiled, revealing his crooked yellow teeth. "Welcome to the Sanctuary! What do you think?"

We were out of the storm, somewhere warm, with electricity. "It's heaven," I said.

"I'm going to make it even better. Don't go anywhere," the guy said and disappeared through a side door.

The thin clapboard walls shook in the storm. High up on the left and right walls, small beveled, framed windows were piled up with snow, and the wind hurled more of it against the panes, shifting the piles as they grew. But no matter how much the wood boards of the church groaned, we were safe from the frozen tempest. Away from AJ and Nico. Finally, a place to rest in peace. Sleep, I meant sleep in peace. The thought of that sent a shiver up my spine.

I gave Alex a small smile. He grinned right back. He wasn't that bad really, for a juvenile delinquent. And he had a pretty great smile when he meant it. The kind that tingled my veins. Obviously, I was delirious with the heat and exhaustion.

Jade took her coat off and lay on it, resting her foot on a pew. "Ah, thank God. Finally," she said and closed her eyes. She was even more exhausted than I'd realized.

Alex sat next to me. "I knew we'd make it."

I whispered to him, "What do you think he meant by expecting more of you?"

"Nothing, he's just ready for whoever gets lost in the snow." Alex rubbed my shoulder. "He's one of the good guys. Relax. We're safe now."

"I guess." I fake-smiled. He was probably right. I'd just had a lifetime of people not living up to my expectations.

I let my head accidentally drop onto his shoulder. He brushed a strand of hair away from my check. I felt so, so, sleepy. I yawned and looked around.

The interior was neatly divided into two rows of pews, with an aisle down the middle. A string of fairy lights dazzled across the podium and trailed from one post to another, stapled on like a temporary celebration. The place smelled musty and damp. There were no Bibles. It didn't seem like this place had heard prayers for a long time. Well, there was mine: *Please help us be safe, please help us be safe, please help us be safe.* I mumbled it in my head, with only lips moving, and knelt, head bowed. I didn't even believe in a god, but I'd try anything to keep us out of danger.

The oak-beamed ceiling reminded me of the cabin, the burnt cabin. It was about the same size, but with a very different feel. The music, the fairy lights, the unexpected welcome made this space seem cozy, safe, and warm. A minor miracle after all we'd just been through.

"You okay?" Alex shifted on the bench.

"I was just getting weirded out by being in a church. It's been so long."

"This is how I feel every week." He rolled his eyes. "I do it for my mom."

"Huh, I never expected that." I swallowed, feeling suddenly like I might throw up. "I'm sorry, I'm"—I shook my head, waiting for the thumping to come back—"dehydrated, I think."

The guy came back with three bottles of water and blankets, soft blue blankets that still had that fresh-out-of-the-dryer smell. "You must be freezing. Come sit over here and warm up. Have this water, small sips. Then what can I get you—tea, coffee, orange soda?"

I salivated so much, I almost choked. "Coffee," I replied.

"Won't it keep you awake?" Jade asked. Not so sleepy then.

"No chance." Every time I blinked it took all my effort to open my eyes again.

I drank my bottle of water down so fast I almost puked it up. "Hey, Jade, put your foot up here if you want." I handed a yellow cushion to Jade, who nodded in thanks. Her foot had turned a deeper purple and had swelled up even more.

"Too bad we don't have any ice, but I know thirsty people when I see them," the guy said.

Jade nodded. "We haven't eaten all day." This was not strictly true, but I'd lost track of time, even with my dad's giant watch on my wrist.

"What am I doing, talking and talking, while you sit there starving? Stay there." He vanished back through the door.

"Oh God, how stupid am I?" I braved the outside for a second to load up my hat with snow. "Here, instant ice pack." I placed Jade's foot on it. It melted quick enough, leaving a puddle of water that Otis happily licked up. At least Jade could wriggle her toes.

Alex and I basked in the glow of the fire, blissing out at the freedom of socked feet, warm cheeks, all fingers and toes accounted for.

The smell of pizza wafted over us, drenching everything with the promise of melted cheese.

"This is such a relief." I took off my ski jacket and fleece and made them into a nest around me.

Alex scratched behind Otis's ears. Otis thumped his tail on the wooden floor, sending dust bunnies flying.

"Thanks to Mr. Soto's awesome store." I watched Jade snuggle under her blanket. "I don't know what we'd have done if we hadn't been wearing all that stuff." And we'd never be able to thank him.

Jade rolled her jacket into a pillow. "I still can't believe he died like that. In the snow." She shuddered. "Poor guy."

"I know." I bit my lip and caught Alex's eye. "I wonder what really happened."

"At least we're safe, and warm, and alive," he replied.

"Too right. This pizza could save your life." I smiled, allowing a slight ray of hope to enter. It wasn't that weird, finding a guy all alone, in a unkept church with no parishioners, waiting for people to save—like a vicar or a priest. I didn't get that selfless feeling from him though. There was a touch of pride. He wasn't just a holdout in an empty church, but a savior of grateful strangers. That had to make him hold his head a little higher.

The guy came out with a mug of coffee and two plates full of pizza. Cheese oozed down the sides. "Here, Excedrin Extra Strength on the side, for you, my dear. That should help with the swelling and the pain. You really don't want to keep your foot cold after being out in that kind of a storm."

Jade smiled and thanked him. She discreetly showed me the E stamped on the oblong white tablets. I shrugged. The E could be for *ecstasy*, for all I knew. But Alex nodded. I obviously needed to educate myself on American painkillers. The only nonprescription ones I knew were the giant bottles of red ibuprofen Mum got from Costco.

I took a slurp of lukewarm coffee and bit into a piece of pizza, struggling to swallow it down. It was either freezer burnt or he'd microwaved the packaging with the pizza, and they'd become one gooey, plastic mess—tasteless red sauce with foam cheese sprinkles, on a cardboard base. I gave Jade my last slice. "You eat it. I'm stuffed."

Otis smacked his lips with his crazy-long tongue as Alex fed him pizza crusts.

"That dog well trained? Not going to be a problem?" asked the guy.

"No way." Alex shook his head.

"I wasn't expecting dogs, only people."

"Us?" I asked.

"Well, not you, exactly, but people. That's what I'm set up for," he said with a yellow-toothed smile. "Lost folks out in the dark on a night like this. Must have followed the lights. You'd think they'd know to come here, but people are strange. Get lost in the simplest of places."

"Dogs get lost too," said Jade.

"Guess that's a fact." The guy looked toward Otis. "Don't know if we have enough food for a dog as well."

My gut squirmed. I gave Otis a hug and tapped at my side for him to sit next to me. "We won't need much." I gave Alex a WTF glance.

"Otis is happy with any leftover scraps, and we'd be really grateful for anything you've got to spare," Alex said, giving his best choir boy smile.

I uncrossed and recrossed my legs. "Just for the night. We'll be out of your way by morning."

"For sure," added Jade.

"Oh no, don't you worry. You're not in my way at all. Not at all."

34

10:57 p.m.

WE SAT, AS INVITED, IN FRONT OF A SPACE HEATER, THE kind that was designed to look like a small fireplace. The fake hearth glowed by the podium, and a paper plate of half-eaten pizza and a plaid blanket lay nearby. It's amazing how reviving something as simple as warmth and water can make you feel. Alex and I exchanged a smile. Maybe I was wrong, maybe we'd be okay here.

"Do you stay here?" Jade asked the old man, who was standing nearby, as she warmed her hands over the orange bars. "As the janitor?"

"I'm not the janitor. I'm the security guard." He pointed at the badge stuck on his bomber jacket. "This is my church. I try and keep it in shape, ready for the time when it's put to full use again."

"Oh, like in the winter?" asked Jade. "When the skiers come?"

"No." The guy scratched behind his ear. "Not those tourists. For seekers like you, that see the lights and search for the comfort of God."

Or maybe we wouldn't be okay here.

Alex widened his eyes at me. There was something odd happening. The warmth, the fire, and the weirdness of feeling safe were colliding into delirium. I was so tired, beyond tired. But my skin was too tight, and my senses were on full alert. The shot of caffeine didn't help, but it wasn't just that leaving me jittery.

"It's a serious responsibility. It takes a special person to fill that role." The guy polished his badge with his dirty jacket cuff. He nodded at Jade. "How did you end up together?"

Jade looked up confused. "Um, I'm not sure what you mean."

I butted in: "We're sisters. We got lost, that's all." I wasn't about to tell him about the fire and everything else.

"And who's he then?" He pointed at Alex. "Don't tell me he's your brother, because that'd be one hell of a mixed-up family."

"He's my..." I hesitated a little too long.

"Cousin," said Alex at the same time as I said *friend*.

"Cousin who's like a friend," Alex clarified.

"I opened my doors up to you. Don't make me regret it." He took his cap off and scratched his head. His greasy hair stuck to side of his cheek. The sharp light made the deep lines appear to be carved into his face. He stared at Jade. "You don't look like sisters."

Jade narrowed her eyes. "What exactly are you saying?"

I squeezed Jade's hand. "Different dad. No mystery." I stared at him full on in his piggy eyes. Always trust your spidey sense.

"Family, huh? Well, I suppose that's okay." He narrowed his eyes. "Don't you try anything. I know your sort." I could say the same about bigoted old white men.

"And what sort would that be?" Jade leaned in, eyes glaring.

He shook his head. "You know, teens, running amok without their parents. If that doesn't happen, I expect we'll get along just fine."

I breathed a sigh of relief. He wasn't about to throw us out. He was just an old, cantankerous white man. A yawn swept through me, from my toes to the top of my head.

Jade caught it and pretended not to, stifling it in her mouth, jaws trembling with the effort to keep it in there.

"Where are you from, Carl?" asked Alex. "Where's your family?"

"Good God-fearing family, American born and bred." His nostrils flared. "How'd you know my name?"

Alex pointed to his badge. "Carl, Infinite Security."

"'You can count on us,'" Jade said, reading the slogan under the name tag. "Let's hope so," she added quietly, but not quietly enough.

"What are you saying?" asked Carl.

"That…I hope we can count on you." Jade arched her brows.

"You think this is a joke?" Carl's jaw tensed.

"We weren't laughing at you," said Alex in a whoosh of words.

I shot Alex a shut-up glare. "We're all so tired, we hardly know what we're saying." I said, hoping Carl would give us the benefit of the doubt, so we could just rest easy for one night.

"I see that." Carl watched Otis snuffling along the pews. "You're welcome to stay and sleep. This is the Sanctuary, after all. We welcome everyone. I'll see if I can find you some pillows." He shuffled to the back of the church, bending low behind the pews.

"Thanks, we really appreciate it," Alex called after him.

"Jesus, I can't believe we stumbled into this place." I wiped my sleepy eyes.

"Yeah, *he's* a bit much though," said Alex.

"For sure," added Jade.

"Yep. We're clear off first thing. Keep telling yourself, warmth, food, shelter, one night," I said. It was hard to keep my eyes open. It felt like I was sleeptalking.

"Easy for you to say," said Alex.

"True," I said, suddenly aware of how stupid that was of me. "We're safer here than out there, is all I mean. We'll leave once the storm's over, so you don't have to put up with his shit."

"So *we* don't have to put up with his shit," Jade corrected.

"Damn right," Alex added.

35

11:24 p.m.

I WANTED TO CURL UP IN THE BLANKETS AND FALL
asleep, but I seemed to be the only one. Jade and Alex got a second
life fueled by warmth and pizza. The tablets seemed to work for
Jade's pain too. I was falling into a coma and they were buzzed.

A cloud crossed Jade's face. "Do you think your mom and Oliver
will find us tomorrow?"

"We'll probably be able to call them." So stupid not to think of
that. "Um, Carl, do you have a phone we could use?"

"I've got my own direct line." He touched his heart. "From right
here, to there," and he beamed at the arched ceiling. "That's how I
know exactly what to do when the time comes. Like now with the
lights. Trust me, I prepared for this."

My heart sunk. "Yeah, but do you have a phone *we* can use?" I
wanted to let them know we were safe, that we hadn't been hurt in
the fire. I wanted to know *they* were safe.

"There was one, but with the lack of funding and everything, it got cut off. So, sorry, not unless you can work a miracle on it." And he laughed like he was so funny.

I sighed. I'd be in so much shit, with the cabin burnt to a crisp, and all the stupid mistakes, starting with me letting Alex in. I glanced at him, sitting there with his lopsided grin, next to Jade, comfortable as old friends. Finding joy even in this weird place.

A familiar sourness churned in my gut. I just couldn't shake my unease; something wasn't right about this place. Something more than a racist old man.

"Yes, you followed the divine path." Carl handed Jade another slice of pizza. I had no idea how she fit it into her seemingly tiny stomach.

"It wasn't divine intervention. It was luck," Jade said between mouthfuls.

"That's where you're wrong. You saw the heavenly lights, and that's why you're here. And I'm here to keep anyone who enters safe, by the grace of God."

"Did you mean the auroras?" asked Alex. "They were amazing."

"They were sent for everyone, but who really *saw* them?" Carl's eyes grew wide. "Who understood what they meant?"

"They were caused by solar flares. Dad would understand," said Jade softly.

"Would he though?" Carl twirled a key ring around his fingers. The keys clattered like metal teeth. "Where is he when you need his explanation?"

"On his honeymoon with my new mom." Jade's voice slowed down at the end, as if each word was heavier. *Mom* being heaviest of all. She stared off to the side, mouth pinched.

"And I suppose you've got a new dad?" Carl looked at me.

I ignored him and turned to Jade. "We should get our clothes dry." I spread out my ski jacket and fleece in front of the space heater and helped Jade spread out hers. She pulled off her hat and let her hair free from its bun.

"I'm relieved, for your sakes, that you found me, ready to save you, ready to give you the true explanation and help you see your paths to enlightenment."

"We're thankful too," I assured him, hoping to cut off any sermons he might be planning.

"Isn't that right, Jade?" I asked.

"Yeah, totes," she agreed. "I'll be even more thankful to leave," she whispered.

"Me too," I whispered back. Mum and Oliver would be tucked up and cozy at their hotel, thinking we were safe in the cabin. They wouldn't know any different if the cell signal was still out. No phones, no news. All they could do was trust and hope that we were okay. And I wasn't even sure about that.

"Everyone ready for bedtime?" Carl asked. "Lights out, no creeping about now."

"Actually, can I use the bathroom, if you don't mind?" I asked.

He could hardly say no. He pointed to the door he'd been coming in and out of. "That way, past the kitchen, last door on the right."

I walked straight into a pew, catching my thigh on the sharp wooden corner, and hobbled to the kitchen door. I'd expected a stinking disaster, based on Carl's lack of personal hygiene, and I wasn't wrong. The tiny narrow kitchen was equipped with an oversized oven and an undersized fridge. There was a note with *11:13*, scrawled in thick black Sharpie sticking out from a KEEP TAHOE BLUE magnet. A time he needed to remember, maybe.

A deep double sink was piled high with dirty dishes. That explained the paper plates. I wondered how long Carl had been holed up here, since the church wasn't even used right now. It could be off-season for the church, and it was being fixed up for the start of the upcoming season. Something made me severely doubt that.

The bathroom door was partially blocked by a stack of boxes covered with a dusty white sheet. It was a one-stall affair, like going to pee in a freezer. An old toothbrush and a scrunched-up roll of toothpaste lay on the brown-stained sink. I rubbed some toothpaste around my teeth; even the minty tang felt good.

I sniffed my pits. Too bad I didn't have any deodorant. Hopefully I had enough layers on to trap the smell. Washing with soap was blissful. I tied my limp hair back into a loose ponytail and peeled off my socks to check my toes for blisters and chilblains. Five blisters and two fat chilblained pinkie toes, not too bad considering. Just being able to spread my toes was a blessing. I opened all the drawers in the chipped yellow cupboard, looking for Band-Aids, but they were full of toilet paper rolls and spare toothbrush packets, the kind dentists give out for free.

I hummed an old English song Dad used to love: *In the Bleak Mid-Winter*. I tried to hold on to the good memories—flying on the swings, running on the beach, but I knew they were only memories of photos, not actual memories.

I squashed the real memories down, all the way down. Dad's

face, all twisted up and angry, before he walked away. Maybe it wasn't anger. Maybe it was regret. It's hard to see clearly through an eight-year-old's lens. Best not to look at all.

Coming out of the bathroom, I passed the boxes and flipped up the sheet that covered them. The boxes were full of cans: Campbell's soup, cream of tomato. A film of dirt sat on the top layer, and the bottom ones had left a crust of rust on the linoleum floor. They must have been there for months, if not years. Maybe it was for the homeless. At least we'd be alright if we got snowed in. The wind howled around outside, showing no signs of the storm calming down. I picked a can up to check the sell-by date: May 2011. If everything was that old, it would explain the strange-tasting pizza. Carl could have been the security guard all along, slowly eating his way through the stockpiles of food for years.

I jumped as Carl banged on the door. "Hey, people are trying to rest out here. Don't need you clanging about the place."

I hurried back to the fake fireplace. Alex was gently snoring. Jade was in full-on REM mode, and Otis was running in his sleep. Carl poured himself a whiskey before shutting off the fairy lights. I slid in between Jade and Alex.

As soon as my eyes shut, I was out, dreaming my bones froze and snapped into tiny pieces, disintegrating into ice crystals before being blown away. I woke with a start. Snow splat against the windows and wind pushed against the wooden boards as it tried to force its way in, but I was still in one piece, untouchable within these walls. I fell back into a deep, bottomless sleep.

DAY THREE
October 27

36

7:05 a.m.

WHEN I WOKE UP, CARL WAS PATTING JADE ON HER head as she slept.

"Those that seek, will all be saved," he murmured. I guess he thought Jade needed reassuring in her sleep. He was lucky she didn't wake up and slap him.

I peered at Carl through crusted eyes. It was dark. Snow was piling up against the opaque windows. "Is it morning?" I wanted him to know I was awake. "Don't touch her."

Carl nodded. "Don't worry, just trying to reassure her. Won't happen again. It's early. You can go back to sleep."

I covered my face with my blanket, but I could hear him shuffling around, stopping, and shuffling again.

"What's he doing?" Alex whispered as Carl disappeared into the kitchen.

"You're awake!" I pushed him with my foot. "He's checking the perimeters," I whispered back. "Is it normal to get up this early and creep around the church?"

"No," said Jade, in what was for her a hushed voice. "And he touched my head when he thought I was sleeping." She shuddered. "I hate that."

"The power should be back on by now," whispered Alex.

"Check your phone," I said.

"No power. Guess I drained it looking at the compass."

"You weren't just looking at tree moss then?" I knew it.

"That does work." Jade turned back to Alex. "Do you have a charger?" There's one at the cabin." She pursed his lips. "Or there used to be." She gave Otis's tummy a tickle. "Maybe Carl has one, or a cell phone we can use."

Somehow I doubted that. "I'll look around for the landline. Maybe he's wrong about it being out of service. After all, people need to call to book all those weddings and funerals." I said. Not that it looked like anything had happened there in the last five years.

I put on my boots and jacket and set off exploring. The church was dark, too dark to see the top of the ceiling. The generator hummed as Carl clattered around in the kitchen, singing a hymn out of tune.

This place felt like it hadn't had electricity for a long time. Everything was dusty, abandoned, old. And that would be why Carl rigged up the generator. I walked along the creaking walls past the podium, to a small desk area at the back of the church hall. I flicked through a pile of dusty envelopes, bills from 2015.

Once I started really looking, it was obvious the church had seen better days. The paint was peeling off the walls. A black spider darted out of a crack. I dreaded to think how many more things lived inside the walls, creeping and scuttling their way around the church. The pews were worn, and the podium's wood-trimming was coming loose. Someone had scratched *11:13* into the woodwork. I had a feeling it was Carl. He might not be the janitor, but it was very unlikely this run-down place had needed a security guard for a long time.

The floorboards creaked. I hoped the noise of the wind was covering my snooping. Next to the desk was a tall metal filing cabinet. I quietly slid it open. Two rolls of duct tape and nothing else but dust. I closed it again and looked at the desk piled with paper. And there, hidden behind a file box, was an ink-smeared beige phone. It had come unplugged from the jack. I crawled on the dusty floor to plug it back in. There was no dial tone. At least Carl was right about something. It was all looking quite sad. But not as bad as being out there in the blizzard.

Alex and Jade were sitting in front of the electric fire when I went back. The wind thrashed about outside, but the hum of the generator soothed the threat to a mere murmur.

"Need any help in there, Carl?" Alex shouted through the door. The bitter smell of coffee was percolating from the kitchen.

"Nope, I got it." Carl emerged with three cups balanced between his hands. "How do you feel about church hospitality now?"

"Great," Jade said, reaching for a cup. Her sarcasm went right over Carl's head.

"We have Swiss Miss too! And since you're early risers, pancakes," and he disappeared back to the kitchen.

"Please don't go to any trouble," I yelled out. We didn't want to owe him for anything.

"No trouble, my pleasure!" Carl called back.

"What is he doing going out there all the time?" I whispered to Alex. "There's a ton of stuff back there. All those cans of soup, frozen pizza. What's he hoarding it all for?" I sat down next to Jade, cradling a cup.

"That's churches for you, full of weird shit," said Alex.

"Yeah," said Jade, "our church used to have tons of packets of crackers from like before I was even born."

"We never went, so I guess I don't know what's normal." I sat crossed-legged, like a schoolkid. "What does a church need that much soup for?" We should leave as soon as the storm dies down. "How's your foot doing, Jade? Is your ankle any better?"

"Stiff, but not as bad." She flexed it in front of me to prove she could still move it. It was swollen, but I could at least see that she had an ankle.

Carl pushed open the door, carrying a cup of Swiss Miss for Jade. "What's not normal?"

"People making unasked-for hot chocolate," said Jade.

"The church having lots of food stockpiled?" I said over her. "I figure you must be using it to help the needy." I gave him a big false smile.

"I've been getting this church ready to receive the saved. That takes a lot of time and preparation. You can't make those plans without a lot of supplies." Carl narrowed his eyes at me.

"I was right, then?" I pulled my blanket around me.

"Why else would I have all this stuff?" His face flushed. He pulled out his chain of keys and swung them around his nicotine-stained index finger. "It's to help people get back on their feet."

"Good to know," said Alex. "We're all for doing good deeds." He grinned at me.

"Doing God's deeds," Carl said and turned up the heater. "There, nice and toasty."

We sat in silence, taking sips from our mugs, listening to the soft patter of snow on the roof. The wind had died down. The storm was finally coming to an end. We could leave.

Otis snuffled around the end of the pews, then sneezed and flicked his drool onto the stone-tiled floor.

"Gross, Otis." His fur smelled of pine needles, dirt, and snow. It was hard not to forgive him. I gave him a full-on hug. "Jade, I see why you cuddle him so much. He's like a giant quilt." Otis licked my nose. I smiled. "Love you too, puppy."

Otis suddenly jumped up barking, startling all of us, and raced to the front door, hackles raised, ears back, pacing up and down as soon as he got there.

There was a loud knock at the door, then another, followed by a silence that echoed through our bones.

37
7:53 a.m.

I STARTLED TO MY FEET.

"It could be anyone. We don't know for sure," Alex said, thinking the worst.

Carl rushed to the door and started to turn the handle to unlock the deadbolt.

"Stop! You don't know who it is!" I ran after Carl, putting myself in his way.

"It's The Sanctuary." Carl opened his arms, fully playing his role as savior. "I let in anyone who needs help."

Nico's voice came through the door: "We're tired and injured. Let us in before we die of cold." He stomped his boots and shook the door. "Please," he remembered to add.

"Don't trust them," Jade pleaded. "They're only here because they're after us."

Alex joined her, with his back up against the door. "Seriously, they're bad news."

Carl shook his head. "Don't be ridiculous." He bellowed through the door, "Welcome, welcome! I knew there had to be more of you!" And he turned the handle halfway, almost unlocking the door.

"Thank you, thank you!" AJ's smirk rang out in his voice.

"They just tried to kidnap us." I said. This could not be happening. My skin crawled off my body. We had to leave now, before they stepped one foot inside.

Carl looked from me to Alex. "But they followed you here to safety. That's my job, to save souls. The more the better. I'm doing this for the good of all." He pushed my hands away.

My heart sunk. "But you're just a security guard."

Carl frowned. "No *just* about it. I'm God's security guard, securing your path to heaven. I knew there had to be a reason I was left here. God spoke to me. And I listened."

He was more unstable than I'd thought. I rushed to the backpacks, ready to flee before AJ and Nico got inside. Jade caught on and did the same. Alex stood rooted by the door.

"Open up, come on. What are you waiting for? Christmas?" Nico let his impatience get the better of him.

"See," I said. "Bad people."

Otis barked.

AJ shouted through the door, "I'm relieved you found a safe place to wait the storm out! We can take you home now. Your mom and dad will be so happy we found you safe and sound."

"He's lying." Adrenaline trembled through me. "You can't let them in."

"Come on," said AJ, "the police are looking for them, search

225

parties and everything. You don't want the situation to be misconstrued, have people thinking that you took advantage of the storm to kidnap children." God, he was good, twisted, but convincing.

Carl gave me a panicked look, stuck between two versions of reality.

"Open up." Nico rattled the door again. "If you don't open this door…"

"They have a gun." I grabbed Alex's arm, making him flinch.

Carl looked less sure of himself and glanced at Jade, who'd ducked behind the pews.

Otis growled low and deep in his throat. His ears were on high alert. Alex grabbed his collar and tried hauling him away from the door.

I whispered, as if Nico and AJ could hear my normal voice over the storm: "I don't think they can get in, as long as the door stays locked. Carl, please…"

Carl called out: "Did you follow the heavenly lights?" Still clinging to his savior complex.

"What are you talking about, old man?!" Nico shouted through the keyhole. "We're only here to take this trio of runaways off your hands and get them back safely to their parents."

Jade shook her head. "No way. No fucking way."

"No cursing," said Carl to himself and wandered over to the podium, ducking out of sight for a second before returning. "Why aren't their parents getting them if they know where they are?" He smiled at me. I gave a nod back.

AJ replied, "Their parents can't wait to see them safe and sound, but with all the roads closed, we have the only kind of vehicle that can get them home." So smooth.

"And where is home?!" I yelled.

There was nothing but silence.

A gust of wind buffeted the building and sent snow smacking harder against the windows. The creaks and strains of the wood moaned louder. Still no answer.

"They're under my protection now. There's no place for you here!" Carl yelled, red-faced at the door, body tense with anger. He turned the handle back to fully locked position.

We'd have to sneak out when we left, or risk that rage being turned on us.

My temples throbbed. Otis padded up and down behind us, guard-dog mode.

We braced ourselves, crouching behind the pews, as if we believed AJ and Nico could somehow storm the church. I searched my pockets for weapons—pens, keys, anything. Empty.

Waiting, waiting, waiting. There was nothing, not even a door rattle.

Carl shook his head. "They've gone."

"Are there other exits?" I darted up looking from one wall to another.

"Maybe we should leave now, before they find a way in. Just make a run for it," said Jade. She gathered up her backpack and put her jacket and hat back on, ready.

"We might have to," I said, doing the same.

"There are no other exits," said Carl finally. "There's only one path to God." Oh, great.

The snow had lessened enough for us to hear the roar of the engine as they revved it up and reversed away. My legs collapsed with relief. Otis barked as if he'd scared them off, and my shoulders wouldn't stop shaking.

"You're right, Jade," said Alex. "Let's get going before they come back."

"Oh no," said Carl far too softly, "nobody's going anywhere."

38
9:15 a.m.

"I'M NOT LETTING YOU RISK YOUR LIVES, RUNNING OFF into that storm. It's crazy to even consider it." Carl stood behind the podium, fidgeting with bits of paper.

The wind kicked up again. So much for thinking the storm was nearly done. A knot of snakes writhed in my stomach. This was never going to be over.

Carl frowned. "Don't worry. No one's taking you from here. I won't let them."

Otis paced back and forth in front of the door, stopping to sniff along the bottom with every second step.

"There's no way they're leaving just like that," said Alex. "They'll be back for sure. We can't sit here waiting for them."

Jade shook her head. "We should blockade the doors so they can't get in."

"They've already tried and failed." What else could they do?

Something, that was for sure. "I don't get why they're even still after us. Why don't they get away while they can?" I asked.

Alex shook his head. "Not really how they operate, and Jade did mention her dad coming after them. And like you said, we're all witnesses."

"Christ." I said. He was right, and we'd escaped like they told us not to. "Shit, they were going to hold us until they delivered the telescope, right?" At least they didn't actually want us dead.

"So now you're saying it's my fault?" Jade scowled at Alex.

"No, but they're running out of time. The storm can't last forever. The power will be back. The telescope will be reported missing, if they managed to get it, and it will be hard to sell once everyone knows it's stolen. There's an easy way to deal with loose ends, especially with all this snow and ice. You never know when you're going to have an 'accident,' roll into a ditch, and not be found until it's too late." Alex paced back and forth as he spoke.

"There's no way in hell they'd rather go down for murder than theft!" I replied. "That would be ridiculous."

"There'll be no swearing in my church," said Carl sharply.

"I told you, AJ will do anything to avoid prison. Do or die." Alex carried on before I could butt in. "And Jade's right. We should prepare for their return and protect ourselves."

I looked around the church. The pews were too big to move, the podium might do, and the filing cabinet would take a lot to shift but could blockade the front door. We could stack up the boxes of canned soup. I took a breath. What was I doing, getting caught up in their paranoia? "I think we should calm down. They can't get in.

We're freaking out that they found us, but Carl's here and he's not going to let them take us. What are they going to do, shoot him?" Oops, I wish I hadn't asked.

Carl nodded, then looked confused. "Why would they shoot me? I'm working for God."

"Nope," said Jade, ignoring him, "barricading is the only way to go," and she started trying to drag the podium over to the door. Alex ran to help her. Carl watched, then went into the kitchen and came back with a box of cans.

"Many hands make light work," said Carl.

"Alright." I went and grabbed a box from the bathroom too, sneezing from the dust, and before too long we were all sweaty from stacking up boxes of food, a chair, and the podium in front of the doors.

"What do they have on you anyway?" asked Carl. Talk about direct.

"It's a long story," said Alex.

"Give me the short version." Carl double-checked the door handle was still in fully locked mode.

Alex sighed. "I gave them a ride."

"That was it?" Carl raised his brows.

"Yeah, well it turned out be something more than a ride. It was a ride, then a wait, and then a get-out-of-there-fast."

"What, you were the getaway driver without knowing? Sweet!" Jade laughed.

"No, not sweet!" I said "God, how did that lead to this?"

Alex's face reddened. He fiddled with his jacket sleeve. "One favor for an old friend became several and then it got hard to walk away; a package here, a bike there, easy. All insured. No victims."

"Theft isn't a victimless crime, you know." I gestured to Jade. "If you'd done what you intended, she would have been devastated."

"Not for me, for Dad. He could have lost his job because of your stupidity." Jade threw another chair onto the barricade.

"Yep, thanks for that clarification." Alex scratched his nose and caught my eye. "I screwed up." Oh, that boy. With his sad eyes, sweet face, and willing ignorance. Seriously, grow the hell up.

Jade switched the fairy lights on. "It looks more hopeful. While we're all here waiting to be hunted down." Like we needed that reminder.

Alex sighed. "Oh God, I'm so sorry. One thing leads to another, and before you know it, you're an accessory and your decisions catch up with you, and you hardly recognize the trail you've left behind. All from one dumb favor."

"Yeah, it was pretty dumb." Jade smiled. "But at least you have a cool dog."

Otis ran over for an ear scratch from her, like he understood.

"These guys are just as caught up as us, born into it, really. AJ's great-grandfather had mob connections from way back. They used to rule South Tahoe, friends with Frank Sinatra and all that. I mean, it's changed a lot now, but AJ can't afford to lose that respect for his family's name. If he doesn't deliver to the bosses what he promised, he'll pay big-time. It's more than money on the line. It's his whole future."

"Oh," I said, fake sad. "I feel so bad for them. They have a gun and tried to kill us!"

"I know, I know. I was just trying to explain. I never meant to put either of you in danger." Alex sat with his head in his hands. "I swear Jade, I had no idea how much that telescope meant to you."

"To Dad." Jade sat on the other side of the aisle. "He never should have brought it up here." She sighed. "Like, how does he explain that? Luckily it didn't get burnt—but now it's been stolen." She stared at her feet, blinking back tears.

I couldn't get that last image of the cabin collapsing out of my head. My heart was suffocating in the smoke. I couldn't undo what I'd done.

Branches scraped against the walls, and snow splattered against the windows. I prayed AJ and Nico wouldn't come back, that the power would come on, and that Carl would stay calm.

"God has bigger plans for you." Carl drummed his knuckles on the podium. "11:13 all will be revealed. You were meant to come here for redemption." Not much chance of that then.

There it was again, 11:13. I shivered. The church had gone from a beacon of hope to a dank, dusty shroud.

"What if they don't come back? What if we just leave?" I knelt next to Alex, whispering in his ear so Carl wouldn't hear the question, or the answer.

"As long as nothing happens to that truck, they'll be back. They're just messing with you, trying to make you think you're safe. I thought if I stuck with you, they'd leave us alone. You know, safety in numbers." Alex leaned forward. His hair tickled my nose.

I rocked back on my heels. "Oh, I get it. You used us as cover. You figured with us two tagging along they'd leave you alone. But they didn't, and now they're after all of us, idiot!" I poked him in the chest. "We risked our lives running after you!"

"No…" Alex struggled to find the words. "I was trying…"

"Yes, you're always bloody trying." God, I'd forgotten my own mantra: people only let you down. I should never have trusted him. Shit, this hurt. I refused to cry and pretended to get some water and lingered in the kitchen until the tears had trickled down my throat.

When I went back, Jade gave me a sad smile. "Everything's a mess, isn't it?"

"We'll be out of here soon." At least we were still a team. But that wouldn't last long. Once we got back to normalcy, we'd go back to being strangers. My chest was thick with sadness. Everything was pointless.

"They didn't know what they were running into coming here, trying to take you from me like that." Carl grinned. "And soon the holy lights will be upon us once more and I will guide you to your destiny." It was hard to stop myself from throwing something at him. I was so tired of being a thing for other people to save, to control, to rescue. I just wanted to be free.

The generator sputtered, and all the fairy lights went out one by one. The electric heater bars faded from deep red, to orange, to pale yellow. A gust of wind shook the church.

"You have more gas for the generator, right?" Alex jumped to his feet. "You must have."

"Ah, God is waiting." Carl held his arms out wide. "We're ready Lord. Here and ready!"

39

9:53 a.m.

"CARL!" I SNAPPED. "WE NEED PETROL. WHERE'S THE petrol?"

"It's a sign. The sign. Not long now." He gazed at the ceiling, willing God to come and take us.

I rolled my eyes at Jade, and we started the hunt, opening cupboards in the kitchen, searching in the back section by the old desk. I made sure not to be in the same space as Alex. I didn't want him to think he was in any way forgiven.

Otis ran from place to place, excited by so much activity. The snow had slowed but the wind was still gusting. The church creaked from side to side. The temperature plummeted without the heater, and the lack of light added a solemn gloom to the proceedings. I put the last of my cold-weather gear back on and Jade did the same. Her foot and ankle were still swollen, but I helped fix her boot, carefully placing her foot into it once she'd cut down the side. We wrapped it in place with the duct tape. Then we looked for the petrol again. Like it would be so hard to find a bright red canister.

"Lottie?" Jade called just loud enough from the kitchen for only me to hear her, putting her finger to her lips when I turned. She held up a wallet. It was a trifold, black, leatherette.

I flipped it open, and there was Carl's driver's license, only it didn't look like Carl, it looked like a guy ten years younger, with glasses and a moustache. It was a together, normal Carl. There was no money, only a folded slip of paper—an unemployment check stub from 2017. He'd been staying here for ages. No job, no pay. No wonder he was having a hard time. Being stuck with Carl was looking worse by the hour.

"Why is he here and what the hell does he want with us?" whispered Jade.

"No idea." Everyone was living a lie. I slid the paper back into the wallet and glanced across to the kitchen. The door was moving. I could hear Alex and Carl talking urgently in there. This disheveled church, shaking in the wind. Jade's question swirled around my head. What was Carl doing here? What was he waiting for?

Alex came bursting out of the kitchen carrying an empty petrol can. "No gas left for the generator."

"What?" said Jade.

His face dropped. "It's not my fault. Stupid Carl used it all on powering his music before we arrived. What now? You're both annoyed at me? You got it so wrong, honestly, trust me."

"Yeah, right."

"You should show him," said Jade, "what we found."

"What did you find?" Carl stood there, leaning against the doorway, trying and failing to look unconcerned.

"Nothing," I said too fast.

Carl narrowed his eyes. He knew. "Sometimes you jump to the wrong conclusions. Salvation is salvation, no matter the circumstances of the person who offers it."

"So, it wouldn't matter if it was you, or a priest, or a security guard, or anyone at all?" I leaned forward, staring into his watery gray eyes.

"God chose me. He forgave all my sins and told me what to do." Carl's jaw tensed.

Jade's eyes widened. "Chose?"

Carl raised his hands in prayer. "The lights led you here, as he told me they would. You are the lucky ones. You get salvation. You get to see the true meaning of the Lord."

"So you're not the security guard?" asked Alex.

Carl shook his head. "It doesn't matter, not anymore. God found me here, ready to take up my new role, ready to save you, and soon one journey will end, and another will begin." He pulled a gun out from his belt. "I will protect you to the end."

"Holy shit." My stomach dropped to the floor. I was rooted to the ground, unable to take my eyes off the gun. This was real. I was going to die right there, in a church. In a bloody church with a deluded guy who thought he was saving our souls. "I think we'll be okay without your protection. Thank you and everything, but…" Shit, this wasn't going to work.

"Shall we?" Carl gestured to the pews with the gun barrel.

"You're safe here. But only if you stay. And I'm really sorry about this." He waved the pistol around. "I was hoping I wouldn't have to bring it out."

"This what happens when it's so easy for just anyone to get hold of a gun." Jade muttered under her breath, grabbing my arm, and pulling me along.

"You're keeping us captive," said Alex in astonishment.

"Only for your own good," Carl said, amazed that we didn't see it that way.

"What is he waiting for?" I murmured to Jade.

Jade shook her head. "I have no idea, but we better get out before it happens."

Alex started to speak: "You can't keep us here…" But he froze when Carl cocked the gun.

"I knew you'd be trouble." Carl released the safety, making a tight click. "Ready or not, when the time is here, we'll go together."

We sat in the pews. Jade and I squeezed each other's hands, not daring to move, while Alex glanced around, looking for a way out of this "salvation" we'd blindly walked into.

40

10:48 a.m.

MY FOOT WAS NUMB, BUT I DIDN'T DARE MOVE. WE hardly dared to breathe, even after spending a good half hour huddled in the pews, watching Carl pace back and forth, muttering to himself.

"For those that follow the lights, shall seek salvation, and those that seek salvation, shall be saved. I shall save them, just show me the sign, Lord!"

We still had no idea what sign we were waiting for, or what would happen when it inevitably didn't come.

That was what I was more afraid of. What would Carl do then?

Otis whined, tail between his legs. An engine rumbled louder and louder, the sound ebbing and flowing with the wind. Within seconds it became a loud mechanical screech that echoed up to the walls. There was a moment of silence then a giant crash.

"Move!" Alex shouted and dropped to the floor.

The church shook. The wall buckled inward, and the black bull bar of the red truck glinted between the flimsy plaster board church wall and the outside world. My heart stopped. They'd come back.

Jade and I raced to the kitchen. "Go out the bathroom window. I'll be right behind you." Then I saw Alex.

He was pulling Otis by his collar, trying to get him away from the damaged wall. Otis growled and rushed to the front door.

"Go out the front!" I yelled at him from the kitchen doorway.

"You can't smash your way in!" Carl shouted at the wall. "I'm armed and ready!" His voice made me jump. I hadn't realized how close he was, standing at the end of the pews, master of nothing.

A rifle poked through the freshly made hole in the wall. "And so are we!" I could feel the excitement in Nico's voice.

Alex was one foot out the door when AJ stepped through the gap. Otis jumped up at him, growling and barking. AJ went to kick him. Otis backed away.

Alex whistled to Otis. He ran immediately to Alex's side.

I gasped. "What the hell?"

"Hi, Lottie, miss us?" AJ smiled, like he was meeting a long-lost pal. "I'm sorry about all this, but you did bring it on yourself, chasing after Alex, when you could have stayed safe at Soto's. Then escaping when I'd told you explicitly not to. You would have been fine, everything would have been taken care of, and you would have been free to leave." He shook his head. "I hate these situations. Still, what can you do? My skin is on the line too."

I grabbed my backpack and scuttled backward, smacking up against the edge of a pew.

"Alex, aren't you going to save your girlfriend?" AJ threw his head back and laughed. "Can't save your dog. Can't save your girl. Not much use, are you?"

Alex ran at AJ, who spun to the side so that Alex's fist missed his face.

"Really, Alex, is that how you treat an old friend?" AJ seized Alex by the hair and dragged him in front of Carl, before throwing him to his knees. My heart was on overdrive.

Carl aimed his gun at AJ's head. "You let him be. He's mine."

"I'm sure you realize we can't let you keep these people." AJ glanced at Alex and then at me. "One person short."

Otis growled but dared not get closer.

"Go, Otis!" I could at least get him out. He took one look at me then ran out the front door into the storm. I hoped to God that Jade was out there too.

Nico climbed through the gap in the wall. "Guess what we found?" He brandished Einstein's telescope in his hand. "It's amazing how reflective the lens is when you shine a flashlight on it. Oh yes"—he winked at me—"we found it even without your help." He turned to Carl. "A shoot off, eh? I thought you were a man of God."

Carl was caught off guard for a second, before raising his gun again in his slightly trembling hands. Not knowing who to aim at—Nico to his right, or AJ, straight ahead.

Alex was trapped, caught in the crosshairs between the three of them. Fresh snow blew in from the gash in the wall and the wind howled.

I glanced back at the kitchen. Jade's face peered around the door.

My heart dropped. She'd come back for me. I mouthed, *Get out.* She got the hint and vanished, before anyone noticed.

I should have fled with her. But I couldn't make myself move. There was abandoned and there was condemned. I couldn't leave Alex behind.

Alex shook his head at me, like I was going to try something crazy. As if I had a plan. I edged toward the kitchen, figuring I could grab anything—a can, a knife—to throw as a distraction. Long enough to let Alex escape.

"You're not taking no one." Carl fired a warning shot at the ceiling. "The next one's gonna hit one of you." He grinned. "But which one? Eenie, meenie."

Nico frowned and pointed his rifle at Alex, who looked more like a ghost with every passing second. "You're not making this easy, old man. We've got no business with you, but we can't let you keep them. Don't be a fool and sacrifice yourself for nothing."

"No." I rushed forward. "You don't need to harm him. He's not part of this. You don't need any of us. You've already got the telescope."

"Yeah, we do, but now we've got to deal with you," said Nico, "and we're running out of time. You created this mess by bringing him into it."

"Where's the other girl?" asked AJ, without taking his eyes off Carl.

"Bathroom, girl business." My voice trembled. Be outside, Jade, be safe with Otis. "Alex and I swear not to say anything, and neither will Jade. Who'd believe us anyway? As for him," I nodded at Carl, "we don't even know each other's names."

"You swear not to say anything? What do you think this is, high school? We're not talking about a slap on the wrist here." Nico took a step toward me. "Call her out and no one has to get hurt."

The gun aimed at my face did little to help me believe that. I swallowed hard and stared at Alex.

"Jade?" I called weakly, praying she'd gone this time.

"These are my souls to take, not yours. God will not allow it!" In the gloom, Carl's voice took on a new urgency, a conviction of power. "The Angels of Death are coming."

Alex's eyes grew wide, as he realized what Carl was saying. "Souls to take?"

We were screwed every way we looked. A gust of snow came in through the gap in the newly created jagged opening and the wind whistled in. Things were getting colder fast.

Alex mouthed *Go!* I had no idea if he had a plan. I took a large step backwards to the kitchen, then another and another until I could touch the door.

"Get out of the way, old man." Nico aimed the rifle back at Carl.

"The first was a warning. Next one's for real." Carl spoke low and steady. "My church. My rules. You sit there, no talking, no moving, unless I say so." He glared at AJ.

AJ raised his brows at me. "Where are you going, Lottie?"

"Come back here." Nico motioned with his rifle.

I was trapped like a rabbit, head against the kitchen door, pulse hammering a thousand beats per second. I had no escape; my legs didn't work. AJ and Nico were both focused on Carl, and he was glancing from one of them to the other, unsure who was the bigger threat.

This was not good. Sweat dripped down my back. I glanced at Alex. He shook his head. No big ideas on how to escape either.

There was a blur of black and white and a growl as Otis came hurtling in the newly created gap in the church wall. He raced for Alex.

Nico trained his gun on Otis.

"No!" AJ held his palm up. "Grab the dog. Don't shoot it."

Nico lunged toward Otis, but the dog darted back out of his reach, cowering behind Alex.

Carl fired his gun above AJ's head. "Enough! Last warning. Now get out of my church!"

"Hush, old man, or I will put a bullet through your skull." AJ trained his gun on Carl.

Carl's face paled and his hand trembled, but he held on to his gun.

"No one has to get hurt," AJ said calmly. "We'll just take what we came for and leave."

Otis growled.

Nico turned back to AJ. "Sure I can't just shoot it?"

"Run, Lottie, run!" Alex bolted between me and Nico, shielding my escape.

I raced through the kitchen doorway. As I turned to see if Alex was following, a gunshot rang out.

The echo filled every corner of the church, and everything went into slow motion.

Chips of wood exploded from the corner of the pew.

A shard flew into my hand as I shielded my face.

AJ shouted something incomprehensible.

Alex gasped and staggered in front of me, clutching his calf, as a bloodstain spread along his jeans. Otis whimpered as Alex fell to the floor.

"Shit." My mouth dropped open.

The bullet must have ricocheted off the pew and into Alex's leg.

Tears welled in my throat.

He had risked his life for me, and I couldn't even move.

41

11:03 a.m.

CARL STOOD, PISTOL IN HAND, READY FOR WHENEVER Nico poked his head up again. He paused like he was thinking of aiming at us, but AJ moved, so Carl fired at him, missing again.

As I managed to make my way to Alex, Carl looked at me. "I could have saved you. You could have seen the light. Now you get nothing." And he spat in my direction, his face screwed up with hate and pain. To think we almost stayed.

"Go, Otis, go find Jade," Alex murmured in his ears.

Otis ran outside. Smart dog.

I grabbed Alex under the arms, scooting him backwards, staying low to the ground, like that would make us harder targets. Fortunately Carl had turned back toward Nico and AJ. But our slim escape window was closing. "Come on. You can do this," I told him.

A trail of blood mapped his progress across the floor. His eyes watered. His breathing was shallow. He winced with pain every time he moved. "I can't make it."

"You have to. I'm not leaving without you."

Alex gritted his teeth and made a last lunge for the door and into the kitchen.

That's when I noticed another *11:13*, crudely etched into the door of a kitchen cabinet. Carl had given meaning to completely random signs. Making up his calling from nothing.

A shot went off again. Nico yelled with pain. It must have been Carl doing the shooting. We had to get out fast.

"I can't believe he got me," said Alex, his voice fading in and out.

"Carl was trying to stop Nico. But he missed and the ricochet got you. And who needs a leg anyway?" I blinked away my tears. "You could have died shielding me."

"I might still."

I helped him get through the kitchen and into the bathroom, locking the feeble door behind us, knowing it would only take one kick to bring it down. I kissed his cheek. "You have to climb out the window. We'll patch you up outside."

Jade shouted through the window, "I'm here!" It was so amazing to hear her voice.

"Alex is coming through the window. He got shot in the leg, but he's going to be fine." If I said it enough, it might be true. "Is Otis with you?"

Otis barked.

I actually grinned. "Good boy, Otis!"

"Come on, hurry!" Jade's exhausted eyes fixed on mine.

The snow had drifted into a slope almost up to the window. "It's a tiny drop. Alex, you can do this easy."

Alex slumped against the door. "I can't make it."

"Yes, you can." I shoved him up to the window and pummeled him until he moved and stuck his torso and then his hips through the small space. His face was so pale. He sucked his breath after every slight move. "I'll be right behind you."

There were two more shots, then five more rapid ones.

I clambered out the window, scratching myself on the splintered wood as I wriggled my shoulders through the tight window frame. My jacket tore on the latch. I made a final heave and hurtled myself into the white nothingness.

A thick ice quilt smothered me, sucking the air from my lungs. I'd felt this before, back in the car—waiting as snow covered the windows and ice creeped into my veins. And the hollowness of hope fading, until I knew Dad wasn't coming back. Trust turned into nagging doubt, then resignation, stamping out that flicker of hope that he thought I was worth coming back for. I was left alone until the morning, when Mum finally realized something was wrong, very wrong. Would she realize that this time? Would Oliver?

Snow softly plopped all around me. The wind had died down. The church was quiet. Deathly quiet.

I rolled over and stared at the sky. Blushed clouds hovered over the treetops, painting a violet glow over everything. Even the drifting snow was brushed with pink. I squinted to make out the shapes between the sharp gray spikes of trees, a flash of red, or blur of black and white.

A bright blue blob appeared at my side—Jade. A rush of joy brought tears to my eyes. I hugged her tightly and she didn't even flinch. "I thought we'd never make it out of there. But we're okay. We're going to be okay."

"Yep, we are." Jade spoke through chattering teeth. "All of us."

I glanced back at the church, frightened by the splintered wall groaning in the storm, that it would collapse, that they'd come after us. That behind that precarious wall, Carl, AJ, and Nico were locked in a battle that could break out of the church at any second.

I staggered to the tree line with Jade, where Alex and Otis were waiting. Deep red splats marked Alex's trail. Jade whipped out the duct tape and wrapped it around Alex's wound. Alex grimaced with each additional wrapping but grinned whenever Jade looked up to check she wasn't hurting him.

"It looks like it didn't go in. It's a graze, not an entry. Could have been a lot worse," Jade said, giving the bandage a light pat. "That should hold for a while."

"And you know that how?" I saw from her face I shouldn't have asked.

"Friday nights, we'd deliver pizza to the ER. Mom would be rushing around fixing up gunshot wounds. I wish I remembered her face like I remembered those injuries." Jade blinked back a tear. "Dad says I'm exactly like her, but how can I be sure, if I don't remember anything about her at all?"

"Shit, I'm sorry." There was nothing else to say.

We sheltered silently in the canopy of a pine trees while we figured out what to do next. Snow fell in soft, floaty feathers, drifting around the tree trunks, like it was searching for us.

"At least I won't bleed to death." Alex held out his leg, puffed up around the calf with the duct tape. "You fixed me like a pro nurse, like your mom."

"Doctor," said Jade. "She was a doctor. Smart, funny, and successful, not too much to live up to." She nodded at him. "But thanks."

I glanced back at the distant church. "We should get away from that craziness. It's going to end badly in there."

"Yep, find a safe place fast." Jade flicked the snow from her face.

We couldn't go far, not with Alex's injury. The cloud's tint of pink had turned charcoal. "Let's follow the road and hope to find another car, or a cabin, or a store—anything to get us away from them." It was like wishing for a magic lantern. Not going to happen.

Another gunshot rang out.

My heart skipped a beat.

From our hiding place we could just about see AJ appear at the church doors. "It was self-defense, right?" That was all we could make out from what he was shouting. His shoulders sagged, as if he couldn't quite believe what had happened.

Nico came out nodding, rifle in one hand, telescope in the other. His wiped blood from his cheek then limped to AJ, shaking his head. "It's done."

They grabbed hold of each other, hugging like they were actually shaken.

I gripped Jade's arm and Alex gripped mine, and we ran, and we didn't stop running until we couldn't see anything but white all around us. And then we crouched, silently behind a knotted tree trunk, squinting to make out any shapes in all that nothingness. And then something came, large and black-and-white and shaggy. Otis.

He'd kept up with us. Thank God. Jade's smile was priceless as she hugged Otis, and I didn't even mind when his tail smacked me in the mouth.

"What now?" asked Alex. "My leg is killing me."

"Mine too," said Jade. God, I'd totally forgotten her damaged foot and twisted ankle.

"I could leave you guys here, with Otis, and scout ahead?" I suggested.

"No," said Jade, "we stick together."

I tucked my hands into my armpits and shrunk into my jacket.

"Shh," said Alex, holding Otis to keep him still.

The rumble of the engine came so close, I could feel the air move. They'd managed to reverse it out of there. No skidding away this time. The beams cut through the trees, swaying from side to side, on a mission to find their prey. Thank God it was snowing hard enough to partially cover our tracks.

"Duck," I said, and we flattened ourselves into the snowy ground.

Within a few minutes they'd slowly driven past us and away, until the taillights were just a red glow and then nothing.

"We go back to the church," said Alex. "That's the last place they'd look for us."

I shook my head. Whatever was in there, I knew it would be

nothing good. Nothing I'd want to see. "There's was no way I'm going back to that hellhole. You heard what they did to Carl." My voice trembled. "Did you notice the time?" I showed them my watch. "11:23. We've been running at least ten minutes. *11:13* was scribbled all over the church. It's like Carl predicted the time of his own death." A chill ran across my spine.

"No"—Alex shook his head—"you don't even know the exact time he got shot."

"It was probably a Bible reference. It's sad, but just a coincidence." Jade glanced in the direction of the church. "But maybe it's best not to go back."

Alex nodded. "Okay, let's find out where we are. This whole situation is kind of hopeless."

"Yeah, so hopeless. You saved my life, shielding me back there." I choked on my words. Tears rolled down my cheeks as reality sunk in. I wiped them away as fast as I could. "Don't want them to freeze," I joked and gave a small smile.

"I'll always be there for you, I promise." He took a deep breath. "We all stick together, the three of us, no matter what."

"All for one, and all that." Jade grinned.

We laughed and hugged, as if we were a team, friends even, and not three bedraggled teens lost in the snow, with nowhere to go, and no way to get there.

The deep engine rumble cut through our pledge, destroying it in an instant. The beams were blinding. We scattered between the trees, fumbled our way out of the light and into the shadows. Nico and AJ were still hunting us.

42

11:44 a.m.

SNOW SPIT INTO OUR FACES. BUT IT ALSO COVERED our tracks and hid our outlines as we zigzagged from one black tree to the next. AJ and Nico couldn't keep up. The trees were too thick for them to navigate, even in a 4x4. They were forced to stop, leaving the engine running and the lights blazing.

I fell over myself trying to escape, my feet tangling with each other. I lost sight of Jade and Alex. Arctic wind slapped my cheeks, rubbing them raw. I wished I'd had a balaclava. I would never laugh at Jade for wearing hers again. And there she was, not far ahead of me. I didn't know how she managed that with her limp. She must have had a rush of adrenaline from fear.

"We can find Alex and Otis once we've lost these guys," I said between puffs. Jade nodded and pushed us on farther away from the truck.

We stopped to catch our breath, listening to the sound of

footsteps pounding through the undergrowth. We froze, praying we blended in with the trees and spiraling snow-globe air, invisible forest dwellers fading into nothing, a glimmer in the whiteness.

"Lottie, I know you're out there." Nico called my name instead of Alex's. My guts clenched. That was not a good omen.

Jade and I hid behind a thorn bush that waggled in the wind. The shadow shape of Nico came toward us, like static fuzzing against the landscape, unreal and unwanted.

"We might have to run," I whispered in Jade's ear.

She nodded.

The clumps came closer, paused, one step forward. "I know you're there." But he didn't. If he did, he'd be looking in our direction. He stumbled forward, swearing under his breath. "I've got a gun," he called out. As if I we weren't aware of that. I held Jade's arm tight—don't move, don't breathe. We waited for Nico to head away again, before silently slipping from our hiding spot.

We stumbled in the opposite direction from where Nico had gone, falling into snowbanks, clambering out of them on our hands and knees, staggering in the wind, in an effort to walk upright, before stepping back into another deep divot. Holding hands was the only way not to lose each other. Progress was excruciatingly slow.

My cheeks were raw, frostbitten. I couldn't feel the difference between my foot and my boot. My legs were wooden stilts. I didn't know where the ends were. I stumbled on a root, twinging my ankle. At least there was some feeling left down there.

I panted, out of breath. If we'd stayed in the cabin, none of this would have happened. I wouldn't have found Mr. Soto or been chased by AJ and Nico. We wouldn't have seen the horror show at the church. Alex wouldn't have gotten lost and injured. Of course, if I hadn't let Alex in, none of this would have even gotten started, except for those weird lights and the power outage. I never would've met him, and he would have never seen the telescope. My heart faltered at that thought. The whole situation wouldn't have happened. He wouldn't have used us, and he wouldn't have needed to save me. It was an endless list of what-ifs. Not worth thinking about right then and there, with the iciness of death catching hold of our veins.

Snow turned to sleet, firing ice bullets into my face, each sharper than the last.

Jade held up her gloves against her face for protection. "My whole body hurts."

"Keep moving. Stopping is the worst thing we can do."

She huffed. "There's no point. Everything looks the same. My foot's frozen." She sat on a lump of rock.

I tugged the boot off and rubbed her foot between my hands. "Can you feel this?"

She shook her head.

I plucked off what was left of her sock. Her toes were dark purple. I took off my gloves and rubbed her foot between my hands until I couldn't feel my hands anymore. I stuffed my glove over her foot and tucked my hands under my arms to warm them. The fingertips were bloodless already. Shaking caused them to sting, as if the cold was literally biting them. Nothing kept the warmth in; there was no warmth there to keep.

Jade's eyes locked onto mine. "You didn't even want to come this weekend. Dad told me. You hated the idea."

"True, not my first choice, nor yours either." I raised my brows.

"True," she agreed.

"But my hating the idea of coming here wasn't about you. It was about me and Mum, and our history." Her broken promises.

"Yeah, well it was about you being forced on me, as if I needed a sister when me and Dad had been doing just fine. Sounds stupid now. Anyway"—she squeezed my hand—"I'm glad you came."

"God, me too. I really like Oliver, and you're not so bad." I nudged her. "I'm sorry it turned out like this." It had to be hard on her too, losing her mum, meeting mine.

She shrugged. "You're not as bad as I thought you'd be."

"Cheers, thanks." I nodded my head. "Feel so much better now." But we were both grinning. I put her boot back on. "This mess, I want you to know, it's all on me. I'm the crap one. I shouldn't have let Alex in. I shouldn't have thrown the pine cones on the fire."

"You shouldn't have opened the door to those idiots that first night."

"No," I agreed, "I shouldn't have." Everything went wrong because of my bad decisions. "I promise we'll get us out of this." We had to.

"What about Alex and Otis?" Jade sniffed.

"We'll find them, but first it's you and me, okay?" I stamped my feet.

"Thanks, Lottie." Jade smiled. "But we're a team, so we'll get us out of this together, okay?"

"Sure." My teeth chattered. We'd freeze sitting here in the snow. "How's your foot feel now? Can you move it?" I poked her. "Try a little marching on the spot."

She took a step forward and doubled over, breathing heavily.

"Asthma?" I asked.

"No, just tired." She let out a little wheeze.

"Are you sure? How many puffs left?"

"Two. But I don't need it. Plus I've still got Mr. Soto's inhaler for backup. I can always squeeze a few more puffs out, even after the counter hits zero."

I wasn't sure if I believed her. "How much was left in Mr. Soto's inhaler?"

"Two puffs. Yeah, don't worry." Jade stopped still. "Can you hear that?"

Soft footsteps were padding right toward us.

43

1:04 p.m.

THEY STOPPED, WITH THE WIND. THERE WAS A TENSION in the air, a stillness. The hair rose on the back of my neck. No stomping boot steps, something wilder.

There was a rustle and a rabbit hopped out in front of us. Jade and I beamed at each other as it jumped out of sight, leaving little paw prints behind. The snow landed gently around us, plops and sighs, rather than spits and rattles. There were no other sounds. Jade and I were the only ones here, yet I still had a sixth sense that we were being watched, like captives in a snow globe, with someone on the outside deciding when to give us a good shake-up.

Nothing felt real. It was as if the cabin and the church never existed. It was just us two, and the never-ending mountains. I knocked the snow off my hat and tightened my scarf.

Jade tugged at my sleeve. "Lottie, what is it?"

I blinked myself back to reality. "Sorry. Listen, can you hear anything? Anything at all?"

A branch snapped. My bones froze. We stood silently waiting, knowing it was coming. The air was thick with expectation.

I felt it before it leapt, the frisson of power, as it sprang right across our path—thick, golden, black-tipped tail, muscles rippling, tufted ears back. A mountain lion. Our backs stuck to the tree trunk as the lion seemed to bound out of nowhere and disappeared as fast.

"Bigger, you have to make yourself look bigger, and wave and scream." Jade's words came tumbling out all at once. "And whatever you do, don't run!"

"It's gone. It's gone. It must have been after that rabbit." My heart raced after that rabbit too.

"Hare," said Jade.

"Yeah." I swallowed. "Wow, that was close."

Jade nodded. "Too close!"

"America is bloody scary. The animals here might actually eat you. The worst thing that's going to happen to you in Britain is you step on an adder."

"Yeah, but Scotland has nipping pike and all those midges that do eat you."

I laughed. "Yeah, midges, far worse than mountain lions." My pulse still raced a thousand beats per second.

"They are," said Jade, with absolute conviction. "Mountain lions rarely attack humans. Midges can't stay away!"

I swept my hair from my face. Snow churned in all directions. No sun, no sky, no sound, no shapes. "Which way?"

Jade rubbed snow from a tree trunk, revealing the moss beneath. "North? I think the road runs that way."

I shrugged. "I honestly don't know. I guess it should be downhill. So that way?" I pointed vaguely to the left. "Can you walk alright on that foot?"

"Yep, if I go slow." Jade squinted at the sky, like she was trying to find the sun. "If we keep going the opposite direction from that lion and where we last saw the truck, we'll at least be walking away from them."

"Sounds like a plan."

We traveled silently, stopping to listen to every other step, freaking out at every cracking branch, every plop of snow. My eyes ached, but the outlines of things looked clearer; snowflakes were settling on my gloves, millions of them. The fur cuff of my snow boot iced into a thick ridge.

Dad might have had that sensation of clarity, walking into thin air, no external threats, just internal angst. One misplaced step forward, too late for regrets. Lost in the void. He was always leaving, sometimes for months, but he'd always return with hugs and trinkets, like the heart-shaped rock he'd found for me on Ben Nevis. There were good times. Me-and-him times. Walks in the woods, past Shire horses, and foxes that popped up from nowhere and dashed away just as fast. The tides and the stone-skimming; his tall, thin legs and his big, calloused hands; his soft voice and his watchfulness. Climbing over TRESSPASSERS WILL BE SHOT signs, and walking way past exhaustion, so he had to carry me for the last leg back to the car. But not after that last time. After that, there were no more smiles. No more anything.

"Lottie." Jade's teeth chattered as she wiped the snow crystals forming on the edge of her hat. "It's getting hard to see."

I grabbed her arm and locked it in mine. "Do you think this is what Oliver meant when he said we should hang together and get to know each other better?"

"Yes, get lost in the snow and hold on to each other." She wheezed slightly at the end of her sentence. "Stop a sec." She breathed steadily and slowly, in and out, in and out. With only a hint of one tiny wheeze.

A faint sound came from behind us. And again. A bark, a definite bark!

We slip-slid toward it.

44

2:17 p.m.

I'D NEVER BEEN SO HAPPY TO SEE THAT CRAZY DOG.
Otis smothered Jade with exuberant licks, and there was Alex. He
stopped for a second, as if to check it was okay to be there, as if we
wouldn't want him to find us. My heart danced for him.

"I'm so sorry. I didn't think, I just..." He took a tender step
toward me.

"Ran. Us too." I smiled. "It's so good to see you. How's your leg?"

"Still there. It's not too bad as long as I don't have to..."

"Move it?" I asked.

"Yeah."

We hugged, like siblings, and then not, then hung back slightly
embarrassed, until we couldn't take it and hugged like we'd never
let each other go.

"Jeez, get a room!" Jade grinned and hugged him too.

"So," Alex finally said, shaking the snow off his hat, "what now?"

"Find a road. Or a mythical cabin," I suggested.

"Or even a bus shelter or a shed," added Jade.

Otis was swimming in snow, no belly sighting at all. No racing around for him. He looked as exhausted as the rest of us.

Alex caught hold of my hand. I smiled. It took a while for the world to stop spinning.

"We almost got eaten by a mountain lion," said Jade, turning to Alex. "It was so cool!"

"Seriously?"

"Yep. It went after a rabbit instead, but it could have been us…"

"Do you think we're safe with Otis here?"

"Totally," said Jade. "It was never really after us."

"You could have told me that at the time!" I wriggled my nose. It was getting colder. "Best get moving before dark."

We walked on, slowly, leaning on each other, pretending it was for warmth. I scanned the tree line ahead. I was sure I'd heard something, like a twig crack, but maybe not. Still, the hair on the back of my neck tingled. And there it was again.

I held up my hand and placed my finger on my lips. We crouched down and waited. I prayed it was another mountain lion.

A shape staggered from the trees, barely twenty feet ahead—a human wearing a beanie. Nico had caught up with us. He stood still, as if he hadn't actually seen us but could sense we were close.

"How the hell did he find us?" I whispered.

Jade and Otis crashed through the undergrowth, too far ahead to see him, too far away for us to warn them. Shit. *Keep going Jade, keep going.* Alex and I crept low and backwards. I tripped, pulling Alex over, making him yelp in pain.

A warning shot filled the air—he'd heard us.

The air stilled. There was a pressure on my ears, a sound vacuum, and then a soft *whumph,* followed by a roar that filled the air. The ground exploded under me. I threw myself to the side.

"Lottie!" Alex's voice came from everywhere at once.

A sheet of snow glided past like a wave, smothering everything in its path. Alex clung to a tree, a freaking moving tree. I reached for him, leaning as far forward as I dared to without getting caught in the snow tidal wave. He passed within inches from me. The tips of our snow gloves touched before the avalanche sped past with him.

"Jump!" I yelled.

Alex pushed himself from the tree and disappeared. A tsunami of snow thundered down the mountain, rolling past me, leaving nothing but a cloud of powder-icing snow.

"Alex! Alex!" I charged to the place I last saw him, where he could have jumped, if he'd jumped, if he hadn't been thrown and tossed like a limp rag doll to the bottom of the mountain. Hold back that thought. Breathe. "Shit, stuck under an avalanche, needs air, a breathing hole."

"Lottie!" It was Jade, not so far ahead after all. She pointed to a mound of fresh snow at the side of the flattened stretch of the post-avalanche mountain, right beneath the ledge that had saved me. "Is that Alex's hat?"

I broke off a stick and poked a hole as far down as I could

reach without falling in, and twirled the stick to make the air hole bigger. "Alex?"

"Here, in here," he called back.

"Hang on. We're going to get you out."

As long as he could breathe, as long as we could dig him out with our hands before Nico found us, he stood a chance. My stomach lurched as I thought of him freaking out down there.

I dug. My hands became robotic shovels. Dig, dig, dig, no pause button. My only thought: *Don't die, don't die, don't die.* Jade dragged herself to me on her belly and joined in the digging effort using stones and sticks—anything to help scrape away the snow and speed up the rescue.

I lay on my stomach, digging a trench as deep as I could at the edge of the snow mound. The trench became a burrow, twisting its way to Alex. I worked at making it wider, rotating the stick around the sides, until it fell in and dropped. I had no idea how far down the stick had fallen.

"Alex!" I shouted into the hole.

There were gagging, coughing sounds, then a feeble "Still here!"

"Don't worry, we've got you!" Jade shouted down to him. She squeezed my hand. "We can totally do this."

I nodded, and scooped frantically, chucking the snow behind me. The wind drove the snow into my eyes and nose and built an ice shelf on my neck. My hands were frozen stiff. Shaking them did nothing. Sod it, better to use them as shovels and not feel, than to not try at all. Once we'd made a hole big enough for Alex's shoulders to get through, the biggest challenge would be hauling him out with his injured leg.

"Jade, listen out for Nico too, okay?" I said. The last thing we needed was for him to sneak up on us. He could kill us, and no one would know until the snow defrosted in spring and our bodies were found. That would be the last image Oliver and Mum would have of us, frozen, blue-tinged skin, or animal-ravaged. That thought kept me digging through frozen tears and trembling limbs. There was a bark, a scatter of ice, and Otis pounced at my side.

Better late than never. "Dig, Otis, dig."

Otis sniffed around the hole I'd started and dug like crazy.

Jade crawled beside me. "We're so close."

"Lottie! Jade!" Alex called up, his voice much clearer. "Otis?"

Otis yelped and carried on frantically digging until he'd created a huge hole that we could look down and clearly see Alex's upturned beautiful face.

A new burst of energy pulsed through me. "Almost there!" I yelled back down. I turned to Jade. "Do you have a belt?"

"No, I have something better." She tugged it out of her backpack. "Parachute cord, from Mr. Soto's. Dad always takes it on hikes, 'cause you never know."

We both smiled. That was so totally Oliver. I looped it around Otis's collar. I wasn't sure if Alex could reach it, but it was worth a try. Jade got Otis to lay as close to Alex as he could without falling down the precipice.

"Alex, grab the loop!" she shouted.

"I can't see it."

"Reach for it." I leaned over, dangling the green cord down, bopping him in the face.

"Got it." I felt him tug at the end.

45

3:27 p.m.

IT WAS SLOW GOING, CLASPING ALEX'S HANDS AND trying not to be dragged down, pulling him up along the snow. Him with one dangling foot, trying not to cry out when it hit anything, and using the other to push off against anything to nudge him forward.

Jade and I lay on our stomachs and grabbed a hand each, while Alex tried to climb out with one leg. After five tries we managed to get him close enough to the top that he could flop over the edge and push himself up with his arms. He slumped, half in, half out of the hole. Otis gave him a face wash. We dragged him by the arms, over the ice, until he was able to pull himself and lean on me and stagger away from the danger zone.

Alex shook violently all over. His blood had drained away from the surface of his skin, as if it had been sucked out down there in the hole. He held his leg out stiffly in front of him. I had no idea if that was the right thing to do. It needed a good clean, or it would get infected.

"You're going to be okay." I gently brushed the snow from his face. "I promise." I knew I couldn't, but I had to. My face crumbled every time I pictured the alternative.

He nodded but couldn't speak for trying to get his breath back.

"Here." I sat him down, rubbing his shoulders and arms until some kind of warmth could make its way back in.

Jade hobbled over and hugged him, wheezing faintly as she breathed.

"Jade, you're wheezing." I said it very gently.

She shook his head. "I'll be fine."

"It's not worth the risk. Take it so you feel better sooner."

"What are you, my mom?" She rolled her eyes but rummaged in her pockets then fumbled in her backpack. She took one puff and then, seeing me staring at her, another. "Alex looks bad."

"Don't we all." This the kind of survival situation Dad warned me about, where bad luck and bad decisions led to bad outcomes. That's how people die.

"Nico's shot probably started the avalanche," said Alex. "Idiots."

"I think they've gone." Jade shook from the cold. Her brown eyes were bloodshot with sleep deprivation as she limped along on her twisted ankle. "Maybe they got struck by the avalanche."

A silver lining. "I hope so," I said. We could do with some good luck. "But we can't assume anything. We need somewhere safe to hide, somewhere they wouldn't expect."

There was nothing but waves of undulating snow leading

to a faint line of trees on the far horizon, where a road might be. Hopefully that's where they headed in their truck, fleeing away from the scene with the telescope. I hoped to God we never crossed paths again.

"We should make a snow cave," I suggested. "Two birds with one stone, hide from them, and give your legs a break. Oh, that sounded awful. You know what I meant."

Alex nodded. "You're right," he murmured through cracked lips. "We should look for a sheltered spot. Snow-cave building is part of Eagle Scout training. Easy as mud pies."

Jade looked dubious.

"Seriously, Jade, we can do this," said Alex. And Otis nudged Jade along, just for backup, belly disappearing in and out of the snow.

I took it one tiny step at a time with Alex leaning against me, pretending each one was bringing us closer to the mythical sheltered spot. Alex was incredibly heavy for a skinny guy. His injury left a blood trail, again.

Jade dragged herself along, zapped of energy after all that digging. Her asthma probably didn't help either. How were we going to get through this? Otis slipped between us, stepping out of the way before we tripped over him. Trees lurched as we passed. The wind howled, hurrying us along, teasing and twitching, pulling at our frozen clothes and slapping our cheeks. My whole face felt as if it had been rubbed off by snow.

Alex's shallow breathing grew fainter as we walked. He struggled to keep up with my slow pace. Every three steps we stopped for a few seconds before carrying on.

"I can't…" Alex muttered.

"Yes, you can." I looked away from his tired, sunken eyes, determined to hold on to my crumbling hope. I stumbled, bumping into Jade. My arms felt like weights tethered to my shoulders. My feet floated away. Shadow monsters lurked in the edges of my vision, waiting to steal Jade and Alex away as soon as I stopped twitching around to keep them in sight.

It was so exhausting and pointless. Opening my eyes. Breathing. I hadn't realized I'd stopped moving. Alex hung limply by my side.

"Don't stop." Jade squeezed my hand. "Come on, don't leave me alone with your mum."

"Fair point." I smiled and forced myself onward.

And there they were, two pine trees leaning together, making a narrow arch, like a doorway to another place. A well formed around the bottom of the tree trunks and stopped the snow from gathering. Up close, I could see right down to the dark dirt. There was space for two people to squeeze below the snow line and shelter under a snow roof. Three of us, and a dog, was pushing it, but as long as I could dig, we stood a chance.

I listened for AJ and Nico, but the only sounds were the pelting of snow and waves of wind ripping through the branches. I could be at the ocean. The Northern Pacific Ocean. Riptides, whisking me away, tumbling under the sea, rushing along with the current; limp body thrown up miles away. I had to stop focusing on death. Alex was alive. Jade was alive. I was alive. It was going to be okay.

Alex slid down into the tree-well while Jade ripped off the underside of the trees' skirts and placed them on the floor of the well, a slight protection from the frozen earth. Her whole body quivered from the cold.

"Climb down to Alex. Keep each other warm," I ordered.

Jade slumped on the pine floor, head disappearing beneath the deep green branches of one of the base trees. Otis snuggled against her. At least his doggie heat would help her warm up.

The snow was too fresh and powdery to stick together easily. I pushed heaps of snow up to the edge of the well and packed them together to make a wall. A crumbling wall was the best I could do. I shoved more snow against it to make it thicker. The wind drove the snow flurries sideways. I spent more time shaking my head free from the ice crystals forming around my eyes than building the walls. They were uneven and patchy but were holding. At least they'd created a wind-free zone inside the tree-well. My bones cracked with ice. My hands fuzzed, and I couldn't feel my knees.

I ripped the bottom branches off a nearby pine tree and lay them over one end of the shelter to make a roof. The snow would fall on the branches and cover the roof in snow-icing. Nico and AJ would never find us. We'd be completely hidden.

46

4:18 p.m.

I SQUEEZED DOWN INTO THE TINY SPACE, LEAVING A gap at the end to keep the air circulating. It felt cozier seeing the branches whipping around without being out there, even if I was encased in frozen mud, snow, and ice. Alex and Jade were comatose. Otis huddled between them, watching me with his sad puppy eyes. They would need more warmth than that. I fumbled in Jade's backpack for matches.

She stirred, opening her eyes.

"We should build a fire, near the entrance," I said.

She nodded.

I made the entrance opening larger. Shaping the snow walls cut out the wind. The area was far enough away from the trees not to catch fire but sheltered enough by the canopy that a small fire might stay alight.

I stripped off weedy branches and poked Jade with them. She

took them and I passed her a handful of damp sticks as well. "Get going fire-master, do your worst. I don't think it can get out of control up here." I doubted we could even start a fire, but it was something to focus Jade on.

"I'll try," said Jade, tightening the mess of twigs into a tight nest to burn.

"Come on. You can do this. They're counting on you." I gestured at Otis and Alex. "I'm counting on you." I'd turned into a raging dictator. Whatever it took to keep them alive.

"You need a hole." Jade pointed to the roof I'd made out of branches.

"What?" I crinkled my nose. My head throbbed faintly like a warning.

"To stop us suffocating from lack of oxygen. Trust me, I know what I'm talking about."

"I know you do." I rearranged the branches in the roof to make a small opening above our heads that was still beneath the shelter of the trees. "There. Thanks for saving us from suffocation." I grinned at her. "Pretty good team, huh? The three of us."

"All for one." Her smile was limp, but it was still there.

"One for all." I gave Otis a hug. He could barely be bothered to move, but he licked my hand and snuffled up closer to Alex, like a portable fluffy heater.

I blew on my fingers. God, I hoped this worked. I could hardly move. I was a stick doll, ready to snap in two. "Do you think it's okay to let him sleep?"

Jade shrugged. "No idea. Let's hope so. The main thing is not to freeze to death."

The first match crumpled in Jade's hands. The second spit and caught hold of the twigs, like Jade promised it would. She built a weedy fire from a few twigs and some energy bar wrappers. The plus side of not littering. It wouldn't last ten minutes, but the glow reflected in the snow tunnel was all our tired hearts needed right then.

We had a cramped shelter, protected from the wind by the trees, with walls of snow that we could barely sit up in. We could hardly move without knocking into each other. My skin tingled like crazy, and my cheeks were completely dead. It didn't matter; sleep was all I craved.

"We should use the rocks," said Jade, "warm them in the fire. That's what Dad does. Keeps everything warmer longer without burning things."

"Great plan." I felt along the ground for rocks, and Jade passed me two smooth ones she'd been sitting on. I crawled out and placed them in a small ring around the fire. There were only four, but it was better than nothing. The flames wavered but held out bravely against the wind. It would only take one plop of snow to drop from the branches and snuff it out. The cave seemed extra dark when I sunk back in.

Alex coughed. He'd flopped against Otis's back. There was barely enough room for us to sit scrunched up with our knees bent. Otis's tail stopped wagging. He'd face-planted in the pine-covered dirt. I patted his head, and he licked my nose. Dogs, always so optimistic.

I passed Jade a flashlight. "For emergencies only. Like peeing in the dark."

"Or if we hear someone outside and need a weapon." Jade hadn't forgotten those guys could be close.

"Don't worry. They'll never see us tucked away here." I rummaged around Alex's backpack. Surely an Eagle Scout would have something useful like—"A pair of socks!" There were three pairs. He'd taken a pair for each of us. What a thoughtful thief. They still had their tags on, Tahoe, Soto's Shakes & Supplies. "Penguins, stars, or snowmen?"

"Penguins, obviously!" Jade managed to get them on over her still-tender-but-not-quite-as-swollen foot and ankle.

I tried taking off Alex's boots, but I didn't want to wake him, and his feet felt warm in his Sorels. Trust him to have chosen the Arctic-ready gear at Soto's. He was very skilled at high-end "borrowing."

As the snow piled on top of our roof and the tiny fire reflected its feeble glow, it was almost cozy. The snow dripped around it. We had a cup from a camping flask taken from Soto's, and we set it on the rocks to turn snow into drinking water. Magic. If the snow cave held up until the storm passed, and the rescue parties came out, we'd be okay.

I crawled back out to the fire and threw a couple of pine twigs onto it. Smoke poured into the tunnel. Jade coughed then wheezed, gasping for air. I tried blowing the fire out, and when that didn't work, I smothered it with snow. It went out with a fizz. At least we had the hot rocks.

Jade coughed sharply, as if something was caught in her throat. She sat up, fighting to catch her breath.

"Where's your inhaler?"

She looked so dazed.

"Inhaler. Jade. Where's your inhaler?" I nudged her.

"Empty." She coughed some more.

"Shit, since when?"

She doubled over wheezing.

Alex sat up bolt upright, completely awake. "Jade, look at me." He held his arms out to his sides. "Come on. Copy me. Like this—no, look at me, nowhere else. Look at me. Move your arms like this, up and to the side. Breathe in"—he held his arms up—"and out." Then he put them to the side. "Come on, you've got this. Stay near the air hole. There you go. Now in and out, and slow and calm, and we are breathing. Good job. Keep going. Lottie, find the inhaler."

I nodded and swept the floor with my flashlight. "There." I slapped the orange canister into her hands. "Any fumes left?" I asked shakily.

She shook the inhaler and took a deep puff from it. She shook it again. And again. It was empty. "All gone now. They're both empty." said Jade. She took a deep breath, wheezing lightly, but sounding better than before, and that would have to do.

I squeezed her hand. "Cuddle up with Otis and try to sleep. You'll feel better in the morning." At least, thanks to Alex, she could breathe again.

47
5:22 p.m.

IT TOOK A WHILE TO NOTICE ALEX STARING AT ME.

"How did you know to do that? You saved her," I whispered.

"Remember I told you about Izzy, my sister? When she gets asthma attacks, I try to keep her calm and focused on me so she can focus on breathing. Sometimes it works, sometimes not so much."

I nodded. "Thank God it worked."

"Yeah, as long as she keeps away from smoke and cold." He flicked his hair from his eyes. I listened to Jade's breathing, slow and steady now as she slept.

"Feeling any better?" I tapped his leg.

He nodded. "It hurts like hell, but anything is better than being out there."

I whispered, "I didn't think we'd get you out alive."

A gust of wind pushed a cloud of snow into our cave, reminding us how lucky we were to be hidden away from the full force of the storm.

Alex started to say something, then paused before starting again. "When I was buried, I kept thinking I'd never be able to tell my family I was sorry. They'd never know that I loved them. I knew even when I left what a giant idiot I was being, but I couldn't seem to stop myself. Things just gained momentum and rolled out of control." His leg trembled as he lay it across mine.

"Sometimes you have to decide you're not taking it. That's how I felt in the church. All that talk about who owned us, it's bullshit. No one owns us." I paused and hugged myself. "Before all this, I'd decided I wasn't going to be dragged around by my mum anymore. As soon as I finished high school, I'd go to England for university, even if it meant getting a student loan, to be free."

"And leave Jade? You're only just getting to know each other, aren't you?"

"Yeah, well, I don't think Jade would exactly be devastated." I shivered. "She's way cooler than I thought. I mean, funny, smart, and interesting. This Tahoe weekend has been bonkers terrifying on so many levels, but weirdly amazing, when you think about it. I'd never have given Jade a chance. And there's no way we'd have met. You would have stolen that stupid telescope and given it to AJ and Nico, if my migraine hadn't forced you to stay with us." I laughed. "So, now you're both injured and we're hiding in a snow cave, and I've found people I want to be with." I rested my head on his shoulder. "I didn't expect to find two new friends, that's for sure."

"Yeah, about that." He puffed his cheeks out. "I know I haven't been the best, but I'd never have hurt either of you. I really thought I'd found the victim-free answer to everything."

"The telescope?"

"Yeah. If I'd gotten it, there would have been a huge payoff. Big enough for them to let me go. No more surprise next jobs. I'd be free."

I wriggled in closer. "So, they kind of owned you?"

"I guess they did. Or maybe I let them. No more." Alex tilted his check to rest against mine. It was safe and quiet and peaceful in the cave.

I watched Jade's shadow breathing in and out. "What amazing things were you going to do with the riches from selling Einstein's telescope and breaking Jade's heart?"

"Don't put it like that."

"It's true." I tilted my chin at him.

Jade coughed. Alex shifted his weight slightly away from me. "I got accepted to the Academy of Art University. I couldn't believe it at first. It came with a scholarship, but not enough for me to move to San Francisco without taking out a very big loan. It was a lifetime of debt as a starving artist or give up my dream. This last job fixed everything."

"And your family couldn't help?" I dreaded that question. Families were the worst.

"They don't even know I applied. They think I'm starting spring semester at UC Berkeley. Which I wouldn't have a hope of getting into with my 3.5 weighted GPA." He laughed. "No matter how amazing my mom thinks my drawings are. I lied about my SAT results, so they wouldn't worry about me."

"It's sweet that they worry. Do your parents even know you're in Tahoe?"

He shook his head. "Oh, and there's no aunt, but you knew that. There, all lies on the table. No more, I promise."

I closed my eyes and felt the soft flutter of his breath on my skin. "Do you know how much I'd give to have a family that wants the best for me and actually knows I have test results?"

Alex tucked his knees up and his whole body tensed with the pain. "You're right. I've never noticed what I had, and now it's too late. And Izzy will forever think I find her annoying and stupid and never realize how much I loved her."

"Stop that." I punched him lightly in the chest. "You can tell her how you feel when we get out of here. Don't give up. You're going to be fine." I really thought that in the moment.

"I'm trying." He yawned and snuggled closer.

I pulled out a very crumpled drawing from my back pocket and crushed it into his hand. "I saved it—actually, stole it. Sorry. You totally freaked me out when you showed up. You were scary, sneaking about with those guys and everything, but I kept this because it's good."

"You did look freaked out when I turned up. I tried so hard not to scare you." He opened his jacket and pulled out a crumpled-up journal. "I only read one poem, but I figured you'd want it saved from the fire."

"Oh God, my journal." He'd found my soul. "Seriously, you only read one?" I grabbed it from him and flicked through the damp pages. It was mostly intact.

"Is that good or bad?"

"I don't know." I closed my eyes and listened to his heartbeat.

"Both?" I drew circles on his chest. "Thank you for saving it. I'm glad you're not the devious guy I took you for."

I could feel his smile in the dark. "Thank you for those stellar words of praise."

Otis huffed in his sleep, paws patting the snow-cave floor in his dreams.

The wind tossed the trees and snow thudded against the feeble roof, but we were together and almost warm. I leaned into Alex, tracing his lips with my finger. He pulled me closer. Our lips met.

"Hey, I'm still awake." Jade had been listening the whole time. "You're pretty cool too, for the record, before we die and stuff," she murmured.

"Shush, go to sleep." I listened as her breathing slowed again. Otis snored softly. I spooned against Alex, as he wrapped me in his scent of earth and honey, and I listened to the softening patter of snow, until I drifted away to another place and another time.

48
11:05 p.m.

THE FOG TWISTED ITS WAY OVER THE TOP OF THE mountain, reaching out long tendrils to wrap around my bones. A thin layer of snow lay on the ground, crunching beneath my boots' steps. My boots were too tight, pinching my little toes and squashing my big ones. My blisters cried with every step. We'd been walking forever. It was always just one more corner, just one more hill, just to that tree, and we'd get a view that would amaze me. He promised every time. Only we never did. I was too busy looking down, watching my feet, trying not to mess up and trip.

"Come on, Lottie." Dad grabbed my hand. I ran to catch up, stumbling on my screaming feet. And his face, so easy to read: How could he have such a clumsy, uncoordinated daughter? His gray eyes fierce, mouth twisted with annoyance: "Go back then. Wait in the car, if you're really that cold." I walked to the car, a tiny blue Fiat, and watched his broad back disappear into the fog. And I waited.

As the fog shrouded the car, I imagined I was in a cloud floating above the mountain. I heard voices but couldn't see anything, so I curled up to keep warm and hid under a scratchy blanket we used for picnics. My shivering woke me. The fog had lifted, but there was no Dad, nobody around. There was a crack of a branch, a huff of breath, and right outside my car door was a deer, an albino deer, pure white, as if it had stepped out of the snow. My eight-year-old brain added a unicorn horn. I could never see it as anything else. She stared at me with her bright-pink eyes, blinked her enormous lashes, and leapt away. The most magical and most awful experiences of my life happened on the same day.

But the dark always takes over, and I'm always lying there awake but asleep, unable to move, covered in flashing red and blue lights, voices calling my name, all of them scared. All of them with flashlights and dogs, lots of dogs, snarl-teethed, red-eyed, and howling with grief.

Sweat trickled down my back. My skin was clammy. Night terrors.

Alex squeezed my hand and whispered, "Are you okay?"

I nodded. "It creeps up on me, once a year, that same dream. Those same feelings."

"What dream? It might help to talk about it."

I shook my head. "It doesn't. He never comes back."

"Your nightmare is about your dad? What happened?" He stroked my hair. "It's okay if you don't want to talk." He held me for a while in silence.

"He disappeared." I sucked back my breath. Soft waves whooshed outside our cave. The storm was finally dying down. "They said it must've been an accident. It's so remote out there, no wonder they couldn't find his body, or perhaps he didn't want to be found. Do you know"—I turned to face him—"hundreds of people drive to state parks to purposefully disappear?" I took a moment. "It's worse when there's no body. You just never know."

"But if he was alive, that would be good?"

"It would mean—" I choked, swallowed, and started again. "It would mean, he'd abandoned me, deliberately, for good."

"Do you really think your dad meant to abandon you? Couldn't he have got lost, or something, like…"

"I don't believe that. Why take your kid for a walk and then off yourself? It doesn't add up. They said it wasn't a suicide, because there wasn't a note, or a body, but then what? He'd climbed to the top of Everest, but somehow fallen off a stupid little Welsh mountain?"

"Maybe"—Alex cleared his throat—"maybe it was a spur-of-the-moment, I-can't-face-anymore kind of thing. And he just wanted to disappear, start a new life?"

"What, because he had such a lame-arse daughter?" I moved away from Alex. I couldn't go over this again with another person who I wouldn't know in six months' time. My heart was cracking, caving, swallowing me whole. I clutched it, rocking back and forth. It was my fault anyway. Hard to love, hard to like, obstinate, selfish, stubborn, disagreeable. My shoulders shook from holding everything inside.

"Hey." Alex wrapped his arms around me. "You were eight, just a kid. There's no way your dad disappearing had anything to do with you."

I sniffed. "Mum says…"

"She knows it wasn't you. You think you chased your dad away, but you've got it wrong. You hate him for leaving you, that's understandable, but you don't know what happened, and whatever did, it is not your fault."

My head throbbed. "What do you know?"

"Your poems." He brushed the tears from my cheek. "You keep it all locked up inside. It's too much. Let it go. Don't carry that burden anymore. It's not your weight to carry."

I sniffed. "That's easy to say." I wiped my nose on my sleeve. "Families are crap." I blinked back more tears. "I don't have anyone…"

"You have me, and your journal. Pour it into your poems if you don't want to talk to me. But let this guilt go."

"You said you'd only read one."

"I didn't tell you which one. You're changing the subject because you know I'm right."

"You're wrong." I rubbed my face, pulling down my cheeks, hiding my eyes. "I don't know anymore." I hated my Dad, and I yearned for him.

"It's tearing you apart." Alex hugged me tighter. "I'm here, if you need me."

Jade mumbled in her sleep.

"Did she hear me?" I whispered. "I didn't want a new family, before I got to know her. It's easier to be alone."

Alex held me tighter. "It's okay. She'll understand. You're allowed to change your mind. You told me that. You're shaking. I'm sorry.

I didn't mean to freak you out. But now? Things are better with Oliver and Jade. Your new start?"

"Who knows, maybe it will work this time. Maybe Mum's tired of moving around too." I closed my eyes. "I'm just so tired of everything."

He kissed the top of my head. "Everything?"

I smiled. "Maybe not everything."

"See, now you've given me hope." His voice trailed off. He was exhausted, mentally, physically, and emotionally.

I lay with my eyes open, listening to Alex's heartbeat again. The wind dropped. A heavy hush fell over the snow cave, as if it were waiting to rejoin the real world, where parents come to the rescue, and you don't fall asleep and never wake up. Maybe he was right, and I should accept that it wasn't my fault. I might never know what happened to my dad. I'd always carry the pain, but it could be a snowflake instead of the whole storm. My lungs felt lighter, the air clearer.

Alex stirred and pulled me closer, wrapping his arms around me in his sleep. His steady breath was like a feather on my cheek. I traced the outline of his floppy fringe, pushing it aside, to reveal his fluttering lashes and dreaming eyes. He moaned and said something incomprehensible ending in "Lottie."

I pulled his arms tightly around me and kissed his hand. He nuzzled my cheek. I turned my face, raising my lips to meet his.

DAY FOUR
October 28

49

6:05 a.m.

THE STORM HAD DROPPED COMPLETELY. NO MUFFLED snowfall, no wind rustling the branches, just soft, tentative silence. It was chilly but no longer mind-numbingly freezing. I inched away from Alex and Jade and poked my head outside.

A random snowflake kissed my cheek. The predawn light was dim, but the snow had faded to a few half-hearted flutters. The ground around us was piled with fresh snow. If you didn't notice the entrance to our cave, you'd never notice us. Maybe that was a problem. We were alive but hidden. No one would rescue us if we stayed there. But Alex and Jade couldn't walk far. And then there were those two imbeciles out there somewhere, with a bloody gun. It wasn't safe to be seen, it wasn't safe to stay.

Jade muttered in her sleep.

"My *sister*, Jade." Just whispering it made me feel warmer.

The first time Mum told me about Oliver, her eyes sparkled. She was bursting to tell me all about him, how brilliant he was, and his adorable daughter, and how she couldn't wait for me to meet them, how it was love at first sight and they were getting married, and how my stepsister would be my new best friend.

I didn't want to like Oliver. I didn't want a stepsister. Only, Jade meant so much more to me than that. A wave of sadness washed over me. I'd gotten her into this mess, building a snow cave in the middle of nowhere. I had to get her out of it.

My eyes pricked with tears. My face collapsed. And I let myself sob. All the pain and hate and fear whooshed out in so many tears. I hadn't even cried when Mum said we were moving again.

I sniffed back the last of my tears. I don't know why I even cared about Dad anymore. I couldn't remember his face, not really, only Mum's photographs of it. I couldn't remember what he smelled like, or how if felt when he hugged me. Mum didn't handle his disappearance any better than I did. She probably struggled under the weight of guilt too.

Anger was exhausting. Sitting curled up in that cold, dank cave, I knew I had to let it go.

I focused on the sound of Jade's breathing. Smooth in, smooth out. I couldn't see Dad again—but I could make things right. If not for me and Mum, at least for Jade and Oliver.

Alex whispered, "I'm so sorry. This was all my fault."

I shook him gently. "You awake or talking in your sleep?" His hair tickled my cheek, and his breath warmed my neck. Otis rolled partially off Jade, pushing Alex and me even closer.

Alex sat up and cringed. "Leg cramp."

I rubbed it, which made his whole body tense up. "God, sorry."
He needed a doctor fast. "I'm glad I found you," he murmured,
"whatever happens."

"Whatever happens? You don't think we're getting out of this,
either?" I shook my head. I'd been pretending I'd got this, that I was
going to miraculously lead them to safety. But I had no clue what I
was doing. And with Alex's leg, and Jade's stupid asthma, we were
totally stuck.

"You're saying sorry?" I stared at Alex. "You got shot!"

"If you'd never met me, it wouldn't have happened."

"Don't worry." I gave him a pathetic smile. "You're actually the
silver lining."

That's when I heard it. A mechanical whir coming from the sky,
a shudder of blades. A helicopter.

I shot out of the cave and raced into the clearing, jumping up
and down with arms waving, waving, waving. To a retreating black
speck in the sky.

50

7:15 a.m.

GOD DAMMIT.

"Did they see us?" The noise had woken Jade, or my rushing out and nearly treading on her had. She came out to see what I was up to. "Sometimes they look like they're flying away, but really, they've seen you and send out a rescue party, especially if they can't land."

"Lottie?" Alex's voice was faint, coming from the cave. "Water?"

The water from earlier was long gone, so I scooped up some snow in my flask lid.

"No," said Jade. "He'll get hypothermia."

"He'll dehydrate if I don't." Damned if you do, damned if you don't. The situation of impossibilities, with just a sliver of survivor's instinct to push you through despite the odds, knowing the odds. I could start a fire, but that hadn't worked out so well.

I went back inside. It seemed so much smaller, as if it shrunk as people exited. "They won't find us." Alex's eyes were glazed. How could he be worse than he was an hour ago? Water, he needed more water, and warmth. "We're too remote."

I rubbed his arms up and down. His whole body trembled with cold. A scarf or five would have been good. I gave him mine. "You're going to be fine. Rest, but don't sleep. I'll be back in a sec." I kissed his cheek. He was almost asleep already.

Jade shouted through the breathing hole, "Is his leg going to be okay?!"

"Yes!" I answered sharply. "Yes. Can you stay with Alex? Keep him warm? He needs to stay awake." I couldn't have him drifting off, never to return.

"Yes." Jade came inside, head bent against the low roof.

"Good. Have Otis stay next to him if you can, and if you need fresh air, sit just outside the entrance. Stay close. I'll make a fire farther out and heat the rocks again. And melt some snow." I smiled at her then turned to Alex.

He gave me a thin, pathetic smile and closed his eyes.

"How's your leg?"

"Fine." He lied.

Jade's voice was cracked and parched. "Can we signal for help?" She looked so desperate. "There's got to be something we can do."

"They'll see the fire." There was nothing else to signal with. "And I'll make a massive SOS sign with branches. And I'll think of something." And it had better be fast.

The clouds were faintly backlit by a pale sun failing to break through. The wind whispered among the trees, *Almost gone, almost gone.* They had to know we were missing. If there was a helicopter, there had to be power, communications. There were clues, like the burnt cabin and the letter at the store. Carl, AJ, Nico, if they were still alive and coherent and told them we were out here. But would they?

I got the fire going, not too close to the camp, but close enough for the helicopter to easily find us as soon as they spotted it.

Rescue teams had to be out searching for survivors. But we'd have heard the shouts if they'd called for us. A sinking dread had rooted in my bones. Alex didn't have time. I listened for another helicopter or snowcat. Nothing. Otis would have barked if anyone had been close.

"Hello?!" I shouted. It echoed back to me. I wrote SOS with branches and rocks, drawing in the snow, when those ran out. Sweat tickled down my back, my head throbbed, and my fingers burnt, the side effect of actually feeling my extremities again. Even with no snow and no wind, it was freezing.

I crawled back inside the cave. Alex's breath was soft on my face. I kissed his forehead. It felt warm, too warm. His wound had to be infected. He'd fallen asleep. I shook him, slapped his cheek, lifted his leg, but he was out of it. Asleep or unconscious, it was impossible to tell. At least he was still breathing. "Stay alive, Alex, stay alive."

His chest rose under my hand, falling, falling, slower, slower, slipping away. How could he be slipping away when he was drinking water and eating snow moments ago?

Jade hugged him, then tried some gentle and not-so-gentle shakes, anything to wake him.

"Jade, keep him as warm as you can."

She nodded. "I'll get Otis to stay next to him."

"Do that. Be here when he wakes, and get him to drink some water."

A ray of sun shone down—a God Ray, as Dad called them, lighting up the entrance.

I squeezed Jade's hand. "Promise me you'll stay here with them." I was the only one who stood half a chance of finding help, and half a chance was better than none. I had to find the road.

Jade swallowed. "What if you don't come back?"

I stared into her tired eyes. "I promise I'll come back."

She reached up and brushed my cheek. "Take care, Lottie."

"You too." I flicked her #blackbirders beanie.

I filled the flask with snow and stuck it into my waistband and bundled up as best as I could: boots, socks, hat, mittens, and jacket. "Here, last half of a Energy bar." I tossed it onto Jade's lap. "Chocolate Brownie."

She ripped it open and tore it in two. "For when he wakes up."

I nodded, taking a mental picture of her sweet face. Even exhausted, wheezing, and freezing, she was thinking of others.

I headed out. My boots crunched and slipped, compressing the snow into ice with each step. I focused on not falling at first, then I remembered Alex looking for moss on the north side of trees. After brushing a patch of snow from the nearest tree, I set off, heading what I hoped was southwest, using the sun and the trees to guide me. It was a hundred times easier to hike through snow without the wind and ice slapping my face. A blue jay screeched encouragement, a flash of sapphire against snow, a flash of hope in the wilderness.

51

8:09 a.m.

MY DEEP FOOTPRINTS WERE STARK BLUE AGAINST THE perfectly iced ground. The beams of sunlight sent the whole forest into a glittering frenzy. Snow crystals glittered at the tops of trees and glowed ice blue in the shadows. Shadows became snow-covered rocks, fallen branches, bushes, and small trees. A crow cawed as it flew overhead.

I looked up and finally found the landmark I'd been hoping for—a line of trees standing like sentries at the top of the embankment. The road had to be down there, only six feet away.

I scrabbled to the edge and peered over the side. Twenty steep feet below me was a crashed vehicle. Red metal glinted from gaps in the snow.

I crouched at the top of the embankment. The pickup truck had crashed sideways into the trees, taking out the railing in its path after skidding around the corner too fast. Judging by the snow covering it, they'd been there a while. The wind had blown a thick wedge of snow over the mashed-into-the-trees side of the truck. The other side was still covered in a layer of snow, but the back window had a small bare patch. The kind you'd get from condensation if someone inside was breathing.

I waited, shivering in place. They had a gun, and if they were alive in there and saw me, they'd use it. No movement didn't mean they weren't watching. I sat frozen like the rabbit, waiting for the mountain lion to pounce. But Jade and Alex would have zero chance if I bolted.

I scrabbled down the slope, clinging to the shrubs to stop myself from slipping. If I was quick, they might not spot me. I crawled to the back of the truck. Still no movement. Branches swayed in the wind, whispering to each other. No noise came from inside the truck.

I took a deep breath and snuck a quick peek into the rear window. It was too dark to see anything from that small bare patch. I'd have to scrape some snow off. I crouched close to the back door, listening. Something moved inside. I jumped back. Shit, I didn't have time for this.

Sweat trickled down my spine. Come on, you can do this. I clenched my gut, stood, and knocked off a chunk of snow from the back window. AJ was slumped on the wheel, completely still, dead or unconscious, or faking so he could pull the gun on me. Nico was motionless in the back seat. Face pressed against the far window. A corner of ice fell, revealing more of the red truck's exterior. Red, bright red, much easier to see against all that white snow, even from the air. If the helicopter ever came back.

My heart thumped so hard, there was no room for my lungs. I leaned over as far as I could to push the snow off the truck. Stretching up, I hardly reached the top. I stepped alongside the double cab, jumping up to knock away more, but it was useless. I grabbed a stick and managed to shift a bit more snow with that, but I was too short to reach all of it. At least it would melt quicker, if the sun stayed out.

If there were helicopters searching, there had to be snowmobiles and snowplows, rescue teams looking for people who needed help. People like us. I just needed to guide them here.

I knocked more snow off the front windshield. A dazzling glint hit me from inside—the sun reflecting off the telescope lens. I blinked away the imprint that flashed behind my eyes. Just like Nico had said—it was amazing how brightly the lens reflected direct light.

I swallowed and yanked open the driver's-side door. AJ's silence filled the air. Don't move. Don't move. A clump of snow fell off the roof. I clutched my heart as I saw that AJ's skin was waxy and ice white. I prodded him. His whole body was frozen over the steering wheel. I looked back at Nico. His eyes were closed. His head lolled on the headrest. I held my hand to AJ's mouth, checking for any warmth or breath. I gauged before feeling for a pulse on his cold, limp wrist. If he had one, I couldn't find it.

I glanced at Nico again. The telescope lay on his lap, pointing to the front windshield. His arm hung over it, clinging on even in death. They could have got away if they hadn't chased us. It was hard to feel sorry for them, so I didn't. I got to work.

I pushed the front seat back as far as it would go and gave AJ a hard push. He fell forward but wouldn't let go of the wheel. I accidentally touched his face, shuddered, and buried my head in my fleece. I lifted his head and let it fall hard onto the horn. It honked loudly. The vibrations sent slivers of snow skidding off the truck. Hopefully that meant the sound traveled far.

Nico slumped down farther to the side. The movement must have knocked him. I climbed between the front seats and into the back. AJ's lap was covered in blankets, stained blankets. They were still wet. Blood. He might have died bleeding out from an injury. His face was untouched, totally calm, peaceful, even. I reached out for the telescope, gripped the ends of the brass legs, and tugged it gently toward me.

A hand grabbed hold of my arm and held it vice tight.

Nico opened his eyes. "What the hell are you doing here?"

52

8:39 a.m.

MY THROAT WAS BONE DRY, BUT I COULDN'T LET GO OF the telescope. "That's your best chance of getting out of here." My voice quivered. I swallowed twice.

He squinted at me. "And what makes you think *you're* getting out?" He pulled his other hand from under the blanket. Carl's gun glinted in delight.

I pushed away, breathing fast, panic breaths. I could slam the truck door and run for it. But then he'd win. Everything he'd done, everything he put us through, would be worth it to him, because he'd scared me into abandoning my help-finding mission to save our lives. I couldn't do it. I couldn't walk away. I was going to take that telescope, knowing he was going to pull the trigger.

Sweat trickled down my spine. "How long have you been here?" I asked, eyeing the telescope. "Waiting for help that isn't coming?" I repeated his words back to him: "Wrong place, wrong time."

He stared at me with glazed eyes. "I'm the one with the gun, girl. Don't you forget that."

I shook my water bottle so he could hear the tantalizing, lifesaving drops.

He tilted his head. I held it out to him. He reached for it. I snatched it away.

"Not until you hand over the telescope."

He shook his head, "You're crazy. Give me the water or I'll shoot you, crawl over, and get it from your writhing body." He grinned. "Very stupid of you to enter the lion's den, when the lion's not dead."

"We're all going to die, if you don't give me that." I stared at the gun and held out my shaking hand. Dead here or dead there. It didn't matter. He was probably scared too.

"Maybe. Or maybe just you." He flicked the gun up. "But your friends, I guess they're dead already."

My muscles tensed as hate burned through my veins. "That's it! I'm sick of your shit. AJ's dead and you're dying. You won't make it another hour without my help. Rescue teams might find you eventually. But by then it will be too late. What are you going to do, kill me too, so you can add to your body count? Infamy in death, or do you want an actual shot at living?" I held the flask out to him. "Want this, you have to trade."

The gun quivered in his hand, glinting dark and deadly, like it had a mind of its own.

"I don't want the gun, just the telescope," I added.

"And how else can you pay me for it?" He looked me up and down and winked.

"Oh yeah, because that's such a tempting offer!" I snatched the telescope from his lap and threw the steel flask at him. There was only so much bullshit I could take before fear turned to fury.

We glared at each other.

"Shoot me. I don't care. But I'm your only chance." The underside of the telescope was covered in blood. I wiped it off on my sleeve. "Looks like you might bleed out before too long."

Nico never said a word, just gulped greedily from the flask, letting the water dribble down his chin and the gun rest in his lap.

I closed the door on him. God, make this work. I unscrewed the lens as quick as I could. Watching as the clouds gathered around the sun, blotting it out. "Please, please, please." It peeked out the other side. I had to be fast or this whole thing would be pointless.

"What are you doing?" Nico called out.

"Saving your arse." I carried on dismantling the telescope.

The seat creaked from him moving around in there.

I clambered onto the truck bed. "Remember," I shouted at him, "kill me and you're killing yourself!"

53

9:03 a.m.

THE TELESCOPE'S LENS WAS WEIGHTY IN MY HANDS, green, thick, perfectly smoothed glass. I bet Einstein never used it for this. I kicked off the driver's-side mirror, smashing the glass into long shards. I lifted the telescope lens to the sun and focused the beam onto the mirror. Tilting the mirror back and forth created an eye-burning flash. What was SOS? I closed my eyes, trying to recall Dad's SOS lesson. *Three short, three long, three short. Lessen your chances of staying caught.* Or was it three long, three short? It wouldn't matter as long as there was an obvious pattern.

Nico pushed his door open with a thud, rocking the truck. I almost lost my balance. He almost fell out. I kept going: flash, flash, pause, flash, pause, flash, flash. I flicked the wet off my palm. Blood. I'd been so focused on my task I hadn't realized the shards had cut me. I carried on flashing to the empty sky, to the trees, to the empty road.

Nico puked up the water, then slumped back.

I signaled again, wondering if those light rays went anywhere except space, where no one would notice us for light-years. Clouds lingered around the sun. I flashed the signals again. And once more. Come on, come on. Someone had to see them. It was sunny. It had stopped snowing. Everyone should be out searching for us.

Some kind of signal was better than none, but there had to be more I could do. I looked around the back of the truck. A snow-covered tarpaulin hid a stash of boxes, electronics, cables, TVs, DVDs, game consoles. AJ and Nico would be on the fast track to jail if they were found with this lot.

I jumped off the truck bed. "Is there a first aid kit back there?"

Nico looked up at me with his bloodshot eyes. "How would I know?"

I took a breath. Every second here was time lost helping Jade and Alex. "Look for it."

"Are you sure he's dead?" He kicked the driver's seat.

"Absolutely."

"AJ wasn't who you thought he was."

"Who is?" I looked him straight in the eye. No fear.

Nico passed me the red first aid bag he'd been squashed up against. "AJ, Alexis Jermille." He smiled. "We're cousins, you know."

I shook my head. "No, but it makes sense. Blood ties and all that crap."

"He wasn't always like this. He was only eight when he lost his dad."

"Yeah, well so was I."

It was as if he hadn't heard me. "He could be a son of a bitch, but he looked after me. And I looked after him." The yearning in his voice was so real, for a second, I felt sorry for him. And then I didn't.

"By trying to kill us. Didn't work out too well, did it?" I stuffed my pockets with bandages, medical tape, Advil, and two emergency blankets, and handed Nico a red plastic whistle. "Keep blowing that. Someone will hear it." They'd better. "This isn't your truck, is it?"

He shook his head. "Some family in NorthStar. Found it in their garage."

"It's totally screwed up."

"Yep." His red blanket was now a deeper red across his legs.

"You still bleeding?"

"Yeah." He groaned. "But it's slowed."

I should not be doing this. Every single second was time wasted, lives slipping away. "Do you have a belt?"

He nodded.

"Pull it off." I wasn't going to help him do that.

Every tiny movement caused him to grimace with pain. He had to stop, breathe through it, and carry on. I never took my eyes off his hands. He could be faking the pain, luring me in so he could grab me and…I couldn't even go there.

"Hurry up." I picked up the remains of the telescope, ready to leave. I tied the belt around the top of his left leg, where most of the blood was coming from. It might stem the bleeding for a while.

He reached for the telescope—a last-ditch attempt that left him gasping in agony.

"You've got to be kidding." I held out my hand. "The gun." I didn't want to touch it. But I didn't want to risk being shot in the back either. "I'm not going to use it. I'm going to put it in the back, so it looks like a hunting gun that you haven't used."

He slowly passed it to me. My hand shook.

"So, you are scared."

I ignored him and threw the gun under the truck. He'd have to make a miraculous recovery to get to it. I hoped I never saw a gun again. "This is over, all this stuff with you and Alex, it's done."

He nodded.

"I don't trust you." I stared at him hunched up before me.

"I don't trust you." He shivered and drew himself up tighter against the seat back. "You're leaving me here to freeze to death?"

"Better blow that whistle then. The louder you blow, the sooner they'll find you." I tucked the telescope under my arm and crawled back up the embankment.

My heart sunk lower with each foot. Nico's whistle was shrill, but this far from civilization, only the birds would hear him.

The telescope kept slipping from my arm. The dark wood and brass would show up nicely against the pristine white snow. I unscrewed the legs from the body and lay them just below the top of the embankment, in a large, clear expanse of snow, making a large V of spindly legs, topped by the telescope's body—a giant arrow pointing in the direction of the snow cave. If anyone found the truck, they'd see that for sure. I drew another arrow pointing the same way and carved a message in the snow: PLEASE COME SAVE US. If Nico kept blowing that whistle, there was hope. I'd done all I could do. The rest was up to luck.

54

9:45 a.m.

THE SOUND OF THE WHISTLE GOT WEAKER WITH EVERY
step I took, until I could only hear it faintly, and finally not at all.
Nico had given up already. A puff of dove-gray cloud hovered
halfway over the sun. Sweat dripped down my back. How could I
be so cold and so sweaty at the same time? I'd need to build up our
fire, keep it going all day, and pray the snow didn't return. No one
would come looking after dark. I couldn't even cry—my eyes were
too cold.

A raven landed on a nearby branch. Its bright, beady eyes tracked
my slow progress, my death trail. I'd forgotten how huge they were,
so silky, black, and watchful.

My head fuzzed. I could hear music, leaves whispering, and
flowers falling, soft, white snowdrops. No, it was me sinking into
white quilts up to my ears, lying in a lovely pile of feathers. It was so
soft and cool on my sweaty neck. I took off my gloves and scooped

up some ice to suck on. Oh no, that was bad, because…it would make me too cold. I *was* too cold. Trembling cold. Where was I going? I sat up on my heels. I couldn't get up. Darkness would fall, bringing indigo shadows, and I would merge into the trees. Become a wood elf. *No stupid, you'd be dead.* I snapped myself back, forced myself to stand. It was so painful, pins and needles in every limb.

I squinted against the bright snow, tripped, and scraped up my hand. I'd forgotten to put my glove back on. I swooped around the icy ground for it. Gone. I'd lose my fingers, all of them. No more pinkie promises. I wriggled my little finger to an imaginary Jade. I promise to do better.

"Ah, there you are." My glove lay right beside me. It felt as cold wearing the glove as not wearing it. I tucked my hands under my armpits and carried on. Each step felt like walking on glass shards. My feet bled. I must have had glass crumbs inside my boot from that mirror. I took my boot off to check. No, just blistered, numb feet. Feeling something, even pain, was good. My foot was too big to go back in. I looked up at the horizon. There were swirls at the edges, ice mirages. No sign of the snow cave, only trees and hillocks and white and black. And monochrome triangles and jagged arcs, flickering at the corner of my vision.

"Jade! Alex! Otis!" My voice froze in the air. I crawled on my hands and knees because it was easier, like swimming. I lay down, so peaceful. My arms and legs were so heavy and tired. I could rest for a while. I closed my eyes and smelled the air, the lovely, pine, mountain air, and slid into blue, calm, nothingness.

Wet slobber hit my face, warm and sticky. Not in my eyes! A bolt of fur fell onto me, rolling over, smothering me. Black-and-white fur. "Otis!"

His tail beat against a tree stump. I shook the ice from my face and pulled myself slowly from the ground. His back legs disappeared into snow as he bounded ahead. I staggered along trying to keep up with him.

Otis stopped at the pine trees. I hardly recognized the site. No one would have ever found us, buried under the snow like that.

"Lottie!" Jade's weak voice called out. She hobbled toward me. "I kept a fire going. I knew you'd come back."

"Jade, you're brilliant." How could I tell her that no one would see it? "Where's Alex?"

"Asleep inside. I think."

Asleep, unconscious, or dead? Each step I took, my imagination went wilder.

"It's alright. He's alive." Jade squeezed my hand. "Trust me, I do know what vital signs are. And," she said, seeing my foot, "you'd better put your boot back on!"

I hugged her. "It's *so* good to see you."

Alex was curled up in the corner of the snow cave. "Lottie?" he asked though squinted eyes. "You're back."

"Of course." I took his hands in mine. Tears ran down my cheeks. "How are you?"

He smiled his lopsided smile. "Fine, now you're here."

"We don't have to worry about those guys anymore." I lay the back of my hand on his forehead. "You don't feel as hot as you did before. Thank God. You scared the crap out of me." I brushed my tears away and tried to smile, but my face crumpled, and I fell onto his chest. Alex was my safe place.

He pulled me close, and we kissed, short and sweet. Then he smiled. "Just testing to be sure it wasn't all a dream."

"I'm still not sure." I held his face between my hands. The next kiss was nose fumbling, cheeks squashing, hearts racing, skin tingling, bliss.

We lay beaming next to each other. My whole body fizzed.

"So, drugs?" I pulled the first aid kit out and handed Alex some Advil. "And a superhero cape!" I pulled out a silver foil blanket. He wrapped it around his shoulders and let me guide him out of the cave, like foxes who'd been hiding from the hunt.

It might be enough if we were rescued in the next hour or two. If not, I'd lead them back to the truck before nightfall. Alex sat up against a tree, by the fire, taking little sips of water.

Daggers stabbed my temples.

"Your turn." Jade cleaned my cut hand with an alcohol wipe, which stung like hell, then bandaged it up with way too much gauze. "Are you okay? You still look kind of pale."

"I'm fine. Sit by the fire with Alex. You've done great." I grinned at her, and my face almost cried with the effort. I was so damn tired.

It wasn't much of a fire, more of a scrappy nest of glowing twigs cowering before the wind. It wasn't producing much smoke, which was good for Jade, but bad for being rescued.

Alex closed his eyes. His chest moved slowly up and down. I took his hand and rubbed it between mine. "Hey, Alex. You still there?" I could hardly tell. My vision was shutting down.

Everything was five-dimensional, a cubist forest. I dry-swallowed the last two painkillers.

Alex wiped his clammy forehead and undid his jacket. "So hot." Otis licked his face.

"No, no, no, leave that on. Here." I pressed my flask to his mouth. "Drink this. They will come…and find…save…" I was losing words. My migraine was back.

Alex was still trying to remove his jacket. Sweat beads pearled on his upper lip. His forehead was burning up.

I pulled the emergency blanket tighter around him and hugged his body, rubbing his arms up and down, and then his legs. I pushed a rock Jade had heated close to Alex's feet. I hugged myself tight to keep everything from spilling out. We had to survive. They had to come and find us. There had been a helicopter. Civilization was out there working again. I'd done everything I could, and it wasn't enough.

55
10:29 a.m.

THE PAINKILLERS HAD CALMED THE ZIGZAGS, SO I could watch us dying clearly. It was the only time I'd ever wished my migraine auras would come back. I brushed my hands across my face. I had to smile, keep positive, pretend to the end. My new mantra. At least the storm was finally over. But there should be search teams out, people on skis, snowmobiles cruising the area looking for survivors. If only my phone worked, I could at least say goodbye, and sorry.

No, I shook my head, we had to be found. We couldn't go back in the snow cave another night. We'd never come out.

"They'll send another helicopter," said Jade. "Someone will see our fire. The darker it gets, the brighter it will glow." She didn't believe it any more than I did.

If rescue teams were out, they'd have found us already. The fact there were no more helicopters meant they didn't expect us to be out there. All I could hear was Alex's faint breathing and Jade's soft wheezing. No traffic, no planes, not even birdsong. Even Otis had flopped into the snow, with a look of pure resignation. The storm was over, we were bathed in sunlight, but we were still on our own.

My heart twisted. Mum and Oliver must have realized we were missing. Maybe they weren't okay. God, let them be okay.

I so wanted to sleep. I bit my tongue and squeezed my cut palm—pain with purpose, anything to stay awake. Alex watched me like I was a stranger. His skin was clammy and waxy. God, how was I going to keep that boy alive? At least his eyes were open. Otis slumped at his side, refusing to leave him, even for Jade.

"No one's coming." Alex spoke with shocking clarity. "No one's coming. This is it."

"They have to find us." But they wouldn't. My soul knew that. There was only one option left. I jumped up. "We'll go to the truck, share the heat, beep the horn, listen to the radio."

"With those madmen?" asked Jade.

"One's dead, the other's exhausted." Like the rest of us.

"Truck?" Alex raised his head a little. "We're that close to a truck?"

"Close enough, as long as you can use those floppy things called muscles to get there."

"I can crawl." It was muted, but his determination had come back.

Thank God. Last chance at the No Hope Saloon. I nodded to Jade. "Ready?"

She nodded, all set and ready to go.

"For the record, you're pretty awesome." I smiled at her.

"Great, a dying commendation." She grinned. "You're not so bad either."

The wind changed direction and whipped up snow chips from the ground, straight into our faces. It was the snow cave or the truck. There were no other options.

Die here or die there. Might as well try a change of scenery. "Let's go."

Alex couldn't walk by himself. But there was no way were we leaving him, as he kept insisting, so he leaned all his weight on me and hopped along. Jade staggered by my side. And Otis straggled along with his tail sagging, eyes drooping. I longed for his happy, wagging tail.

The snow had melted earlier, creating a layer of thin ice on old snow as it froze again. We must have made a strange sight, three shadows, heads bent, eyes focused on our footsteps, huddled together, not saying a word. The air was thick with thoughts we dared not share. One more step, just one more step, and then another, and then finally the line of trees and the embankment.

"I knew we'd make it," said Jade, as she slid down.

"You're so positive." I gritted my teeth as I thought of the dead body and Nico sitting inside. It was the only choice, but an awful one.

She gave a tired smile. "You're the one that never gives up." If only she knew.

We all held hands, slipping down the last bit of slope together, landing next to the truck.

Jade eyed it warily. "Are they…?"

My heart sunk. I nodded. "It's okay." I rapped on the rear window. "It's just Nico." Crap. I braced myself for the worst and pulled open the door.

It was empty. Deep caterpillar tracks marked a path alongside the pickup, coming in one way and turning around and leaving the other. The rescuers hadn't seen my giant arrow, or my sign in the snow. No one was coming back to find us. Nico hadn't told anyone we were there. Why was I surprised? I looked up at the sky and saw straight into the future, and its cold, stark reality.

56

11:20 a.m.

I TURNED THE KEY IN THE IGNITION. NOTHING. I TRIED again. "Shit!" No gas, no heat.

"At least it's warmer in here," said Jade mournfully.

"Yes." Yes, cling to that faint hope. The zigzags threatened again. The Advil was not enough this time. Not that it mattered anyway. I'd go out incoherent and brain-fuzzed, the way I came in. I closed my eyes. A cold blue marble rolled at the back of them.

The inside of the truck stunk of stale breath, BO, and socks. Alex lay with his head in my lap on the back seat. Jade claimed shotgun and Otis sat next to her, watching her fiddle with the nonworking radio.

"That's a good thing, right?" Jade turned to me, red eyes brimming, "Someone came. Rescue teams have been here."

"True, someone found them and took them to...be better." Words were failing again. "If anyone saw signals, they'll head here."

"Signals?" Jade pulled her beanie off and freed her hair.

"Yeah." I smiled. "I made SOS flashes with the telescope lens and glass shards."

"Lottie, you rock!" Jade grinned, lighting my heart. At least we'd die as friends.

"Yeah, you do," murmured Alex. And his eyes shut again.

Thank God he was hanging in there. "You okay, Alex?" I stroked his cheek. A sadness welled up from my heart, making it hard to speak or breathe.

Alex nodded and actually looked a tiny bit less frail, as in not quite dead. He yawned. Otis leaned over and slobbered his face with doggie abundance.

We sat in silence, listening for cars, helicopters, anything to show that the blackout was over and people were on the move. The trees murmured in the slight wind, and the melting snow fell in soft plops.

"We should play a game," Jade said. "Never Have I Ever. Kill time before we're rescued." She glanced at Alex struggling to stay awake.

"Yeah," I said way too fast. "Two turns each." I nudged Alex. "Stay awake." Stay alive.

"Me first." Jade held out her hand, wriggling her fingers. "First one to five gets half an energy bar." She pulled it from her pocket. "Never have I ever wanted a sister." She grinned at me.

"Actually, I kind of did." I smiled. "No, really. I just figured there was no way Mum would ever settle down for real." I laughed. "So, here we are, a minor miracle."

Alex tilted his chin. "I love my little sis, wouldn't ever wish her away."

"Me next." I turned to Jade. "Never have I ever watched birds at night."

"You don't know what you're missing," said Jade. It hung in the air, and now I never will.

"Birds," said Alex. "Why?" He flicked Jade's beanie. At least he was waking up.

Jade smoothed it on her lap. "At first it was a way to escape, be alone. Not be poor little motherless girl or have everything I do be so like my mom, even how I look, like I'm just a reflection of a ghost. It's one thing that's totally mine. I can be alone in the dark with the bird-watching. And just be me." She wiped a tear. "Melodramatic, huh?"

"Yeah," I agreed, "but understandable."

"My turn." Alex leaned forward. "Never have I ever touched a gun."

"Me neither, no way," said Jade, shaking her head.

I cleared my throat. "Well, I took the gun off Nico."

"What?" Jade laughed, "You're such a badass! You win hands down!"

Alex laughed too, and Otis licked my nose. For a brief moment, you'd never know we were three former strangers at death's door.

I'd die before I could become part of my new, beautiful family. And all Mum would remember was that stupid argument we'd had in the car before she left. Hate is easier than love. I'd varnished my cold little heart and kept it locked down tight. But love is sunshine, and without it, life is darkness.

Dad had said that if you'd never truly felt sadness, you'd never know when you were truly happy. Right then I was both at once, truly happy, lying there with Alex and Jade, and truly heartbroken that it was going to end that way.

I was all teared out. I wished Dad peace, wherever he was. And I wished Mum and Oliver happiness and peace, though I didn't know how they could ever have either, losing both of us at once. But most of all, I wished that it didn't end for us like this. No goodbyes, no apologies, just silence and cracking ice.

Tears welled up in my throat and drowned me. Everything I'd tried had always come back to the same sign: No EXIT.

At least Jade, Alex, Otis, and I would die peacefully together. Hope wasn't lost until it got dark. Then I'd know for sure.

57

6:09 p.m.

"I'LL CHECK OUTSIDE, SEE IF THERE'S ANY SIGN OF A rescue party." It was a totally feeble excuse. I needed to be alone for one stolen moment.

Jade barely nodded. Alex was asleep. At least, I hoped he was.

My silent scream came out as frosted clouds of air. My body tensed tightly. Every muscle cried out in pain. I walked around the back of the truck, picking up sticks and rocks, and adding the glass shards, to make a giant arrow on the road. If anyone came by, they'd get a flat tire and be forced to stop. Hopefully before it became our grave site. I looked under the truck. The gun was gone.

Alex, Jade, and I squashed together in the back seat with Otis on top of us. Better to be almost suffocating close together, with scarfs and hats and dog fur in our faces, than able to move about and be freezing. Jade's breath was wheezy, even without smoke to bring her asthma on.

My head throbbed. I needed to sleep, but I knew that was bad. You were supposed to stay awake when you were this cold. It didn't matter. We'd be rescued, or we'd die in our sleep. We'd make it through the storm only to die of hypothermia while waiting to be discovered in a truck that had already been evacuated. There was no reason to come back. This would be the final resting place, a truck, our steel coffin. At least Mum would see I never abandoned Jade. She might even be a little proud that I never gave up.

Alex nuzzled his freezing face against my neck. Still hanging in there. I pulled his arms tight around me and kissed every single finger. Jade's whole body shook with cold even with Otis lying over her. I don't think Otis had much warmth left to give.

"Hang on guys. It won't be much longer." I said. Such a brazen lie.

"Any moment," murmured Alex.

"I'm going to design a rescue pack that has everything you need for every emergency situation and extra Twizzlers, and carry it with me everywhere I go," said Jade. "And make loads of money selling it online."

"I hope you never need an emergency pack again for the rest of your life," I said. "I'm going to make sure I have painkillers every-where I go."

"Your head?" Jade asked.

I nodded.

"I'm sorry," said Alex, slurring around the edges of his speech.

"It'll pass."

"No, for me, for being such a pain, stealing and putting you in danger. And being such an idiot to ever get caught up with those guys."

"That's almost as much guilt as I carry." I hugged him closer. Finally, he was coming around, just in time to freeze to death.

"I'm going to get to art school, to make a new life," Alex continued.

"You can totally do that," I said.

"I'm getting a dog," said Jade, as if she'd been deciding whether to this whole time. "And I'm going to college to study ornithology, not medicine."

"Wise choice." I smiled. "Be your own person."

"How about you, Lottie?" asked Jade. "What are you getting?"

"I'm getting a life."

"You have one," said Alex.

"I know, I just never realized."

Jade rested her head on the seat and closed her eyes. Otis snorted around a little, looking for socks or something else to eat. My head throbbed like my brain was trying to escape. The knife had returned to my temple and stabbed in patterns of three. Bile rushed up and down my throat, leaving a lining of acid.

Jade's arm fell limp at her side. I lifted it up. It flopped back down.

Alex whispered, "Whatever happens, you know…"

"Yeah." We tried.

"I really…" he carried on.

"I know."

"No." He pulled me against him. "I mean," he whispered, "I *really* like you."

"I *really* like you too."

Alex fell asleep with his cheek against mine. Otis turned in a giant circle before lying back down, snuggling against Jade.

"Good dog, Otis. Good dog."

Jade murmured "Lottie" in her sleep.

"It's okay, I'm here. I'm not going anywhere." I was happy the three of us, and Otis, were there together at the end. I shut my eyes, but every rustle, every whisper, every light creak, sent my skin crawling. Voices calling my name, hallucinations, calling me to follow...

A whiny engine, like a dirt bike, was coming toward us. Otis sat up right, barking.

"Lottie! Lottie!" A voice. From outside. Death was calling me.

"Who's that?" Jade sat bolt upright.

The truck door creaked open.

"Hi, there. Looks like you needed rescuing."

I stared at his nose and white-blond hair. The rest of his face was blackness.

"Lottie?"

I nodded—it seemed safer than talking—then I puked all over his bright yellow snow boots.

"She's got a migraine," said Jade. "Are you Nordic Rescue?"

"Sure am." He called back into his radio: "They're alive! They're alive!" He grinned down at me, a smile that beamed across his whole face. "Ah, man, you guys are hard to track down!"

I stared into his eyes, the color of stormy seas, exactly like mine.

58
7:23 p.m.

A SNOWCAT RUMBLED TOWARD US TEN MINUTES later. I hadn't said much. I didn't know what to say and could hardly speak, thanks to the migraine. It seemed safer to listen and nod my head, even though that sent the marbles rolling from side to side.

My telescope flashes led a rescue team to find the truck and the gun. Nico was alive, hypothermic, and in custody. AJ, none of the above. They'd found the gun, and there would be charges of criminal homicide, robbery, and motor vehicle theft, with more to come as they continued to connect AJ and Nico to a slew of burglaries in the area. Another team had searched Soto's Shakes & Supplies, found the notes I'd left and poor Mr. Soto. They found the telescope laid out like an arrow, after I'd left the truck, but somehow missed our camp, even with the fire and SOS sign.

"It's bigger out there than you might think, for a couple of guys on skis to cover," explained Lars, the rescuer with the stormy-sea eyes. It wasn't Dad, just my mind playing tricks on me.

"We couldn't stop looking. We knew you had to be around here somewhere. The rest of us figured we'd already emptied the truck once, it was hardly going to repopulate itself, but there you were," said Tara, the second rescuer. "Lucky you took that risk. I can't imagine it was easy."

"Lottie," said Lars, whose face was nothing but eyes. "Your parents have been going crazy trying to find you and your sister!"

I squinted. My head swam with a kaleidoscope of color—aura overload.

My legs gave way. Lars caught me. I thought it was migraine weirdness, but they said it was hypothermia and dehydration. I'd put it down to emotional exhaustion, staring back into eyes that looked like Dad's. But he was just a stranger in a fairy tale that ended badly. Lars wasn't him. No more magical thinking. No more unicorns. Dad never was going to come back for me. I'd cope. I was a survivor.

There was only space for two of us on the snowcat. They wanted me to go on it, due to my recent collapse, but I persuaded them that Jade and Alex both needed more urgent medical attention. And Otis would hitch a ride.

Alex hugged me before he climbed up. "See you soon!"

"You bet." A piece of my heart went with him.

"So, how'd you get stuck out here?" asked Tara.

"It's a long story," said Jade.

"The best ones always are." She smiled at us and held out a

hand. "We'll get you home, don't worry." She helped Jade get up behind her and waited for Otis to jump on. My heart tore a little as I watched them disappear into the night, my family. There wasn't enough room under my skin for all that emotion.

The journey back was a blur. I had to hold on to Lars's waist. He kept shouting at me so I'd know what had happened during the storm. I was terrified we were going to crash. But he talked nonstop regardless. I didn't realize it at the time, but it was to keep me awake and upright.

The power was back on but spotty. The roads were being cleared and they were repairing the electric power transformers as fast as they could. Mum and Oliver had called out Nordic Rescue as soon as they realized we were missing. Two days ago!

There weren't many casualties, which was amazing considering how deep the snow was and how many cars got stuck. "One poor guy got shot in a church, bled out before we got to him, so sad," said Lars. "From his scrawled note, he really thought it was the end of the world."

Poor Carl. He'd never know it, but he had saved us, holding up Nico and AJ so we'd have the chance to flee. He'd actually saved our souls.

"Mostly people stayed in their homes or made it to a shelter. The blackout stretched from Reno to San Jose, with satellites affected across the world." Lars frowned and looked at me. "Was it just you three, no one else with you?"

"No. Mum and Oliver left before it started. I was hanging out with Jade, my sister, when Alex came along looking for shelter."

"I bet he was. Not a great time to be stuck outside. I'll radio Alex's name in ahead. If his parents know he's missing, they'll be waiting for news."

"Alex Youn," I said, "that's his name," and I stared at the ground, watching it slip away. That's exactly how I felt, like everything was flying out of control beneath me. I closed my eyes and leaned into Lars's back, and there it was, the relief that we had finally, truly, made it out.

DAY FIVE

October 29

59

9:13 a.m.

THEY CAME TO ME FIRST.

Mum looked at me from the door. I was convinced she hated me and knew all about the cabin, the danger I'd put Jade in, the stupid choices I'd made, and what a crap sister I'd been. But she hugged me like I was six again, and I cried like I was too.

After that she wouldn't stop squeezing my hand, but gently, because frostbite. She couldn't stop crying, and then hugging Oliver, who hugged me and said thank you so many times it was like a chant. Oliver cried and hugged Jade, like he'd never let her go. Then it was my turn. And finally, Jade and I were wheeled in to see Alex. And he got the hug treatment, even though they didn't know who Alex was, only that he was important to us.

Alex's little sister, Izzy, was really cute, and hugged me and Jade, and suffocated her brother. Alex's parents were a little shier, but all over Alex, and then shook my hand. Alex's mum, Hyejeong, came over and thanked me for saving Alex's life, even though I tried to explain that he had really saved mine, literally taken a bullet for me. But she was convinced it was the other way around. Alex's family almost knocked over his intravenous drip, twice.

Hyejeong hugged my mum, and Oliver shook Alex's dad Henry's hand. Lars came back and stood at the doorway, just to check that we were really doing okay, so he got showered with love and gratitude too. It was lovely and totally exhausting.

I gave Nurse Miles a pleading look. He immediately threw everyone out, politely but firmly. We had to stay one day under observation before we could go home. Wherever that might be. At least he didn't kick me out of Alex's room. Yet.

Alex, Jade, and I faced each other. It was amazing how much space was between us after hours and hours of being scrunched together. Part of me missed that comfort and warmth and intimacy. Alone felt so lonely.

Alex smiled, that stupid, adorable, beautiful, smile. "You okay?" he asked.

"Yeah, it's just…" I couldn't finish.

"Crazy," Jade said.

"Yeah, and spacey." Alex clasped my hand. "Don't forget me, when you go back to your luxury life."

"Okay, three things: One, a month ago I lived in a one-bedroom flat with Mum in San Francisco, overlooking the freeway. Two, Oliver might be an astrophysics lecturer at Stanford, with a popular podcast show on the side."

"And a couple of lucky grad-student start-up investments," Jade added.

"Whatever," I raised my eyebrows, "but I only joined this family a few days ago. So it's not like I'm running back to luxury. And three, it's not that easy to forget the beautiful boy who saved your..." The rest of the words dissolved into tears that fell on his cheeks as our lips met.

"I have a confession," Jade said, as if she weren't interrupting anything. "That was the most intense experience ever, and I'm so happy you both crashed into my life."

"I'm so glad I found you," said Alex. "I can't believe we actually made it out."

"Yeah, of all the cabins, in all of Tahoe, you had to break into ours." I smiled. "We'll always have Tahoe."

"We'll always have each other," said Alex, hypnotizing me with those deep-brown, gold-flecked eyes.

"One for all." Jade grinned. "Come visit us in Menlo Park. You'll always be our cousin."

Menlo Park, her home. She made it sound like a strange fairy-tale land. That's what home had always seemed like, a faraway place where other people lived and had normal lives, watched TV, and ate dinner around the table together.

Was that my future? I didn't know, but I was willing to give it a try. After all, I had a really cool sister to get to know, and Oliver, who already seemed to care about me more than my real dad ever had. And Alex. My lovely Alex. I stared at his mouth while he talked, not hearing a single word he said.

"Lottie," Alex had asked me again, "ever get homesick for England?"

Home. "Not really, I mean, no more than anywhere else." The only home I'd missed was the one with Dad and Mum, before the incident, and there was no going backwards. "I can always go back for university or whatever, but for now, I think there are a few people I'd like to get to know better here."

"I hope so." Alex's smile made my spine tingle.

I couldn't imagine Alex in a normal home, with parents and a sister. He'd only made sense to me there, in the snow—my Alex, my survivor.

He squeezed my hand. "It's crazy, isn't it, coming back to reality?"

"Yeah, I'm not sure I'm ready."

"I'm not sure we've got much choice," Alex replied and kissed my nose before pulling me closer to nuzzle my neck.

"Hey, still here," said Jade.

After
November 20

60

11:01 a.m.

"TEN? YOU'VE GOTTEN TEN LETTERS ALREADY?" ASKED Jade, patting my bed for her dog, Angus, to sit on.

"Just like he promised." I smiled and stroked Angus's soft, curly hair. "Mum will get mad if she sees him on the bed."

"Nah, she won't. Will she, Angus? Will she, boy?" Jade pushed her nose into Angus's and was awarded with a lick of his long, pink tongue.

I grinned. She was right. Mum wouldn't get mad at us again for a long, long time. I gave Angus a big hug. A pile of silvery drool hung from his mouth, softly collecting on Jade's knee. Jade had chosen a Newfoundland—the bigger the better, she'd said.

I looked at the photo of Alex on my mirror. Even with his face covered in mud and torn pants he'd looked pretty darn cute. I hardly recognized him clean, wearing his black leather jacket with his hair combed and flicked off his eyes, and smiling, like some kind of model with his stupid lopsided grin. He looked so vulnerable and alone. No, he didn't. That was just how I wanted him to feel until I saw him again.

Christmas, he was coming for Christmas, before he went off to art school. He'd been put forward for the "exceptional talent" scholarship and won that! So now he could afford to go and he'd be close by. San Francisco was an easy, half-hour drive. A good reason to finally get my license. I'd actually be finishing my senior year on time at high school, and after that, who knows what any of us would be doing. A year was a long way away.

For the moment I was happy to feel like I was somewhere I could call home and mean it. No more rushed packing in the night, no more worries about avoiding the landlord. I'd stopped waking in the night panicking that this wasn't for real, that Alex would stop writing, that Jade and Oliver would leave, and finally felt a sense of belonging, a sense of peace.

The crumpled photo of Dad sat on my bedside cabinet. I'd stopped wearing his watch. I could look at him now, but I wasn't waiting for him anymore. I had my family.

"Lottie," Mum called. "Letter!"

I ran downstairs to grab it. A lovely, thick envelope of paper. I held it to my chest.

"I can't believe he's still writing that much," said Mum, as I inched past her growing belly. "It's not like you aren't texting each other all of the time!"

Every time I thought about my baby-sibling-to-be, my heart tickled. "Well, snail mail. You've got to add more stuff to make it worth sending." I explained.

338

"Young love," said Oliver, grinning as he polished the telescope lens. His boss had let him keep it longer, for all the good publicity it had brought the university. Oliver told the press that me using the telescope lens to signal SOS was a perfect example of the lifesaving properties of a science education. Never in my wildest dreams did I think I'd be praised for using my smarts under extreme duress, but I'd take it.

"I'm so glad some good came out of this," said Mum.

"Hold on, it's the early days." I smiled at her. She was making an effort to be a real mum. It was a start. I gave Oliver a peck on his balding head and ran back to my room.

"Go on you, out!" I shooed Jade and Angus from my room and sat on my bed, propping myself up on my fleece pillows, and settled myself in for the big read.

I slit open the envelope and turned it upside down. A pile of beautiful paper beetles fell out, with a slip of paper.

Dear Lottie, still bugging you! xoxo

I smiled and pinned them on my board with the monarch butterflies, dragonflies, and spiders he had already sent me. I'd have a beautiful insect menagerie all over my walls by the time he was done.

Christmas never seemed so far away. I needed to run, to release this happiness with motion. I got to the bottom of the stairs, before nearly tripping over Jade, who was racing up them.

"Christmas came early." She looked so excited, I almost believed her.

"It's November."

"Special delivery!" Jade beamed.

Angus barked, excitedly wagging his tail. His bark was answered by a deeper bark—a bark I'd know anywhere. I flung open the front door and almost got knocked down as Otis raced in to greet Jade.

Leaving the special delivery alone at the door.

Alex raised his brows and grinned. "I thought I was lost."

"No"—I could hardly speak for smiling—"you're in exactly the right place."

Acknowledgments

***DON'T LET IN THE COLD* HAS BEEN ON A LONG JOURNEY** of its own, through many twists and turns. At times it seemed like it would never survive to publication, and it wouldn't have without the support of so many wonderful people!

First a huge thank you to my amazing agent, Tara Gonzalez, who believed in me and this story from the start, always knew she would find it the perfect home, and never gave up!

Thank you so much to my brilliant editor, Wendy McClure, for her insightful direction, her complete belief in this story and all it could be, and for being an absolute joy to work with! I am so happy *Don't Let in the Cold* found its perfect editor!

Much thanks to the wonderful Sourcebooks and Sourcebooks Fire team, to Liz Dresner, senior art director, and the design department for the stunning cover, and for all the support from everyone at editorial, Cassie Gutman and Kelsey Fenske, senior production editors, and Jessica Rozler for copyediting. Madeline Brown, marketing assistant, and Madison Nankervis, senior marketing and social media associate, and the publicity, sales, and marketing teams, for all the work it takes to get the finished book into the hands of readers!

To Luka for starting this adventure with me, and Pam Turner for the generous loan of her Tahoe cabin, without which the seeds of this story would never have grown!

Huge thanks to my guardian angels and guiding stars, Lou Minns and Lisa Ramee, for being amazing critique partners, writing coaches and friends, and for all the texts, phone calls, and always believing this book had legs!!

To my incredible sensitivity readers for their enthusiasm for this story, and their insightful advice. (Any misrepresentations are my mistakes alone.)

Thanks to expert advisors: Gary Turner, for explaining how guns work in the cold, Tahoe Nordic Search and Rescue Team, for the great information and incredible rescue work, and BJ at East Bay Fires, for his fireplace expertise. Any errors are mine, and mine alone!

Big thanks to Meg Fleming and Cindy Derby, the best on-the-ground support team, for all the advice, walks, laughs, cries, and always hugs! Karen Langford, for being such a great friend and constant believer, and Rachel Sarah, for being there for all the ups and downs and fun in between!

#TeamTara and #EMLA for all the love and support. Special shout out to my agent sibling Kristy Boyce—I love being on this journey with you!

Thanks to my first critique group, The Inklings, way back when, who made me believe I could write: Pam Turner, Deborah Underwood, Nancy Case, and Carol Peterson, who I met at my very first writing workshop and told me I needed a critique group, then welcomed me into this one!

To the fabulous writers and friends at the Panama Math & Science Club—Lisa Ramee, Lydia Steinauer, Sally Engelfried, Rose Haynes Touhy, Kath Rothschild, and Stacy Stokes—for the drinks, food, critiques, and laughter! And to Mina Witteman, Jim Averbeck, and Joanne Scott, for the critiques, support, and motivation!

Many thanks to Gretchen McNeil, Cindy Pon, Dawn Kurtagich, and Sue Fliess, for being constant cheerleaders and suppliers of great advice. And Amy Warwick, for all the check ins, support, and cheers over our Portland drinks! To my early readers, advisors, and friends: Laura Fasman, Tim McCanna, Jen Fosberry, Amy Moellering, Anne Reilly, Alexandra Ballard, Mike Jung, and Amanda Conran, for your feedback, friendship, and encouragement!

And to everyone at #22debuts for so much guidance and support—can't wait to read all your wonderful books! Thanks to Brenda and everyone at #Pitmad and #Pitchwars for helping motivate me to get this story into shape.

Thanks to SCBWI SF North and East Bay, especially Colette Weil-Parrinello, Louise Hendriksen, and Nadia Salomon, for being such a supportive community. And SCBWI in general for introducing me to so many incredible people worldwide. Cheers to Kathryn Evans and Marie Basting, in the UK—who made those SCBWI conferences so much fun!

Thank you to NorCal writers: Misa Sugiura, Randy Ribay, Joanna Ho, Stacy Lee, and Mike Chen, for your friendship and support—can't wait to meet up at Kepler's again! A to Angela Mann and team at Kepler's for building s YA lit community.

A huge thank you to Judy Wheeler and te Books, who are always so supportive and ch

Immense gratitude to my parents fo adventure, and travel, and to m always being excited for me.

And finally, but m who always believe in adventures—love you

About the Author

photo © Adam Morgan

Keely Parrack grew up in England and came to America for fun, twenty years ago. She is still here doing the things she loves: writing YA novels, poetry, and picture books, and motivating kids to love reading and to be confident creative writers. She has been a teacher, retail manager, childcare director, and a social networker for her local indie bookstore. When she's not writing, she loves to read, binge watch horror movies, travel, and take too many photographs. She lives in the San Francisco Bay Area with her husband, son, and a very demanding cat. More than anything, she hates to be cold! Learn more on her website: keelyparrack.com

#getbooklit

Your hub for the hottest young adult books!

Visit us online and sign up for our
newsletter at FIREreads.com

 @sourcebooksfire

 sourcebooksfire

 firereads.tumblr.com